A Harlequin

D JANET AILEY

Collector's Edition

Harlequin

D JANET AILEY

Collector's Editions

A Harlequin
JANET
DAILEY
Collector's Edition

Harlequin Books

TORONTO · NEW YORK · LONDON
AMSTERDAM · PARIS · SYDNEY · HAMBURG
STOCKHOLM · ATHENS · TOKYO · MILAN

These books by Janet Dailey were originally published as
follows:

FOR MIKE'S SAKE
Copyright © 1979 by Janet Dailey
First published by Mills & Boon Limited in 1979
Harlequin Presents edition (#313) published
October 1979

WITH A LITTLE LUCK
Copyright © 1981 by Janet Dailey
First published by Mills & Boon Limited in 1981
Harlequin Presents edition (#482) published
February 1982

ISBN 0-373-80611-6
First edition May 1984
The Harlequin trademark, consisting of the word
HARLEQUIN and the portrayal of a Harlequin,
is registered in the United States Patent and Trademark
Office and in the Canada Trade Marks Office.

PRINTED IN U.S.A.

CONTENTS

FOR MIKE'S SAKE

"OUR FIGHTS ALWAYS END IN ONE OF TWO WAYS."

The smoldering light in Wade's eyes stole the breath from Maggie's lungs. Would his kiss be the same? Curiosity overpowered any thought of protest. Her lips yielded to the possessive pressure of his kiss. That fiery glow she remembered spread through her again, but it was even better now. More wonderful. More destroying.

Then the kiss ended, and she was forced back into the present. Suddenly she had to know. Could it be possible that Wade was going to propose a reconciliation?

"Why are you here, Wade?" Maggie watched a muscle contract along his jaw as he let go of her.

"I came to tell you I'm getting married again."

Thank God that pride had kept her silent, demanding his reasons before stating her desires.

CHAPTER ONE

THE COMPACT CONVERTIBLE zipped down the street, trees leafed out into full foliage to shade the lawns on either side.

The car's top was down, wind ruffling the scarlet gold hair of the driver, dressed in snug fitting Levi's and a blue madras blouse with the sleeves rolled up to the elbows.

Expertly shifting down to make a running stop at an intersection, Maggie Rafferty saw no traffic approaching and let the little car dart across. Ahead was the ball park and Maggie slowed the car to turn into the small graveled lot near the stand.

Stopped, she lifted the smoke gray sunglasses from her nose and perched them on her head. Her green eyes scanned the cluster of young boys as she pressed a hand on the horn.

Instantly one separated himself from the others and ran toward her, a baseball glove in his hand.

He paused once to wave at the group, backpedaling toward the car.

"See ya Friday, guys!" When he hopped into the passenger seat he was faintly breathless, his dark eyes glittering with excitement. "Hi!"

"Hi, yourself." Maggie smiled, tiny dimples appearing in her cheeks. "Sorry I'm late. I hope you didn't have to wait too long."

"That's okay." He shrugged away the apology, absently punching a fist into his glove. "I'm getting used to you always being late," he said with the patient indulgence of an adult.

"Thanks a lot, Mike." She laughed and reached over to tug the bill of his baseball cap low on his forehead.

Punctuality had never been one of her virtues, but she didn't need a ten-year-old son reminding her of it.

"Hey, come on!"

Mike protested the action, removing his cap and putting it back on at the correct angle. Its momentary removal revealed coal black hair, a shade darker than his eyes.

Maggie's gaze skimmed his profile, lighting on the sprinkling of freckles across the bridge of his nose. They were the only thing he might have inherited from her. "I told you not to do that."

"Sorry, I forgot." Which wasn't totally true. Mike believed himself to be too old for hugging and kissing. It embarrassed him.

Maggie couldn't smother the urge to touch him and love him, so she hid it under the guise of teasing pokes and gestures.

"Are we going home or not?" he prompted.

"Yes, right now."

As she turned toward the door to look over her shoulder for traffic before reversing into the street, Maggie's gaze was caught by the man standing on the driver's side of a station wagon parked beside her.

Tall, in his thirties, with light brown hair and hazel eyes, he was very good-looking, as suntanned as a lifeguard.

The look in his eyes was decidedly admiring in his inspection of her. His mouth quirked into a smile, accompanied by a slight nod of his head in silent greeting.

Maggie returned the smile and the nod without hesitation. One of Mike's teammates raced around the station wagon to climb in the passenger seat, and Maggie breathed out a sigh of regret. Why were the good-looking ones always married with a little wife waiting at home?

She flipped the sunglasses down on her nose and reversed into the empty street.

"How was your first practice?" The Little League baseball season was just beginning. Maggie didn't want to think about the hectic summer schedule that would be ahead.

"Great. The coach says I'm going to make a good utility man, 'cause I can play any position on the field . . . except pitcher, of course. Maybe I should practice pitching."

He considered the idea.

"Instead of being good at every position, you should concentrate on one or two and become the best at those."

"I guess," Mike conceded.

"I've gotta improve on my hitting. I didn't do too well today."

"It's only your first practice," Maggie reminded him.

"Yeah, I know. Coach said he'd give me a few pointers about switch-hitting and all if I'd come earlier than the

11

other guys for practice. Do you suppose you could manage to bring me early?''

"You wouldn't have been late today if Aaron hadn't called from the office just as we were leaving." Maggie correctly interpreted the question as a slur on her character.

"Yeah, but you always leave everything to the last minute. Then when something comes up, we're always late."

"We'll get an earlier start next time," she promised.

There was a flash of blue at the end of a side street, the shimmer of sunlight off the smooth surface of water.

In Seattle there always seemed to be a flash of blue around the corner, whether from a lake or an inlet or Puget Sound itself.

"You don't have to take me. I could always walk."

"We've been through that before, Mike." Her mouth was set in a firm line, irritation sparking through her that he should bring up the subject when she had made her feelings so plain on it before. "It's too far for you to walk."

"It wouldn't be too far if I had a bike, a ten-speed. I saw one the—"

"Your birthday is coming up."

Mike groaned.

"Summer will almost be over by then!"

"If you'd taken better care of your old bike, you wouldn't be without one now."

"I only forgot to lock it that one time. How was I supposed to know someone was going to come along and steal it?"

12

"I hope it taught you a lesson and you'll be more careful with your next bike."

"If you're going to get me a bike for my birthday, do I have to wait clear till then? Couldn't I have it early?"

"We'll see."

"Maybe if I wrote dad, he'd buy me one now," he muttered, not content with her half promise.

Maggie gave him an angry sidelong look.

"You just ruined your chances of getting a bike before your birthday. I've told you repeatedly that you aren't going to play me and your father off against each other. If you persuade him to buy you a bike before your birthday, I'll lock it up until your birthday. Do you understand?"

"Yes, ma'am," Mike grumbled, hanging his head, his mouth thinning into a sulking pout.

Concealing a sigh, Maggie let her green eyes look back to the road. God, how she hated playing the heavy-handed parent!

But she had little choice, really. Mike was only behaving as any child of divorced parents would. If she let him get away with his emotional blackmail, he'd be walking all over her. And *nobody* walked over her, certainly not her own son.

"It isn't so bad, is it?" she asked, trying to ease the friction between them. "To have me take you to practice?"

"No, it isn't so bad," he agreed glumly.

"From now on, I'll make sure you're there early so the coach can give you some tips on hitting, okay?"

"Okay."

As she glanced at him, Mike gave her a sideways

13

look through thick black lashes. A sudden, impish light glittered in his dark eyes. "I know why you're going to get me there early. It's the coach, isn't it?"

One thing about Mike, he never held a grudge, a trait that was totally his own.

Maggie smiled. "The coach?" She didn't follow his comment.

"Yeah, the coach." There was a knowing grin on his face. "I saw the way he looked at you."

"The way he looked at me?" She laughed in bewilderment. "I don't know what you're talking about. I didn't even see Coach Anderson at the ball park."

"He isn't our coach this year. We've got a new one, Tom Darby."

"Oh," said Maggie in understanding and repeated the sound in realization. "Oh, your new coach was the one by the station wagon, the tall, good-looking man."

"Yeah, do you want me to introduce you?"

His dark eyes were twinkling with an awareness beyond his years, but then children seemed to grow up quicker nowadays.

Maggie hid a smile at his matchmaking attempt, but there were telltale dimples in her cheeks despite the straight line of her mouth.

"The coach's wife just might object to that, Mike."

"He isn't married."

His grin deepened.

"The boy who got into the station wagon with him . . . ."

" . . . was Ronnie Schneider. Coach was giving him a ride home. You don't think I'd try to line you up with a

14

guy who's married and has kids of his own, do you, mom?''

"You can just forget about lining me up with him. If there's any lining up to do, I'll take care of it." As they turned a corner the wind blew her hair across her cheek, flame silk against her ivory complexion. Maggie pushed the tangling strands back.

"From the look he gave you, it won't take much lining up," Mike declared with decided certainty. "He'd like to make it with you—I could tell."

His candor brought a bubble of indignant reproof, but Maggie swallowed back most of it, releasing a tame reprimand.

"You see more than you should."

"It's a fact of life, mom. A feller can't ignore it." He shrugged, knowing he was being outrageous and enjoying the feeling.

"It's not my fault I have a beautiful mother and that half the guys think you're my older sister."

"Do you mind?"

She slid him a curious glance as she turned the car into the driveway of their home.

"Nah, I just tell everybody that you had a face-lift and you're really a lot older."

"Mike!"

She didn't know whether to be angry or laugh, and in the confusion became capable of neither.

He laughed heartily, finding her astonishment riotously funny.

"I don't tell them that, mom, honest. But you should have seen the look on your face!"

Maggie stopped the car in front of the garage door.

"Wait until you see the look on your face if I ever find out that you have!"

But the threat wasn't made in earnest.

"Seriously, mom—" he opened the door and hesitated before stepping out of the small car "—I don't mind that you look young and beautiful. And I wouldn't mind a bit if the coach was your boyfriend."

"Oh, you wouldn't?"

Maggie switched off the engine and removed the key from the ignition. "Do you think it might help you to score a few points with the coach?"

"It couldn't hurt. It would be pretty hard for him to bench the son of the girl he's dating, wouldn't it?"

"If you deserve benching, the mother might suggest it to the coach."

"Oh, well," he sighed as he climbed out of the car, "you can't blame a guy for trying to cover all the angles if he can."

With a shake of her head, Maggie stepped onto the concrete driveway. Mike took the short flight of steps to the front door two at a time and waited impatiently at the top while Maggie rummaged through her cloth purse for the house key.

"What's for lunch? I'm starved!"

"Homemade noodles." She handed him the key to unlock the door and reached for the letters in the mailbox.

"Can we eat now?"

He was in the house, tossing his baseball glove on the sofa while he headed for the kitchen.

"The glove belongs in your room and we'll eat in twenty minutes, after you've washed and I've fixed a salad."

16

"You're trying to turn me into a rabbit. Salad!" Mike declared.

"The glove and wash," Maggie reminded him, catching him before he reached the kitchen and turning him back to the living room. "And you like salad, so I don't know why you're complaining about it now."

"I don't like it for every meal."

As Mike retraced his path to the living room, Maggie had to admit her menus had been lacking in imagination lately.

She supposed it was a problem all working mothers faced. Cooking for only two people wasn't easy, either.

Still, Mike's criticism was justified and she should do something about changing it in what was left of her two weeks' vacation.

Maggie set the mail on the counter and began rummaging through the kitchen cupboards. There would be time enough to look over the bills later. Right now, she had a hungry boy to feed.

Boy. Dimples were carved briefly in her cheeks at the word. After that observation about his coach, Mike was fast outgrowing the term of *boy*.

And matchmaking yet. Still, it was better that he had no objections to her dating. It would have been unbearable if he were jealous and resentful of her seeing other men.

But Mike had only been five years old when Maggie had finally obtained her divorce, so his emotional scars were few.

Mike evidently liked his new coach. Tom Darby—Maggie remembered the name.

He was good-looking, in a jock sort of way, and she

17

would have been less than honest if she didn't admit that she had been attracted to him. He evidently liked children, otherwise he wouldn't be coaching a boys' Little League team.

Most of the eligible men she had met lately had either been too young or too old, but this Tom Darby was . . . . Maggie took a firm grip on her imagination. The man hadn't even asked her out yet—if he ever would—and here she was assessing his possibilities!

Mike burst into the kitchen.

"My glove's in my room and my hands are washed. Can we eat now?"

Maggie made a brief inspection of him and nodded. "Set the table while I see what I can fix in place of a salad."

"Can't we just forget the salad? I promise I'll eat two helpings of green vegetables at dinner tonight instead. I'm starved! I really worked up an appetite at the ball field."

She smiled crookedly and gave in.

"All right, set the table and I'll dish up the beef and noodles."

Later when Mike helped himself to another portion of noodles, Maggie carried her empty plate to the sink, picked up the mail from the counter and returned to the table.

She sifted through the half-dozen envelopes, a mixture of advertisements and billing statements, until she came to the last.

Even before she saw the Alaskan postmark, she recognized the boldly legible handwriting. Her heart missed a beat, then resumed its normal pace.

18

"You have a letter from your father, Mike."

Her thumb covered the return address and the name Wade Rafferty as Maggie handed the envelope to her son.

"Great!" He abandoned his plate to tear open the flap with the eagerness of a child opening a present. Maggie sipped at her glass of milk, trying to ignore her pangs of jealousy.

Mike read the first paragraph and exclaimed, "Oh, boy! He's coming home!"

Her heart missed another beat. "Why is he coming to Seattle?"

She refused to use the word *home*.

"To see us, of course." Mike continued to read the contents of the letter.

Not us. He's coming to see you, but not us, Maggie corrected him silently.

Wade had no more interest in seeing her than she had in seeing him.

"Does your father say when he's coming?"

It had been six years since she had seen him last, shortly after their divorce, before he'd left for Alaska, a transfer Wade had requested from his company. Of course Mike had seen him regularly, flying to Alaska in the summers and during Christmas holidays.

The first time Mike had gone, it had been awful, with Maggie worrying about him every second. But it had been even worse when he came back, every other sentence containing "daddy." Even today, she still experienced moments of jealousy, although none as intense as that first time.

To say her five-year marriage and year's separation

19

from Wade had been stormy was an understatement. It had been six years of one flaming argument after another, each alternately demanding a divorce from the other until finally their demands coincided.

They had been too much of a match for each other, her fiery temper equal to his black rage. Yet, since their divorce they had managed to be civil to each other for Mike's sake, albeit at long distance.

"He's coming home Sunday the . . . ." Mike glanced up at the calendar hanging on the kitchen wall, notes scribbled on various dates. "Wow! He's coming home *this* Sunday!"

He pointed at a section of the letter. "He says right here, 'I'll see you on Sunday. I'll call you first thing in the morning.' This Sunday. Wow!" Mike repeated with incredulity and delight.

"Does he say why? I mean, didn't you write him in your last letter and tell him how much you were looking forward to coming to Alaska this summer?" Maggie felt uneasy.

It was so much better when there were hundreds of miles separating her from Wade. "Surely your father knows how much you wanted to come, so why would he disappoint you this way?"

"I'm not disappointed. I'd much rather have him come here. Dad knows that, 'cause I keep asking him to come home. Mom, do you suppose he could—"

"He is not staying here!" She read the rest of the question in Mike's expression and immediately rejected the idea.

"And I'm sure your father wouldn't want to, anyway."

20

"It was just a thought." Mike shrugged and tried to hide his disappointment.

There was sudden perception in her green eyes as Maggie studied her son's face.

"Mike," she began hesitantly, "I hope you aren't holding out any hopes that your father and I will get back together again. We both tried very hard to make our marriage work, but we simply couldn't get along."

"Yeah, I know." He neither admitted nor denied that he had been hoping. "I remember the way you used to yell at each other. That's about all I can remember."

"I'm sorry, Mike."

He folded the letter back up and inserted it into its envelope.

"I hate fighting," he declared with unexpected vehemence.

Maggie's head lifted a fraction as she realized that Mike's unwillingness to argue or remain angry for long was a result of the shouting matches he had overheard. She and Wade had inflicted a few scars on him.

"Arguments can be good, Mike. They can clear the air, bring things out in the open and straighten out misunderstandings. It's normal for two people to argue. In the case of me and your father, we were simply never able to resolve our differences. We weren't able to reach a mutual understanding. Sometimes it happens that way." She tried to explain, but it was difficult.

"Weren't you ever happy with him?"

"Of course. In the very beginning," Maggie admitted. "Your father swept me off my feet in the true romantic fashion. He was very masterful. It wasn't until after we were married that I realized that I didn't want to be

21

mastered. And your father couldn't regard me as an equal.''

Mike impatiently pushed his chair away from the table. ''Why do you always have to refer to him as 'your father'? He has a name just like everybody else,'' he muttered.

''It's a habit, I suppose. Something that's carried over from the days when you were younger.'' That wasn't exactly the truth. It was still difficult for her to say Wade's name. To say ''your father'' came easier; Maggie couldn't explain why.

''Well, he's coming Sunday anyway, and I'm glad.'' Mike rose from his chair, ignoring the food on his plate. ''I think I'll go see if Denny wants to play catch.''

Again Maggie took note of the way he had avoided an argument with her.

It was his turn to do the dishes, but she didn't bother to remind him of it.

She'd do them this time.

AT THE NEXT PRACTICE SESSION Maggie kept her word and arrived at the ball park early so Mike could get the extra coaching on his hitting game. One of his young teammates was already there, sitting in the bleachers and tossing a ball in the air.

''There's Ronnie!''

Mike hopped from the car before Maggie could shift the gear into park. Closing the car door, he paused a second to ask, ''Can you stay for a while to watch me practice?''

The station wagon Tom Darby had been driving the last time was nowhere to be seen. Maggie hesitated, then agreed.

22

"I'll stay, at least until your coach gets here."

Maggie stayed mostly because she didn't like the idea of leaving Mike alone—an overly protective attitude, but she admitted to that.

There was also the motivation, though, of wanting to see Tom Darby again. First impressions could be misleading. Perhaps on second meeting Maggie would find him less attractive.

"Great!" Mike responded to her decision and raced off to greet his teammate.

Maggie followed at a more sedate pace.

By the time she reached the tall wire fence protecting spectators from the batting area of the diamond, Mike had persuaded the second boy to join him on the field. Maggie leaned a shoulder against a supporting post and watched them tossing the ball back and forth.

A car door slammed and she glanced over her shoulder at the sound. A viridescent shimmer brightened her eyes as casual, effortless strides carried Mike's coach toward her.

He was good-looking, almost too good-looking, she decided, letting her attention shift back to the boys on the playing field.

"Good morning." His voice was pleasantly low as he stopped beside her.

With the greeting, Maggie let her gaze swerve to him. The hazel eyes regarding her so admiringly had definite gold flecks. On closer inspection, her initial opinion didn't change.

"Good morning," she replied naturally. "It's a beautiful day, isn't it?"

He nodded agreement and added, "The kind of day Seattle people always brag about, but seldom see."

Maggie didn't argue that the perfection of their weather was occasionally overstated. Instead she let her smile widen and remarked, in question form, "You aren't from around here, then?"

"No, not originally. I'm a native southern Californian."

It fitted. With that deep golden tan, he looked as if he had walked straight off the beach. "But I'm beginning to enjoy the change of scenery."

The lazily explicit way he was eyeing her plainly indicated that he wasn't referring to the landscape of mountains and sea. No woman with an ounce of femininity could be immune to that look.

Certainly Maggie wasn't. If she had possessed any doubt that she was a strikingly attractive woman, it no longer existed.

"It's a nice place to live." Her noncommittal reply didn't reveal that she had interpreted a second meaning to his remark.

Her gaze shifted back to the baseball diamond and the two boys. As yet, neither had noticed the arrival of their coach.

And Tom Darby was in no hurry to make them aware of his presence. That fact produced a warm glow of satisfaction in Maggie.

"Are you staying to watch the practice?" The way Tom asked the question seemed to imply that he would like it if she did.

"I'm afraid I can't." A rueful smile tugged at one corner of her mouth. "I have a bunch of errands to do this morning. I promised Mike I'd only stay for a few minutes.''

Maggie didn't tell him that she had agreed to wait only until he came.

She didn't want him to think he had been the sole reason, or even the main reason she had waited, because it wasn't so.

At the same time she didn't want to totally rebuff the interest he was showing in her.

This time Tom was the one to glance at the two boys playing catch. ''Your little brother is a very good ball player.''

''He isn't my brother,'' Maggie corrected him with a laughing gleam in her green eyes.

''Mike is my son.''

Startled hazel eyes flicked a surprised look back to her. ''I beg your pardon, Mrs. Rafferty. You must have been a child bride.''

''No, I wasn't. And the name is Maggie.''

''Tom Darby,'' he introduced himself, his gaze sliding to her ringless left hand.

Maggie saw the question forming in his expression and was about to inform him of her unattached status when a shout of recognition from Mike eliminated the chance.

Both boys came racing to the wire fence.

''You said if we came early, coach, you'd give us some tips on switch-hitting,'' Mike reminded him on a breathless note, all eagerness and enthusiasm.

''So I did,'' Tom smiled indulgently.

''The bats are in the back of my wagon. Why don't you two go get them?''

As they started to dash off to do his bidding, he called them to a halt.

"Wait a minute—it's locked. I'll have to get them for you."

The opportunity for private conversation was gone.

But Maggie wasn't concerned. There would be others.

"I'd better be going," she told everyone in general, but Tom in particular, as she started for her own car. Her parting remark was directed at her son. "I'll pick you up after practice."

"Okay."

He absently waved a goodbye.

THERE WASN'T ANOTHER CHANCE that week for the personal discussion the boys had interrupted. That day Maggie was late getting back to the ball park to pick up Mike, and Tom Darby had already left. At Mike's next practice Maggie brought him early but couldn't stay, and again picked him up late.

It couldn't be helped.

There was so much she wanted done before Wade returned this Sunday. The biggest task was spring-cleaning the house from top to bottom. She intended it to be spotless when he came.

Plus, there was shopping to be done for new kitchen and dining-room curtains. A new outfit in a shop window caught her eye and Maggie bought it, as well. Amid all the preparation, she squeezed in a visit to the beauty salon.

She was perfectly aware that she was doing all this because of Wade.

It was deliberate, if a trifle vindictive. She wanted him to see how very well she managed on her own. She was doing it all to impress him and wasn't ashamed to admit it to herself.

CHAPTER TWO

"HEY, MOM, are you going to sleep all morning? I'm hungry!"

Maggie opened one eye to see Mike standing in the doorway of her bedroom.

She groaned and pulled the covers over her head, trying to shut out her son and the daylight streaming through the window.

"Get yourself some cereal," she mumbled. "You're old enough to get your own breakfast."

"It's Sunday," he protested.

Maggie groaned again. It had become a Sunday-morning ritual that breakfast was a special meal. No hot cereal and toast, nor a quickly fried egg on this day. No, it was pancakes with blueberry syrup and bacon, eaten at leisure with neither of them rushing off anywhere, not to school nor work.

"Come on, mom, get up," Mike insisted when she failed to show any signs of rising. "Dad's going to be calling anytime now."

That opened her eyes as the full significance of the day hit her like a dousing of cold water.

Maggie tossed the covers back and rolled over to sit on the edge of the bed.

She yawned and paused to rub the sleep from her

eyes. Mike was still at the door, as if he expected her to slide back under the covers any minute.

"All right, I'm up. Go and put on some coffee." Maggie waved him toward the kitchen. "I'll be right there."

Mike hesitated, then trotted off.

She slid her feet into a pair of furry slippers and padded to the clothes closet. Ignoring the new robe hanging inside, she removed a faded quilted one from the hook.

"Old Faithful" had seen better days.

A seam was ripped out under an arm. Two buttons were off on the bottom.

But it was as comfortable as a pair of old shoes, cozy and warm and dependable.

She touched an inspecting hand to her hair to be certain all the clips and hair rollers were in place.

Setting her hair had been a precaution to keep the attractive style she had got at the beauty parlor the previous morning.

Sometimes the thickness of her red gold hair refused to keep the discipline of a style after being slept on and Maggie hadn't wanted to take a chance this time.

As much tossing and turning as she had done last night trying to get to sleep, it had probably been a good thing she had taken steps to make sure her hair looked right this morning.

She hadn't been able to forget that Wade was coming. She kept trying to imagine how she would treat him, what her manner would be.

She couldn't make up her mind whether she would be cool and polite or indifferently friendly. How, exactly, did one treat an ex-husband?

29

Even now the answer eluded her.

At the door to the bathroom, she paused. Shrugging, she walked toward the kitchen.

There would be time enough to fix her hair and put on makeup after Wade had telephoned to say when he was coming.

The coffeepot was perking merrily in the kitchen. Maggie inhaled the aroma wistfully and took out the skillet to begin frying the bacon.

While it sizzled in the pan, she mixed up the pancakes and heated the griddle, putting Mike to work setting the table.

As she stole a sip of the freshly brewed coffee she had poured, she noticed the way Mike kept eyeing the telephone extension by the cupboards. She knew he was anxious to receive the phone call from his father, but made no comment.

When she put the food on the table, Mike didn't eat his favorite meal with his usual enthusiasm. He did more playing than eating, his gaze constantly straying to the telephone.

Half a pancake was drowning in blueberry syrup, slowly disintegrating under his pushing fork.

"There's more bacon." Maggie offered him the platter.

He shook his head in refusal.

"Why hasn't he called yet? He said in his letter he'd call Sunday morning."

"It's a little early." The wall clock indicated a few minutes after eight o'clock. "Maybe he thinks you're still sleeping."

"But he knows I'll be waiting for him to call."

30

"He also said he'd be arriving late last night. Maybe your father is sleeping late this morning," Maggie suggested.

"Him? Dad never sleeps late."

Mike dismissed that suggestion as unworthy of any consideration.

Maggie had to admit that Mike was probably right. Wade had always been a disgustingly early riser, constantly chiding her for being such a sleepyhead. Wade had always been punctual, if not early, for appointments, while she had been habitually late.

There was a long list of differences between them and they had been a continual source of conflict during their marriage.

"You'd better eat that pancake before it turns into mush," Maggie advised.

She turned her mind from the long-ago problems that had been resolved by a divorce.

"I'm not hungry anymore." Mike pushed his plate back.

His dark eyes gazed at the beige phone as if willing it to ring.

"You've heard the old saying, haven't you, Mike? 'A watched pot never boils.' I think your telephone is turning into a watched pot that isn't going to ring. Why don't you see if the paperboy has brought the Sunday newspaper yet?"

When he hesitated, Maggie added, "You can hear the phone ring outside and it won't take you a minute."

"Okay," he agreed, but reluctantly.

As Mike walked to the side door, Maggie rose to begin clearing the table. Leaving the dirty dishes for the moment, she covered the butter tray and put it in the refrigerator.

The door closed behind Mike.

Blueberry syrup had trickled down the side of its container. She wiped away the sticky substance with a dishcloth from the sink and put the syrup jar in the refrigerator.

As she picked up the bottle of orange juice, the lid wasn't on tight and skittered off onto the floor. It rolled into the narrow slit between the refrigerator and the cabinet.

"Damn!" Maggie muttered beneath her breath, and stooped down.

She could see the lid in the shadowy aperture. Kneeling, she worked her hand into the slit, just barely, and tried to reach the lid.

Her fingertips touched the edge. She wiggled her arm a little farther inside and hooked a fingernail in the inner rim.

Slowly and carefully she pulled her arm, her hand, and the lid out.

"Hey, mom! Look who brought the paper!" Mike's excited voice cried.

Maggie was on her hands and knees, twisting her head to see the door open. "Dad drove in just as I went outside." Mike glanced upward at the tall, dark man who had followed him into the house. "I thought you were going to call first."

"I was," the familiar, deep-pitched voice answered. "Since you were expecting me anyway, I decided not to bother, so I came over instead." Eyes equally black as his hair looked at Maggie. "Hello, Maggie."

32

The room spun crazily for a moment. She was paralyzed, unable to move.

There was a familiar leap of her pulse as she stared up at him.

Wade looked achingly the same as when she had first seen him.

That shaggy black mane of hair, those virile, rugged features, that self-assured carriage, all made an impact on her.

A cream silk shirt was opened at the throat, hinting at the perfectly toned muscles of his chest and shoulders.

The long sleeves were rolled up almost to the elbows, a look indolently casual and relaxed.

A whole assortment of disturbing memories came rushing back.

Her flesh remembered the evocative caress of those large hands. The warm taste of his mouth was recalled by her lips and the male scent of his body was strong in her memory.

Her ears could hear the husky love words Wade used to murmur to her.

The look of him needed no recalling. He was there, standing in her kitchen, his dark eyes glinting with silent mockery.

There were dirty dishes on the table. Cooking smells were strong in the air, the room smelling of bacon, thanks to the skillet on the stove and the grease splattered over the enameled range top.

The place was a mess.

So was she, Maggie realized. There were curlers and hair clips in her hair. She wore no makeup, and the faded and tattered robe did nothing to improve her appearance. She must seem the caricature of a housewife in the morning.

This wasn't how she had planned it.

The house was to be spotless, her appearance immaculate. Her new outfit, the two precious hours at the beauty parlor, all to prove how beautiful she still was, had all gone for naught.

Bitter frustration sparked her highly combustible temper.

"Damn you, Wade Rafferty!" Maggie pushed herself to her feet, stepping on the hem of her robe and nearly tripping.

She threw the orange juice lid that she had struggled so hard to reach onto the floor in a fit of pique.

"You did this on purpose. You deliberately came here without calling just to make me look . . . . Only you could be that rude and inconsiderate! Get out of my house!"

She was so angry that she was almost choking on her tears.

During the course of her tirade, the glittering light of mockery left Wade's eyes.

They became an ominous, brooding black, narrowing into piercing slits. His mouth had hardened into a thin line, bringing a forbidding quality to his harshly masculine features.

His hand had remained on the back of Mike's neck in a gesture of affection, but Wade, and Maggie, were indifferent to the presence of their son.

Until he called attention to himself.

"How could you do it, mom?"

His wavering voice and stricken look quenched Maggie's fiery temper.

The damage was already done. Her angry outburst had spoiled Mike's reunion with his father and there wasn't anything she could say to make it right. Her fingers curled into the palms of her hands as she strived to obtain some measure of dignity.

"I would appreciate it if you would have Michael back home by ten this evening."

Without allowing Wade an opportunity to respond to her cool statement, Maggie walked from the kitchen, her head held high.

Her cheeks burned with the knowledge of the farcical picture she made, acting like a lady of the house and looking like a hag.

The first thing she did, upon reaching her bedroom, was take off her old, comfortable robe and jam it into the small wastebasket in her room. Then she began tugging the curlers and silver clips from her hair and flinging them on her dresser.

She didn't stop until the door slammed, indicating Wade and Mike had left.

Then she slumped onto her bed, burying her face in her hands.

There was bitter disappointment and frustration in her mouth.

Yesterday she had been positive Wade no longer had the power to incite her to anger. Yet, within five seconds after seeing him she had been screaming at him like a shrew.

Why, oh, why did he always manage to succeed in making her lose her temper? And in front of Mike, too. Maggie groaned in despair.

There was only one lesson to be learned from the incident. Things were just as volatile between them as they always had been. From now on she would have to be on her guard.

In the meantime, she still had the task of facing Mike when he returned tonight.

CHAPTER THREE

THAT EVENING Maggie sat with forced quietness in a living-room chair.

The house was once again spotlessly clean. Not a single dirty dish was in the sink, nor an ash in the ashtrays. Her makeup was on and there was hardly a hair out of place on her head.

She was wearing the elegant jersey pantsuit in lavender that she had purchased for the occasion. Except for the tightly clasped hands in her lap, she appeared calm and completely controlled.

A car pulled into the driveway and she unconsciously held her breath. She heard a car door slam shut, but only one door.

As the kitchen door opened, the car reversed out of the driveway. Maggie slowly began breathing again.

"Hello, Mike." Her greeting was determinedly bright as she rose to meet him.

She glanced pointedly behind him. "Didn't your father come in with you?"

"No. After the way you yelled at him this morning, did you really think he would?" He didn't quite meet her eyes, but there was no malice in his tone, only the hurt of disappointment.

"No, I guess I didn't," Maggie admitted. "I baked a

cake this afternoon—chocolate with chocolate frosting. Would you like a piece?''

"No, thanks." Mike wandered into the room and slumped into the twin of the chair Maggie had been sitting in. "I'm not hungry."

"Did you and yo—Wade have a good time together today? Where did you go?"

She longed to ask if Wade had made any reference to her waspish outburst, but she doubted that he had. He had always possessed much more control over himself than she had.

"Yeah, we had fun." His shrug expressed disinterest in being more explicit. "We went down to the harbor and took a ferry to one of the islands."

"Did your fa—did Wade say how long he'd be staying in Seattle?"

"No."

Mike was usually more talkative than this and Maggie knew the reason for his brief responses. She took a deep breath and plunged into an apology. "I'm sorry about this morning, Mike. I really am."

"How could you do it?" He sounded both puzzled and hurt. "Dad says hello and you start yelling at him. Why? Do you hate him that much?"

"No, I don't hate him." Maggie denied that suggestion and qualified it in her mind that the violent side of her emotion toward Wade surfaced only at times of supreme anger.

"I don't know how to explain it to you, Mike. Maybe you'd have to be a girl to understand." She attempted a teasing smile, but he wasn't put off by it. "It's been five years since I saw . . . Wade."

38

"I know, and the minute you see him you start shouting."

"That's because I had curlers in my hair, no lipstick on, dirty dishes all over the table and I was wearing that horrible old robe. I didn't want him to see me like that. I wanted to be all dressed up with my hair fixed and everything.

"I was embarrassed and because I was embarrassed I became angry. It doesn't excuse what I did, but I hope you understand why."

He considered the explanation for a minute, then nodded uncertainly.

"Yeah, I guess I do."

"Wade has always had a talent for catching me at my worst. I should have remembered that and been prepared." The milk was spilled and Maggie refused to cry about it.

"Yeah, well, the next time you see dad—"

"I'll try to remember. And I'll also apologize." She'd do it for Mike's sake.

"Dad didn't come over deliberately just to catch you looking like that," Mike said, defending his father.

"I know that . . . now. He was anxious to see you, that's why he came first instead of calling. He misses you just as much as you miss him." Maggie didn't have any doubt about that.

"Which reminds me, what are you two planning for tomorrow?"

"Dad's busy all day tomorrow. He said there were some things he had to do."

"Oh." Maggie frowned. "I thought you'd be spending the day with him, or at least part of it."

"I'm not. Why?"

"Aaron called this afternoon and asked me to work tomorrow."

"But you're on vacation," Mike protested.

"I know, but Patty's sprained her ankle and can't come in. Since it's only for Monday, I told Aaron I could. I thought you'd be with Wade."

She did some quick thinking. "I'll call Denny's mother." Shelley Bixby lived next door and kept an eye on Mike while Maggie worked.

"But what about the game?"

Maggie started for the telephone and stopped. "What game?"

"My baseball game tomorrow afternoon. It starts at five and coach wants us to be there no later than four-thirty. You don't get home until after five. If I'm late, I'll probably have to sit on the bench the whole time. I won't even have a chance to play."

"Don't start thinking the worst. Since I'm supposed to be on vacation, I'll simply tell Aaron that I have to leave by four."

She picked up the telephone receiver. "It's a pity Denny isn't in Little League. Then Shelley could take you both."

"You won't forget to tell him, will you, mom? You won't be late coming home?" Mike repeated skeptically.

Maggie's fingers hovered above the telephone dial. "I won't forget, and I won't be late."

BUT SHE VERY NEARLY WAS.

She didn't leave the office until five past four the next day. A traffic light failed to function properly and there was a snarl of cars at the major intersection where she had to turn.

Five minutes before Mike had to be at the ball park, she turned into the driveway and honked the horn. Mike was waiting on the front doorstep and was halfway to the car before she had stopped it.

He was wearing his striped baseball player's uniform, complete with the billed cap, socks and shoes. He looked cute, but he would have blushed scarlet if Maggie had told him so.

Mike shot her an impatient glance as he hopped into the passenger side of the car.

"You're late."

"Only a couple of minutes," Maggie hedged, and put the car in reverse when his door was shut.

"Dad said I should set all our clocks ahead an hour and then you'd be on time."

She felt a surge of anger at the unrequested suggestion, but squelched it.

"I haven't been doing too badly."

Luckily there was little traffic to slow her up. Several other parents were just arriving with their children when she reached the ball park.

There was a faint smugness to the smile she gave Mike.

"See? You aren't the last one here." She stopped the car at the curb so he could get out.

He stood outside by the door. "Aren't you going to watch me play?"

"You said the game didn't start until five. I'm going home to change my clothes, then come back. This out-fit—" Maggie touched the ivory material of her skirt and its matching top "—isn't what I want to wear if I have to sit in those dirty bleachers."

"Okay. See you later."

And Mike dashed off to where his team was congregating.

Maggie smiled wryly as she drove the car away from the curb.

At least he hadn't cautioned her not to be late. There were times when she wondered who was the parent and who was the child!

Parking the dark green compact in the driveway, she climbed out of the car and dug into her purse for the house key.

She unlocked the front door and held it open with her foot as she took the mail out of the box.

Once inside, she let the door shut on its own and walked into the living room.

She sifted quickly through the mail as she went, kicking her shoes off and letting her bag slide from her shoulder onto a chair.

Halfway to her bedroom, the doorbell rang.

Doing an about-face, Maggie walked back to answer it.

With a brief glance at her wristwatch, she opened the door and stopped dead.

It was Wade, and her heart fluttered madly against her ribs.

She had forgotten how overpowering he could be at close quarters.

Not because of his height, although he was tall. Her forehead came to the point of his chin and no higher. Nor because of his bulk, since his brawny shoulders

42

and chest were in proportion to his frame. His hands were large and his fingers long, easily capable of spanning her waist.

No, the sensation was all wrapped up in the sheer force of his presence.

The years had made few changes, adding character lines to his sun- and snow-browned face. They hadn't blunted the angular thrust of his jaw nor softened his square chin.

There was a closed look to his Celtic black eyes, although the shutters could be thrown open at any time and they would be alive with expression.

The background of Alaska suited Wade, a land raw and untamed, demanding a man capable of compromising with the elements.

It required intelligence, keen insight, and a large measure of self-confidence.

Yet these were the very traits needed to succeed in a so-called civilized society. Wade could slip in or out of either world at will.

All these things were assimilated with the lightning swiftness of the mind.

Then Maggie noticed Wade had cocked his head slightly to one side.

She realized she had been staring and hadn't spoken a word of greeting.

The day's mail was still in her hand. She stood in her stockinged feet, her titian hair windblown, her makeup fading. Again Wade had appeared when she was less than her best.

She managed to curb part of the rush of irritation, but some of it slipped through to make her voice curt.

"Mike isn't here. He has a Little League ball game tonight."

"Aren't you going to watch him play? Children like to have their parents there, cheering them on."

Maggie bristled. "What is this? Are you trying to insinuate that I'm not a good mother to Mike? That I'm somehow neglecting him?"

"I merely asked a question." Wade elevated a dark brow. "I can't control the way your conscience interprets it."

"My conscience?" Maggie breathed in sharply at the inference of guilt. "What about yours? I've attended every function Mike has participated in. Can you say the same?"

"I never said that I could."

"Before you start throwing stones, you'd better check to see if your windows have shatterproof glass," she warned.

"I wasn't throwing stones. I asked a question that you still haven't answered."

"As a matter of fact, I am going to watch him play. I came home to change my clothes first. The game starts at five—" Maggie glanced at her watch, the seconds ticking away "—so I don't have time to argue with you.

"Instead of being so concerned about me, why don't you fulfill your duty as Mike's father and go to the game? It would be quite a novelty to Mike to have his father there for once."

"I've been planning to go to the game ever since Mike mentioned it to me yesterday."

"Then what are you doing here? Oh, of course, you don't know where the game is being played, do you?"

Sarcasm crept into her voice. She stepped onto the threshold to point out the direction, her arm brushing his shoulder.

"You go down to this next corner and turn—"

"I know where the ball park is," Wade interrupted.

"What's the point of coming here, then?" Maggie stepped back, the brief contact jolting through her like the charge of a lightning bolt.

"If it was just to make sure that I was going, you've wasted your time and mine."

"I wanted to speak to you privately, although preferably not on the doorstep."

He pointedly drew attention to the fact that she had not invited him in.

A different sort of tension raced through her nerve ends. "I can't think of a single thing we need to discuss, in private or otherwise."

"Mike."

Wade supplied the subject.

"Mike?"

Maggie stiffened. "He's doing just fine. He's healthy and active, as normal as any boy his age. Unless—" her worst fears surfaced "—you intend to sue for custody of him. I'll fight that, Wade. You won't take my son away from me.

"There isn't anything you could say that would persuade me differently."

His mouth quirked in a humorless smile.

"I wouldn't try. That would be like trying to take a cub away from a tigress. You can sheathe your claws, Maggie. I have no intention of trying to get custody of Mike."

She was confused, and still wary.

"Then why—"

"It's in Mike's interest that I want to speak to you. May I come in?"

He smiled a slow smile that melted most of her resistance despite her better judgment.

After a moment's hesitation she swung the door open wider and backed away from the opening to admit him.

With a briskness she was far from feeling she walked into the living room, pausing to pick up her discarded shoes and bag and set the mail on the coffee table.

She didn't glance at Wade, although all of her senses were aware that he had followed her after closing the door.

A glance at her watch showed that she was running out of time. "Your discussion is going to have to wait." Maggie wasn't sorry.

She needed a few minutes alone to collect her wits before engaging in any conversation with Wade. "I have to change my clothes. It won't take long. If you want something to drink while you're waiting there's beer, Coke, and iced tea in the refrigerator and instant coffee in the cupboard. Help yourself."

All of that was issued over her shoulder as she walked across the living room toward her bedroom. Wade's refusal drifted after her.

"No, thanks, I don't care for anything."

"Suit yourself." She wasn't going to force any refreshment on him . . . or serve him.

She ducked into the hallway, sparing a moment of gratitude that the living room was in order and not strewn with Mike's things, or hers. Tossing her shoes and bag on the bed, she walked to the closet and began rummaging through the hangers for a pair of slacks.

Wade's statement kept running through her mind. He wanted to speak to her about something that was in Mike's interest, yet it had nothing to do with custody.

What could it be? School? Perhaps a private one? Not a boarding school—she would never agree to that. If it didn't have to do with his education, what did that leave?

Maggie was at a loss to come up with an alternative idea.

CHAPTER FOUR

A SOUND IN THE HALLWAY caused her to turn around and her pulse rocketed in alarm at the sight of Wade lounging in the doorway, dark and innately powerful like a predatory beast.

She pivoted back to the closet, grabbing the first slack hanger her fingers touched.

Anger had always been her best defense against his subtle domination.

"I told you I wouldn't be long."

"Don't forget I was married to you." He straightened from the door jamb and wandered into the room. "I know how *long* it can take you to dress. Long becomes a relative term. When you say you won't be long, I always wonder, compared to what?"

His blandness bordered on indifference, yet his criticism irked Maggie. "I never claimed to be as speedy or punctual as you. I doubt if anyone can meet your standards."

She glanced at the blue plaid slacks in her hand and began searching through the closet for a coordinating blouse.

"What is this?"

At his question, Maggie looked over her shoulder. He was pulling out the old robe she had stuffed in the wastebasket. There was a hint of mockery in the ebony depths of his eyes.

"You know very well what that is . . . and why it's there!"

She yanked a pale blue blouse from its hanger. The color intensified the green of her eyes, glittering with irritation.

With her change of clothes in hand, Maggie stalked angrily to the bed.

"I promised Mike I would apologize to you for that outburst yesterday, but I don't think I can ever forgive you for showing up unannounced like that. If you knew how much trouble I went to trying to be sure the house was clean, going to the beauty parlor, and buying a new outfit, and you find me looking like something out of a comic strip. It wasn't fair!"

"So in a burst of temper you threw Old Faithful away." Wade gave the quilted robe a considering study. "It has seen some better days."

For a moment Maggie was silenced by the fact that Wade had recognized her favorite robe, even to the point of recalling the name she had given it. She mentally shook away the feeling of surprised pleasure. So he had a good memory. What did it matter?

"Yes, I threw it away."

Her admission was callously indifferent to the memories attached to the garment. "I have a beautiful new robe in the closet. If I'd been wearing that, at least I wouldn't have looked quite so awful."

"I've seen you looking worse." He let the robe fall back into the wastebasket.

"That isn't any consolation!" Maggie snapped.

"Remember the Sunday we went looking at boats and you fell off the dock into the water?" Wade recalled with a husky laugh. "I think you were wearing a new dress."

"I didn't fall!"

Maggie slipped out of the ivory top and tossed it angrily on the bed. With jerky movements she began unbuttoning her blouse.

"My heel hooked in one of the boards and I lost my balance. I don't recall getting any assistance from you. You just stood there laughing!"

"What could I do? I was holding Mike. Good thing, too, or you'd have drowned him." He was still chuckling, maliciously, Maggie thought. "God, you were a sight! Water dripping from everywhere, your hair looking like a red floor mop."

"I didn't think it was funny then! And I don't think it's funny now!"

Impatiently she tugged at the buttons on the cuffs of her sleeves, finally freeing them and shrugging out of the blouse.

It joined the crumpled heap of her top.

"Your sense of humor was missing when you waded ashore. As I recall, you did a slow boil all the way home. We had one whale of an argument when we did get back."

"And you slammed out of the house and didn't come back until after midnight," Maggie reminded him.

"Yes." The faint smile left his mouth. "Our fights always ended one of two ways—either me slamming out of the house, or right here in this bedroom."

"Most of the time you were slamming out of the house."

The waistband of her skirt fastened behind. She managed the button, but in her agitation she caught the zipper in the material of her skirt, then in the silk of her slip.

"Damn!" she whispered in an angry breath.

"No, most of the time the arguments ended in the bedroom," Wade corrected her statement. He saw the difficulty she was having with the zipper. "I'll fix it for you. The way you're going at it, you're going to break the zipper."

Before Maggie could object or agree, he was pushing her hands out of the way.

The touch of his fingers against her spine brought instant acquiescence as a whole series of disturbing sensations splintered through her.

The warmth of his breath trailed lightly over the bareness of her shoulders, his head bent to his task. The musky fragrance of his cologne wafted in the air, elusive and heady.

From the corner of her eye Maggie could see the glistening blackness of his hair and experienced a desire to slide her fingers into its thickness.

His physical attraction was compelling. She was on dangerous ground.

She wished she had objected to his presence in her bedroom, or steered the conversation away from how their arguments had often ended. It aroused intimate memories it was better to forget.

There was a slight tug and her skirt zipper slid freely. In proportion to its downward slide, her pulse went up. There was a crazy weakness in her knees, muscles tightening in the pit of her stomach.

"There you are, with no damage." His hand rested

51

lightly on her hip, momentarily holding the skirt up. Maggie couldn't move, couldn't breathe. "I had forgotten how little there is to you."

In a thoughtfully quiet voice, Wade referred to the slightness of her build and how easily his hands could span her waist.

Maggie searched for a quick retort, saying the first thing that came to mind in order to deny that his touch was disturbing her.

"There was always enough of me to satisfy you," she insisted with a husky tremor, and immediately wanted to bite her tongue.

"Yes."

His hand slid to her waist to turn her around, releasing the skirt and letting it fall around her ankles. "There was always more than enough of you to satisfy me, wasn't there?"

Both hands rested on her waist, sliding up to her rib cage. The silk of her slip acted like a second skin, the imprint of his hand burning through.

The smoldering light in his eyes stole the breath from her lungs.

"And you received an ample share of satisfaction, too," he added.

That look awakened all the sleeping desires that had lain dormant.

As his mouth descended toward hers, Maggie trembled.

Would his kiss be the same? Could it still spark the blazing flame of her passion?

Curiosity and familiarity overpowered any thought of protest. She was caught up in the sweeping tide of the past when kissing Wade had been as natural as arguing with him.

Her lips yielded to the possessive pressure of his kiss. That same fiery glow spread through her, hot and brilliant.

His grip on her tightened, threatening to crack her ribs, as if he, too, experienced the same glorious reaction. Her arms glided slowly around his neck, her fingers seeking the sensuous thickness of his hair.

The sweetly pagan song in her ears was the wild drumming of her heart while the heat coursing through her veins turned her bones to liquid. Her slender curves fitted themselves to the hard contours of his length, firing her senses with ecstasy.

There had never been any lack of skill in Wade's lovemaking before, but it was better now. More wonderful. More destroying.

Because now that Maggie had been without that special thrill for these past years, she realized the worth of what she had lost. Having lost it, it was even more beautiful to find it again.

His kisses were like rare wine, and they went to her head. She was spinning away into a rose-colored dreamworld where only the crush of his hands and mouth held any reality.

Then the kiss was ending, before her hunger was satisfied.

Wade was lifting his head, staring deeply into her slowly opening eyes, which were as yet unwilling to return to the present.

Gradually her vision focused on the frown darkening his face.

"Old habits die hard, don't they?" he mused with a trace of cynicism.

His hands were still supporting her passion-limp body. A flurry of new questions raced through her dazed brain. The fresh memory of his kiss wiped away others that dealt with the bitterness and anger of their divorce. She wondered if she had deliberately blocked out the good times of their marriage, needing to remember the bad to keep from missing Wade.

He had said that he wanted to speak to her about something in Mike's interest. An entirely new possibility presented itself to her. After that shattering kiss, could it be that he was going to propose a reconciliation between them?

Yesterday Maggie would have found the suggestion appalling and rejected it out of hand.

Now . . . . Now, the idea filled her with hope, cloud-touching hope.

Suddenly she had to know.

"Why, Wade?" There was an aching tightness in her throat. "Why are you here? Why did you want to see me?"

He let go of her and pulled her arms from around his neck. A muscle twitched along his jaw, constricting in sudden tension.

Not until all physical contact between them had been broken did he answer her question.

"I came to tell you that I'm getting married again." Maggie went white with shock, but Wade was already walking toward the door and didn't see her reaction. "I think I'll take you up on that offer of a drink while you finish changing."

He disappeared into the hallway.

She thought she was going to be violently sick. That announcement had never occurred to her. To be truthful, she had never considered the possibility that Wade would remarry.

Although why she hadn't, she didn't know. That supremely male aura of his had always drawn women. Besides that, he was eligible and successful. Those two reasons alone were sufficient cause for many women to want him.

Hysterical laughter welled in her throat, and she jammed a fist into her mouth to choke it back. It was all so pathetically funny! She had thought he might want to come back to her.

How arrogantly stupid! Physical desire hadn't been able to keep their marriage afloat before.

What had ever made her think it would bring them back together?

Thank God that pride had kept her silent, demanding his reasons before stating her desire. Imagine the humiliation if she had told him what she felt.

Maggie moaned and buried her face in her hands. She wanted to rush over and shut the door, close out the fact of Wade's announcement until she had the strength to cope with it, to face and accept it. But it couldn't be done.

There wasn't time to pull her scattered feelings together. He was waiting for her.

"Old habits die hard," Wade had said after he had kissed her. Maggie knew that was how she had to regard it.

A kiss between two ex-lovers who had found themselves in familiar positions on familiar grounds. The kiss had been a natural progression of events, but without the meaning it had held in the past—at least, not on Wade's part.

In a numbed state, Maggie finished changing her clothes.

She added a brush of shadow and mascara to her eyes and a coating of tinted gloss to her lips, a splash of color in her otherwise pale face.

She ran a quick comb through her flame red hair. Drawing deeply on her reserve strength, she walked out of the bedroom to rejoin Wade.

He wasn't in the living room. She continued through the dining room into the kitchen.

He was standing at the counter, turning when she entered, a glass in his hand.

"I decided I needed something stronger than beer." He lifted the glass, a lone ice cube clinking against the side, amber liquid covering the bottom.

On the counter behind him, Maggie saw the opened bottle of Scotch.

Wade caught her glance. "You still keep it in the same place—behind the flour canister."

"Yes." Was that raspy sound her voice?

"Do you want me to pour you a drink?"

"No."

God, no! Maggie thought vehemently.

As wretched as she felt, one drink wouldn't be enough. She'd want to drown herself in the oblivion of alcohol and it would probably take more than one bottle to dull the pain.

"I'd rather have coffee, thanks."

Walking to the sink, she partially filled a saucepan with hot water and put it on the stove.

Then she reached into the cupboard and took out the jar of instant coffee.

Normally she disliked it, but she kept it on hand for mornings that she overslept and didn't have time to make coffee in her percolator. Now, she realized she was using it for a different kind of emergency as she spooned the brown crystals into a cup along with three teaspoons of sugar.

"You never used to sweeten your coffee," Wade observed.

His memory was much too good.

"It's the only way I can stand drinking instant coffee," Maggie lied.

In actual fact, she had heard that black, sweetened coffee was good for shock, and at the moment she felt numbed to the bone.

CHAPTER FIVE

SHE FELT THE PENETRATION of his gaze between her shoulder blades, but she hadn't yet the composure to face him squarely.

There was an indefinable tension in the air, even a second's silence hanging heavy. Bubbles formed quickly in the pan of water on the stove. Maggie removed it from the burner before it came to a boil and poured the steaming water into her cup.

As she stirred the coffee, she took a deep breath and exhaled the words, "So you're going to get married. It looks as if congratulations are in order, then."

Although she turned to lean her hips against the counter, she again avoided directly meeting his steady gaze, holding the cup in one hand and continuing to stir the coffee with the other.

"We agreed five . . . six years ago to seek our happiness elsewhere."

"It was obviously the right decision, wasn't it?" Maggie countered, much too brightly. "I mean, you've found someone else. She must make you happy or you wouldn't be planning to marry her."

"That's right."

There was a certain grimness in his answer as he lifted his glass to his mouth.

But the admission brought a sharp, stabbing pain in the region of Maggie's heart. It glittered briefly in her jewel green eyes before she lowered her lashes to conceal the reaction.

"Who's the lucky girl?"

Maggie sipped at the coffee and nearly scalded her tongue.

"Her name is Belinda Hale."

"Belinda," Maggie repeated, and lied, "that's a pretty name. Is she from Alaska?"

"No, from Seattle, but I met her while she was visiting some friends in Anchorage."

"It sounds like a whirlwind courtship." As theirs had been. She couldn't help questioning dryly, "Is that wise?"

"Don't worry—" there was a wry twist to his mouth as he swirled the liquor in his glass "—I don't intend to make the same mistake twice. I've known Belinda for over a year now."

"Oh. Well, I'm glad." The coffee had cooled sufficiently for her to drink, but Maggie nearly gagged on the sweetness. "I understand that you're doing quite well. Mike mentioned something about you getting a promotion."

"Yes, I'm a vice-president in the firm now. I have total charge of the Alaskan operation, pipeline, terminals, new drillings, everything."

He explained with no attempt to boast or impress Maggie with his importance.

It had always seemed foredestined to Maggie that such a thing would happen.

Wade had always enjoyed challenges and responsibilities.

59

Since he was aggressive and ambitious, as well, it was a natural outcome of his efforts.

"Your fiancée must be very proud of you. Of course, being the wife of an executive isn't an easy job. I hope your Belinda is up to the task." She couldn't care less. In fact, part of her hoped his new wife would prove inadequate.

The jealous part of her.

"Belinda is well versed in the role of an executive's wife. Her father is chairman of the board."

Her eyes widened at the announcement, the bitterness of sarcasm coating her tongue. "How convenient. Did your vice-presidency come before or after you put the diamond on her finger?"

Black anger burned in his gaze. "The promotion came a year ago. It was at a cocktail party celebrating my new office that I met Belinda for the first time. I'm not attempting to marry into power. I stand or fall on my own ability."

"Sorry, that was a cheap shot," admitted Maggie. She took another sip of the heavily sweetened coffee and began to feel its bracing effect.

"I do wish you every happiness, Wade. You know that." In a more rational moment, she would mean it very sincerely, even if the words did stick in her throat now.

"I didn't come here this afternoon to obtain your blessing." His voice was mockingly dry. "If all I wanted to do was inform you of my coming marriage, I could have accomplished that with a long-distance phone call from Alaska."

Maggie stiffened, resenting his implied criticism.

"Why are you here?" Then she remembered. "You said you wanted to speak to me about Mike."

"Yes. I haven't told him yet that I'm getting married again."

Her interrupting laugh was short and bitterly incredulous.

"I hope you aren't planning to ask me to tell him."

"No. I'm telling you first because I want your support. I know it won't be easy for Mike to accept the fact that I'm marrying another woman.

"From some of the things he's said, I know he isn't going to welcome having a stepmother," Wade corrected her in a clipped, precise tone.

"And how am I supposed to change that?" she demanded.

Didn't he realize it was going to be difficult for *her* to adjust to the fact that he was getting married to someone else?

"By remaining calm. And, for once, not reacting emotionally."

"You've never been able to accept the fact that I'm an emotional person!" Maggie accused.

"I've accepted it. I've just chosen not to live in your tempestuous teapot."

Maggie turned away. That remark had hit below the belt.

She took a large swallow of coffee. "That was unnecessary, Wade," she said tightly.

"Yes," he sighed heavily, "it was. Look, Maggie, we've managed to have a fairly civil relationship since our divorce, and I don't want my marriage to change that. Maybe I'm asking too much, but I'd like you to extend the same distantly friendly terms to Belinda. For Mike's sake, I think it would be best."

"Oh, yes, the four of us can be just one great big happy family."

She mocked his ludicrous suggestion.

"Don't exaggerate," Wade snapped. "I'm not suggesting anything of the kind."

Maggie pivoted around to challenge him. "What are you suggesting?"

"That you provide some moral and physical support for my marriage," he explained with considerable exasperation.

"What do you want me to do? Walk down the aisle with you and give you away?" she quipped, hiding behind a black wit to conceal the pain of this conversation.

"Don't be flippant."

"Well, I'm sorry."

She wasn't. "But I don't know what you expect me to do. I have no intention of interfering with your marriage in any way. As for Mike, I'll encourage him to welcome your bride into the family. I don't see how I can do more than that. And I doubt if your Belinda would like it if I interfered more than that in your personal life."

Wade shook his head and downed the rest of his drink. "One thing is certain—" he set the glass down hard on the counter, his control stretching thin "—Belinda is a hell of a lot more open-minded than you are."

"I suppose you've discussed me with her." That thought didn't set well. "As well as all my little shortcomings."

"Naturally I discussed with her my first marriage and

our incompatibility, but I didn't go into detail. Belinda is an intelligent and sensible young woman.''

''And I don't possess either of those qualities.'' Maggie stated what she felt he had implied.

The line of his jaw hardened. ''I didn't say that.''

''No, you didn't have to.''

''Once you meet Belinda, I know you'd like her if you would let yourself—'' there was undisguised irritation in his voice and the glittering black of his eyes ''—and not become jealous.''

''Jealous! I would never be jealous of your new bride!'' The denial leaped angrily from her throat. ''Don't forget I divorced you because I didn't want you anymore.''

It was lies, all lies. Maggie knew she still wanted him, and probably had ever since their divorce. Only she hadn't permitted herself to admit it. Subconsciously she had compared every man she met with Wade, and they had all been lacking.

Moreover, if his darling Belinda were in the room at this minute, Maggie would be physically or verbally clawing at the woman like a jealous cat.

It angered her that Wade had been so accurate in guessing that.

''Don't pretend you won't be jealous. It's a normal reaction for anyone whose former mate remarries.'' Wade swept aside her denial with swift, slicing strokes, the precise cutting thrusts of a rapier striking coldly and ruthlessly. ''It's a natural emotion to feel under the circumstances.''

''Don't be so damned logical!'' Maggie turned and set her cup so violently on the kitchen counter that it overturned.

In agitation she grabbed for the dishcloth and wiped up the spill.

As she started to throw it angrily into the sink, Wade's hand closed around her upper arm to check the display of temper. His grip was firm, yet controlled to imply gentle rebuke.

"One of us has to be," he said. "I was hoping both of us could be logical about this."

Maggie jerked away from his hold, rejecting his impersonal touch.

"How dare you suggest that I haven't been?"

Her eyes were blazing with green fires, the toss of her head making her hair ripple like liquid flame around her shoulders.

"I'm more than aware that you're free and can remarry or not, as it suits you. I've even offered you my congratulations and wished you every happiness with your soon-to-be bride.

"As for Mike, I've even agreed to help him become adjusted to the fact that he'll not only have a mother but a stepmother, as well. What more do you expect from me? Should I throw an engagement party for you?"

There was a flashing glimpse of the thinning line of his mouth before he was turning his back to her, his hands on his hips.

Maggie sensed rather than saw the control he was exercising over his own temper.

He shook his head and emitted a sardonic silent laugh. "I'd forgotten how easily you can rile me. When we weren't making love, we were fighting, weren't we? Did we ever share a peaceful moment together?"

The embittered question deflated Maggie's anger. The stiffness of defiance and challenge left her shoulders and spine, and she felt the sagging weight of defeat. Tears stung her eyes, acid and burning.

"Of course we did . . . in the beginning." But she didn't want to talk about that.

At the moment, the memories of that time were too poignant and too vivid. "When are you planning to marry? You haven't said."

"Soon. Within the month."

Her mouth dropped open.

She had expected his response to be autumn or Christmas, not a date that could be measured in days instead of weeks or months.

The pain of loss splintered through her, followed by a thankfulness that he hadn't seen her reaction to the announcement.

"That isn't much time," she recovered to say. "You're practically presenting Mike with an accomplished fact." But it wasn't Mike she was thinking about, it was herself. "You should have told him sooner, let him know there was someone you were seriously interested in."

"How?" Wade glanced over his shoulder, his mouth twisting in a cynical line. "In a letter? Over the telephone? No, that's too impersonal for something that's so important in his life. I wanted us to be face to face when I told him.

"And I wanted him to meet Belinda, get to know her before the wedding. I couldn't do that from Alaska."

"You shouldn't have waited so long," Maggie persisted in the thought.

"Unfortunately I couldn't get away before now. I considered having Mike visit me, but I knew he would want you around once he learned I was engaged. I did the best I could to arrange to spend this time with him before the wedding. As it is, our honeymoon is going to have to be postponed. But Belinda is very understanding about that.''

''She sounds like a paragon of virtue,'' Maggie muttered sarcastically. She simply couldn't help disliking his bride-to-be.

Wade shot her a piercing look before glancing at the heavy gold watch on his wrist. ''Speaking of time, Mike's ball game started ten minutes ago. My car is outside. Do you want to ride with me? There's no point in taking two cars.''

''No, thanks, I prefer to drive my own. Besides, it will save you having to make the trip back here after the game,'' she refused his offer briskly.

Common sense told her that it was better if she didn't spend too much time alone in his company. The time would be too bittersweet.

CHAPTER SIX

A SILVER GRAY MERCEDES was parked in the driveway behind her small car, the luxury model a sharp contrast to Maggie's economy one. She eyed the Mercedes somewhat resentfully.

It seemed to emphasize the chasm that gaped between them. They were poles apart, as they always had been.

"Your company is generous to it executives, furnishing them with a car like that," she remarked dryly as she walked ahead of Wade to the driveway.

"It isn't a company car. It belongs to Belinda," Wade corrected. "Since I was without transportation, she offered me the use of hers."

"What's she driving, then? Her father's Rolls-Royce?"

Maggie sounded catty and she knew it.

It wasn't that she envied the obvious wealth of Belinda's family.

On the contrary, she envied the woman because she would soon have Wade, something all the money in the world couldn't buy.

"She's probably driving her mother's Rolls." His mouth quirked briefly in a mocking smile that didn't make Maggie proud of her remark.

She tried to change the subject. ''At which hotel are you staying? In case there's an emergency and I need to reach you,'' she tacked on so he wouldn't think she was asking for a personal reason.

''I'm staying with the Hales in their home, not a hotel,'' Wade corrected her with a glint of amusement in his dark eyes.

''Oh.''

How foolish of her to have fallen into that! Where else would a prospective son-in-law stay but in the home of his fiancée's parents? Maggie tried not to think how much time that gave him to spend in Belinda's company.

Their paths diverged as they walked to their respective cars.

Maggie's was closest, so she reached hers first and had to wait until Wade had reversed out of the driveway into the street. Jealousy was a demeaning emotion, she realized as she followed the silver Mercedes to the ball park.

Mike's team was at bat when they arrived. Wade waited to walk with Maggie to the bleachers, occupied by only a scattering of other parents. The rest of the boys on the bench with Mike were shouting encouragement to their teammate at bat.

Mike watched him but was silent, a faintly disappointed expression on his face. His gaze strayed to the bleachers.

When he saw Maggie, and a second later Wade, he immediately broke into a wide smile and waved. Maggie returned the salute as she sat down on the second row of the bleacher seats.

Excitedly Mike poked his teammates and pointed to his parents in the stands.

With all the emptiness in the bleachers, Maggie wished Wade had sat somewhere else other than beside her. It was natural that he would, though.

After all, they were both there to see Mike play. He was their son. Not even Wade's approaching marriage changed that.

At the end of the inning Mike dashed to the protective mesh fence near where Maggie and Wade sat. The rest of his teammates were taking the field.

"Hi!" His shining dark eyes gazed at the two people he loved most in the world. "You're late."

"My fault," Wade took the blame.

"I had something to discuss with your mother and we lost track of time."

"That's all right."

Mike shrugged away the explanation as unnecessary now that they were here. Glancing over his shoulder at the ball field, he added a hurried, "I gotta go. I'm playing first base." He raced to join his teammates and take his position.

"You do it, too," Maggie murmured. She caught the lift of a black eyebrow in question and explained, "Mike gets upset when I say your father and keeps insisting you have a name. You just said 'your mother.'"

Wade paused.

"It's easier."

"Yes, I know," she responded quietly.

Their gazes locked for a long span of seconds, each knowing why they wanted to forget the first-name intimacy in referring to the other. It kept the memory of their once shared love at bay. Just for that moment, they remembered it together.

Maggie felt the tugging of her heartstrings. Her heart hadn't forgotten that song of savage ecstasy, not a single note of it. Had Wade?

He turned to watch the game before Maggie could find the answer in his dark eyes.

She chided herself for being so foolish. What did it matter if he did remember? He had found another woman whose love played a sweeter melody, and he was marrying her.

It was best if Maggie's heart forgot the love song.

The ball game was close, but in the end Mike's team lost.

In contrast to the marked jubilation of the winning team, there was noticeable silence among Mike's teammates.

The corners of Mike's mouth were drooping and his shoulders were slumped by the defeat as Maggie and Wade walked around the wire fence to the team bench.

"It was a good game," Maggie offered in consolation.

"We could have won," Mike grumbled, "if I hadn't struck out every time I was at bat."

Tom Darby approached as the last, defeated words were spoken. He smiled briefly at Maggie before clamping a hand on Mike's shoulder.

The coach was as handsome as Maggie remembered, but he stood in Wade's shadow—as every man would, she suspected.

"You'll have to work harder at batting practice, Mike, so you can change that," he said. "But you did a very good job at first base. If it hadn't been for you there, the other team might have scored higher."

The words of praise bolstered Mike's spirits and he managed a smile. "At least they didn't clobber us, did they, coach?"

"They sure didn't," Tom agreed, smiling down at the baseball-capped boy.

He glanced at Maggie. "Mike played a good game. All the boys did." His gaze strayed to Wade, swift and assessing in its sweep of him, as if measuring the strength of his competition.

Mike caught the look, as Maggie had, and quickly supplied the information.

"This is my dad," he declared with a considerable amount of pride.

In the blink of an eye, Tom's startled gaze darted from Maggie's face to the ringless fingers of her left hand. Then his surprise was hidden by a mask of professionalism as he extended a hand to Wade.

"How do you do, Mr. Rafferty. I'm Tom Darby," he introduced himself.

Maggie stole a sideways glance at Wade as the two men shook hands.

She saw the aloofness in Wade's expression, his dark eyes so cool and withdrawn. Yet behind that chilling veil of indifference they were just as sharp and assessing as Tom's had been.

"It's a rare treat for Mike to have his father attending one of his games," Maggie heard herself saying. "You see, his father works in Alaska and is only here on a short vacation."

She realized she was talking about Wade as if he weren't standing there beside her, but she couldn't seem to stop herself.

Her explanation brought a cloud of confusion to Tom's hazel eyes. Maggie cleared that up with an abrupt, "We're divorced."

There was a moment of awkward silence in which Maggie silently cursed her tactless announcement. Why had she done it so bluntly?

To prove something to Wade? Was it her pride trying to show how eager she was to disassociate herself from him so Wade wouldn't know how his coming marriage hurt?

"Don't mind her," Wade inserted dryly. "She's always said exactly what was on her mind. One of the reasons I married her was because she was so refreshingly honest. After a few years it became one of her irritating traits."

The way he put it sounded like a joke and Tom laughed, but Maggie knew there was more than a measure of truth in it.

She felt the stinging accuracy of his arrow, but forced a smile onto her face as if Wade had said something witty.

"If you have no objections," Tom began, "I thought I'd treat the boys to some ice cream before they go home. Parents are more than welcome to come along."

"Will you?" Mike asked eagerly, wanting to be with his father yet wanting to be with his teammates, and hoping Wade would say yes so the two pleasures could be combined.

"Of course," Wade agreed, a slow smile spreading across his darkly tanned face.

It only took a second for Maggie to consider her answer.

"Not me," she refused.

72

She didn't want to spend any more time with Wade, certainly not with the complication of Tom Darby around.

She wanted time to be alone and think, to come to grips with the fact that Wade was getting married. "I have some housework to do." She turned to Wade. "You will bring Mike home afterward, won't you?" At his nod, she glanced at Mike. "Have a good time."

"I will."

He was sorry, but not disappointed that she wasn't coming. Why should he be when he saw her virtually every day and his father so seldom?

"I'll see you, Maggie."

Tom's goodbye sounded like a promise, now that he was assured she was free.

"Yes. Goodbye, Tom."

It was only when she was in her car on the way back to the house that Maggie wondered whether Wade had noticed how easily she had used Tom's name.

She supposed he had. Nothing escaped Wade's notice for long. What had he thought? Especially in view of the fact that Tom hadn't been aware she was divorced until now.

Sighing, Maggie shook away such questions. Wade couldn't care less.

His only interest in her was as the mother of his child. Any interest in her private life stopped there. He was getting married; that was still a difficult thing to accept.

There was housework to do.

Also, Maggie hadn't eaten. A cold sandwich and a helping of cottage cheese were singularly unappetizing, but she forced herself to eat them. She washed the dishes and put them away—not that there were many to do, a couple of juice glasses and cereal bowl from this morning, a plate from tonight, and the cup from her instant coffee and Wade's glass.

With the dishes done, she had eliminated all trace of Wade from the kitchen, but she couldn't banish his specter from the rest of the house, especially the bedroom. She found herself glancing out the windows for a glimpse of the silver Mercedes bringing Mike home. The telephone rang and she answered it impatiently.

"Is Wade there?" It was a feminine voice on the other end of the line.

A chilling portent shivered through her. "No, he isn't. Who's calling, please?" She knew what the answer would be.

"This is Belinda Hale. Are you . . . Maggie?" the polite but falsely friendly voice inquired.

"Yes, I am."

She was stiff, on guard, disliking intensely the cultured, musically pitched voice in her ear.

"Has Wade . . . mentioned anything to you about me?"

Again there was an infinitesimal pause, calculated to be secretive.

"About your engagement? Yes, he has, Miss Hale. Congratulations." Her teeth were grinding against each other, but Maggie was determined not to sound like a bitchy ex-wife.

She would be pleasant and nice, even if it killed her.

"Thank you," Belinda answered, so very graciously that it grated. "Wade had said he was going to speak to

74

you about us before he told Michael. But I wasn't certain if he'd had an opportunity.

"He also mentioned some baseball game or other that Michael was playing in, so I didn't know whether he'd talked to you privately yet."

"Yes, we spoke before the game started." Maggie's fingers tightened around the receiver.

If it had been the woman's throat, she would have been strangled by now.

As it was, there was little Maggie could do to silence her, short of hanging up.

Wade had said his future wife was blond. Hearing her voice, Maggie could almost picture her. Blond, probably with blue eyes, always wearing the right clothes with just the right amount of makeup, always poised and prepared for any contingency.

Wade would never find his Belinda with rollers in her hair, wearing an old bathrobe, on her hands and knees.

He had said Belinda was the opposite of Maggie, and listening to the cool, unflustered voice, Maggie believed it.

"Oh. Is the game over?" Belinda Hale asked smoothly, with the proper note of innocent surprise.

"Yes." Maggie's answer was curt.

"I imagine Wade is on his way home, then, and it was needless for me to call."

Maggie wondered if the other woman knew how stinging it was to hear Belinda's home referred to as Wade's. She decided it had been deliberate.

"As a matter of fact, I don't believe he is," she said with a trace of smugness.

"Oh?"

"Mike's coach is treating the team to some ice cream, and Wade went along. He promised to bring Mike home afterward. Shall I have him call you when he does?"

"Would you, please, if it isn't too much trouble?" So polite, so courteous, so pseudowarm. "One of my very dearest friends stopped by this evening. I'm hoping that Wade will come back in time to meet her."

"I'm sure he will if he can."

"Yes. Wade can be such a darling at times, and," Belinda added with a throaty laugh, "so infuriatingly stubborn at other times. But, of course, I don't need to tell you that. You were married to him."

Again Maggie felt the prick of a sharp blade, jabbing at her while her assailant smiled benignly. "Were married"—but no longer.

"Yes, I was married to him, but that was a long time ago."

It didn't seem that long. Maybe because it hadn't been very long since he'd held her in his arms and kissed her and all that old magic had come racing back, more potent than before.

"I really am looking forward to meeting you, Maggie. I know that must sound strange, but I do mean it. It's just that I don't see any reason for there to be any enmity between us. Obviously we aren't in competition for anything. Both you and Wade wanted the divorce. For Michael's sake I think it would be very important for us to be friends."

"I'm looking forward to meeting you, too, Belinda." There was a saccharine quality to her tone. For once, Maggie held her usually candid tongue and didn't voice

76

her opinion about becoming friends with Wade's future bride.

A suspicion was beginning to form. Openminded, Wade had described her. Almost ridiculously so, Maggie concluded.

Not for a minute did she believe a hand of friendship was being extended to her.

More than likely the gesture was part of Belinda's act to impress Wade with her unselfishness, her lack of jealousy and possessiveness.

While it cemented her relationship with Wade, it put Maggie on the defensive. If she rejected the attempt at friendliness by Belinda, Wade would view it as spite and ill temper on Maggie's part. The woman was clever, very clever.

"Wade has promised we'll meet sometime soon," Belinda informed her. "And I can hardly wait to meet Michael. Wade has talked about him so much that I almost feel I know him already.

"After Wade and I are married, I naturally want Michael to continue to visit us, just as he always has visited his father in the past."

"Mike has always enjoyed those visits," Maggie returned.

"You and I should get together for a private little chat. I want to learn what Michael's favorite foods are and the things he likes to do, his pet peeves, and so on."

The woman was determined to be the perfect wife *and* stepmother, Maggie decided. It was an admirable thing, unless all this interest was forced.

That was something difficult to judge over the telephone.

"Mike is a very normal boy, easier to please than most."

Maggie wasn't certain if she knew his favorite foods.

They tended to change with his mood and age. She knew his pet peeve—his mother's always being late. And it was one Maggie had no intention of relating to Mike's future stepmother.

"I'm certain he's a darling. Every photograph I've seen of him, Michael has had a striking resemblance to Wade."

"Yes, he has Wade's dark coloring," Maggie agreed. "His personality is very much his own, though."

"After Wade formally introduces us, we shall have to get together and have that little chat. You can sort of forewarn me about the things that irritate Michael . . . and Wade, for that matter.

"I don't mean any offense, but I don't want to make the same mistake you did in your marriage to Wade. Perhaps you can steer me right."

"I doubt very seriously that you would make the 'mistakes' I did," Maggie dryly answered the suggestion.

From the limited information she had been able to glean, Belinda didn't seem the type to let her emotions run away with her tongue, as Maggie was prone to do.

"I hope not." Belinda laughed, and again it was that practiced laugh that sounded in the throat, rich and husky like velvet. "But you probably do know more about Wade's darker side than I do. I'd be grateful for any tidbit you would want to share."

"Of course." Maggie couldn't tolerate any more of the phone conversation. "I'm sure you want to get back to your friend. I'll have Wade call as soon as he brings Mike home."

78

"Thank you, I do appreciate that. I hope I'll be talking to you again very soon, Maggie."

"Yes—me, too, Belinda," Maggie lied through her teeth, and waited until she heard the disconnecting click before she slammed the receiver onto its cradle out of sheer frustration and jealousy.

There was no solace in the fact that she hadn't lost her temper. All she felt was a growing sense of despair.

The only way to cope with the situation seemed to be to get through it with as much grace as possible, which wasn't one of her fortes, and to take each day after that as it came.

A CAR DOOR SLAMMED outside. Maggie guessed it was Wade bringing Mike back.

Remembering the last time when he had simply dropped Mike off and left, she was tempted not to go to the door and tell him about the telephone call he had received.

She had to, of course. She didn't want to be accused of being too mean to pass on messages from his fiancée.

Wade was just stepping out of the car when Maggie opened the front door. "There was a telephone call for you, Wade."

An absent frown creased his forehead. "Was there a message?"

Maggie hesitated for a fraction of a second, aware of Mike slowly making his way up the sidewalk to the house. "Miss Hale asked you to call her."

"May I use your phone?"

To call your fiancée? No! Maggie wanted to scream,

but she controlled the impulse and nodded. "Of course. Come in."

At that moment Mike ducked under her arm and slipped into the house. Automatically she prompted him, "Change out of your uniform into some everyday clothes."

"I will," was his desultory murmur.

Her nerves grew taut as Wade drew closer, his nearness vibrating them like a tuning fork when he walked past her into the house. She closed the door, fighting the weakness in her knees.

"You may use the extension in the kitchen if you'd like some privacy," she offered, but Wade was already walking toward the beige phone in the living room.

"It isn't necessary." He picked up the receiver and began dialing the number with an economy of movement. Maggie wanted to make herself scarce, but his indifference trapped her into listening to a one-sided conversation.

"This is Wade. I want to speak to Belinda," he said into the mouthpiece.

While he waited, his sharp gaze swerved to Maggie. "Did she say why she called?"

"Something about a friend she wanted you to meet." Her answer was deliberately vague.

His gaze narrowed briefly as if he sensed Maggie's resentment. Then his attention was diverted by a voice on the other end of the phone.

"Hello." He was returning a greeting, his voice intimately quiet.

A pain twisted through Maggie at the sensual softening of his mouth, almost into a smile. "Yes, she

80

did," Wade replied to a question put to him. "I'm here now—" he glanced at his watch "—about twenty minutes, depending on the traffic." With penetrating swiftness his gaze slashed back to Maggie. "You did? I'm glad."

There was a skeptically mocking lift of one eyebrow, and it didn't require much deduction for Maggie to guess they were talking about her. "Yes, I'll be there as soon as I can, darling."

Her fingers curled into her palms at the parting endearment. Waves of jealousy and envy washed through her, nearly swamping her control.

She turned her back to Wade, her stomach a churning ball.

"Belinda said she had a 'nice' conversation with you. The adjective was hers, not mine," Wade commented.

"What did you think I would do? Hang up on her?" Maggie snapped.

"I wouldn't have been surprised if you had," he countered dryly.

She spun around.

Her temper had been held in check too long, and it flared now as fiery as her red hair. "That was one thing I could always count on, wasn't it? Your unwavering support."

"You've never been known for your tact."

"Neither have you. But your darling Belinda is diplomatic enough to make up for it," Maggie declared with decidedly biting emphasis on his fiancée's name. "She sounds too good to be true. You'd better hang on to her."

"A compliment like that, coming from you, always makes me suspect it's an insult."

The remark was totally unfair because it was the closest Maggie had come to sincerity since she had learned of his approaching marriage.

She didn't like Belinda; she never would, but she didn't doubt that the woman was going to attempt to be all things to Wade.

"Did it ever occur to you that you're the only one who brings out the worst in me?" Maggie retorted in self-defense.

A nerve twitched convulsively in his jaw. "*I* bring out the worst in you?"

The ominous black of anger was in his eyes as he took a step closer.

Although intimidated, Maggie held her ground. "Then explain why you're still single. I don't see anybody beating a path to your door. From all that Mike has said, you date men very infrequently. Why? Because they know a shrew when they see one. I was too blind!"

"I have as many dates as I want, when I want them and with whom!

"After wiggling out from underneath your thumb, I value my freedom."

"No commitments, is that it?" He towered above her, male and dominating.

"That's it!"

"Men like Mike's coach must like that. You make it easy for them."

Maggie was trembling with rage.

"You above all people should know I'm not easy!" she hissed.

"No, you're not easy," Wade agreed, his hand shooting out to imprison her wrist and twisting it behind her back.

The sudden physical contact changed the volatile atmosphere to something as elemental as time eternal. Maggie was trapped by that searing desire and couldn't escape its velvet snare. The black coals of his eyes burned over her face, catching that breathless look of expectancy in her expression.

"I may have brought out the worst in you," he growled, "but I also brought out the best."

"Yes."

The admission crumpled some inner defense mechanism and Maggie's head dipped in defeat to rest against the solid wall of his chest. "I never meant to argue with you, Wade. How do we always manage to start shouting at each other?"

His hand released her wrist and hesitated on her back, his touch not quite a caress nor totally impersonal. All she wanted was for Wade to hold her in his arms for a little while.

But in the next second he was withdrawing his hands and walking away.

"I have no idea how any of our arguments have started."

The indifference of his tone said it didn't matter. His gaze was hooded when he glanced at her, the fires banked or out completely. "Belinda is waiting for me—I have to leave."

Her backbone stiffened. "Of course."

Wade started for the door and paused. "I was late bringing Mike because we stopped somewhere to talk. I told him about Belinda."

"What did he say?"

"Nothing. Not a word. He didn't say he was sorry or glad. He didn't ask when I was getting married. Nothing." Wade breathed in deeply. "Absolutely nothing."

"It was a shock."

She, too, had been speechless when Wade had first told her.

She'd had time to recover.

"I hadn't realized what a shock it would be," he murmured.

"I'll talk to him," said Maggie.

"Tell Mike I'll call him tomorrow afternoon. If it's nice, we'll go boating. I've arranged . . . oh, hell, what does that matter?" Long, impatient strides carried him to the door.

Without glancing back, he repeated, "I'll call him tomorrow."

The door slammed shut before Maggie could find her voice to acknowledge his statement. She stared into the emptiness of the room, still filled with the ghost of Wade's presence.

When the powerful engine of the Mercedes growled outside, she slowly turned toward the bedrooms of the house.

CHAPTER SEVEN

MIKE'S BEDROOM DOOR was closed. Maggie hesitated outside, then knocked once.

Silence was her only answer. She knocked again, more loudly the second time. Several seconds later she received a reluctant response.

"Yeah?"

"It's me. May I come in?" She waited, holding her breath, dreading these next few minutes probably as much as Mike was.

"Yeah."

Turning the doorknob, she pushed the door open and walked in.

Mike was lying on his bed, his hands behind his head, staring at the flat white of the ceiling. He was still dressed in his baseball uniform, the cap on his head, dirty tennis shoes on his feet.

He didn't glance at her.

"I thought you were going to change your clothes," Maggie reminded him.

"I forgot." Mike didn't make any move to correct the oversight.

Maggie didn't want to force the subject, not yet. She walked to the foot of the bed. "The uniform can wait, but these shoes have to go." She began untying the laces.

"You already know, don't you?"

His gaze ended its study of the ceiling to dart accusingly at her.

"If you mean do I know that your father is planning to get married—yes, I do." She kept her voice calm with effort. "He told me before the game. That's why we were late."

"Why? Why does he have to get married? Why can't things stay the way they are?" Mike protested.

"You don't want things to stay the way they are."

"Yes, I do!"

"If they did, you'd never be able to improve your hitting," she reasoned. "You'd never grow up. Everything changes, people, places and things. That's part of growing up. So is accepting those changes."

"He doesn't have to get married. You haven't."

"That doesn't mean I might not someday." She pulled off the tennis shoes and set them on the floor at the foot of his bed. "Your father has met someone he loves very much, so it's only natural that he would want to marry her."

"I don't care!"

"You want your father to be happy, don't you?"

"Getting married doesn't mean he's going to be happy. He was married to you and neither of you were happy," Mike reminded her, a low blow in Maggie's book.

"It isn't fair to assume that if your father and I weren't happy, neither will he be happy with his new wife. It isn't all that much of a change."

Maggie diverted the subject. "It only means there'll be a woman living all the time with your father. You might even like her after you meet her."

"Have you met her?" Mike wanted to know, skeptical.

"No."

"Do you think you're going to like her?"

"How do I know? I haven't met her." Maggie avoided the question, knowing that she, too, was already prejudiced against the woman.

"Dad says she's young and pretty. They might have kids of their own," he speculated. He stared again at the ceiling, eyes troubled and increasingly dark. "They'd be living with him all the time."

Maggie was beginning to understand some of Mike's uncertainties.

"Your father would continue to love you, no matter how many children he and his new wife might have." That, too, was a thought that didn't bring joy into her heart.

"Besides, when you go to visit him, you would have a brother or sister, or both, to play with. When they get older, you can teach them how to play baseball and things like that."

"Aw, mom, that's boring!"

"How do you know? It might be fun," she argued.

"I just wish he wasn't getting married."

"He is, so you might as well accept that." *So had I,* Maggie thought.

"I don't have to like it, though." There was a stubborn set to Mike's chin as he unclasped his hands from behind his head and sat up, curling his sock covered feet beneath him.

"No, you don't have to like it," Maggie agreed, "but you should keep an open mind about it. You haven't even met the woman your father wants to marry."

87

"Stop calling him that!"

Mike began unbuttoning the shirt of his baseball uniform, his head bent to the task.

"All right." Maggie accepted the reproval. "You haven't met the woman *Wade* wants to marry. You could like her. She might be a lot of fun."

If the impression Maggie had gained from the telephone conversation was accurate, with her poise and sophistication Belinda would not easily relate to a ten-year-old's idea of a person who is a lot of fun. There were enough negatives buzzing around in Mike's head without adding more.

"Why couldn't he marry you?" It was more a protest than a question.

Mike tugged his shirttail from the waistband of his pants.

"Because he loves somebody else. Besides, maybe I wouldn't want to marry him."

It was a tantalizing thought, one she didn't dare think about.

"You were fighting again, weren't you?" It was almost an accusation. "I heard you and dad talking, and you sounded angry."

Maggie wasn't certain how to handle that, so she decided to avoid it.

"Which reminds me, your fa—Wade said he would call you tomorrow afternoon. He mentioned something about going boating."

"Boating! Oh, wow! That's great!" Mike declared exuberantly, completely diverted from his previous subject.

Maggie understood his enthusiasm. Most of his friends

went boating almost every weekend. It was a symbol of status in the community not to be a two-car family, but a two-boat family. Mike probably wasn't aware of that, but he did know his friends were always talking about what they did. Now he would have a story of his own to tell the others.

"That's tomorrow." Playfully Maggie pulled the bill of his cap low on his forehead. "Tonight, it's out of that uniform and into the tub."

"Cut it out," he grumbled in protest, but there was a grin on his face as he pushed her hand away.

THE NEXT MORNING Maggie was in the utility room, folding the clean clothes from the drier.

The washing machine was in its spin cycle, and its thumping roar combined with the music from the radio and the whir of the drier drowned out all other sounds.

It wasn't until the washing machine stopped that Maggie heard the phone ringing in the kitchen. She dashed quickly to answer it.

"Rafferty residence," she rushed, half expecting to hear a dial tone to indicate the caller had hung up.

"Maggie? It's Wade."

Her already racing pulse redoubled its tempo. Determinedly she tried to check its thudding rise. "Mike's outside. I'll get him for you."

Before she could put the receiver down, Wade was ordering, "Wait a minute."

"Yes?"

A self-conscious hand touched the flaming silk tumble of hair on top of her head, secured there by a green ribbon.

89

It was crazy—Wade couldn't see her.

"Did you talk to Mike last night?"

"Yes, I did." She marshaled her scattered thoughts. "He was upset, naturally. It was such a surprise to him. No child likes things to change unless it's instigated by him. It makes him insecure."

"Mike's life isn't changing that drastically because of my marriage."

"But Mike sees that it potentially could," Maggie pointed out. "His main worry seems to be that you might have other children and forget him."

"Maggie, you know . . ." Wade began impatiently.

"I'm not saying it would happen," she interrupted. "I'm saying that it concerns Mike. He isn't an impulsive boy. It's going to take him time to adjust to the idea of a stepmother.

"You've known her for more than a year, Mike hasn't even met her. One or two meetings aren't going to be enough for him, either."

"No, it will take time," Wade agreed in a grimly resigned voice. "How was he after your talk?"

"Eager for today to come so he could go boating with you." Then Maggie realized the time. "You haven't had to change your plans, have you? You said you'd call this afternoon."

"I haven't changed my plans. At least, I'm not canceling the outing," he qualified his statement. "I thought Mike might like to leave sooner, have lunch aboard the boat."

"He'd love it."

"Do you mind?"

"No, I don't mind," Maggie insisted, and wondered

where the silly lump came from in her throat. "You'll want to talk to him. I'll tell him you're on the phone."

"There's no need." Once again Wade stopped her. "Just tell him I'm leaving now and for him to be ready when I arrive."

"I will."

"Maggie? Thanks," he said simply.

She hesitated.

"You'll have to do the same for me someday when I decide to get married." The idea seemed so remote at the moment that it was laughable. Instead, Maggie felt tears pricking her eyes.

"You can count on it," Wade promised.

It was several minutes after he had said goodbye before Maggie had enough composure to walk to the back door to call Mike inside.

She had judged his reaction accurately. He was ecstatic over the change of plans.

When he ran to his room to change shirts and put on a clean pair of tennis shoes, Maggie freshened her makeup and took the green ribbon from her hair.

Then it was back to the utility room and the clothes in the drier.

As she was pairing the socks, Mike poked his head around the door.

"I'm going outside to wait for dad."

"Have a good time." Maggie smiled to conceal her envy for his day.

"You bet!"

"I'll see you tonight." But Mike was already gone and parting words bounced forlornly off the walls of the utility room.

Trying not to dwell too much on what she was going to do with herself all day, Maggie methodically folded the socks and put them with the stack of clothes in the wicker basket.

When it was filled, she picked it up. It was heavy and she hurried in order to bring a quick end to the weight tugging at her arms.

As she rounded the archway into the living room, she was hit broadside by a tall, hard form. The collision wrenched the basket from her straining hands, flipping it upside down and dumping the folded clean clothes onto the floor.

The force of the collision staggered her, but a pair of large hands immediately steadied her.

Wade's hands—her senses recognized his touch immediately.

On impact, she had issued a startled cry. Her heart was lodged in her throat as she stared at Wade and not a sound could get past it.

A white knit shirt, unbuttoned at the throat, contrasted with the navy pants and Windbreaker he wore. The dark blue color intensified the jet blackness of his attractively unkempt hair, looking as if it were freshly rumpled by a sea breeze. A concerned look was etched in his harshly vital and male features, his dark eyes piercing in their scrutiny.

With an effort Maggie forced her gaze from his compelling face, fighting the breathless waves of excitement that engulfed her.

Her glance fell on the once neatly folded clothes scattered over the floor. They would all have to be folded, separated, and stacked in the basket again. Angry exasperation at the wasted time she'd spent overtook the rest of her tangled emotions and her hands slid to her hips in an attitude of temper.

Before she could speak, Wade was saying, "I'm sorry, I didn't know you were going to come racing around the corner at that moment."

Racing around the corner! The phrase indicated the blame was hers.

What had been a mere spark of anger blazed into full flame.

She turned on him, her green eyes flashing. As her mouth started to open, his fingers closed it.

There was a wicked twinkle in his dark eyes. "I said I was sorry," he reminded her. His thumb lightly caressed the curve of her mouth before he took his hand away and glanced at his son.

"Come on, Mike. Let's help your mom pick up the clothes."

That vague caress had turned away her anger. Maggie was left standing there, impotent, while Mike and Wade bent to begin picking up the scattered clothes. It was several seconds before she recovered sufficiently to help them.

"We were just coming in to tell you we were going," Mike explained.

"You'll be home before dark, won't you?" Maggie hadn't asked Wade how long they intended to be gone.

"We'll be back to the marina before dark." He satisfied her mind on that worry. "Don't wait dinner for Mike, though. We'll probably have something to eat before I bring him home."

"Oh."

That meant two meals she would have to eat alone, lunch and dinner.

"Dad, are we going out on the boat alone, just you and me?"

Mike bunched a group of socks together and stuffed them in the basket. Maggie rescued them and tried to sort them into pairs.

"Yes, it will just be the two of us."

"Why can't mom come along?"

CHAPTER EIGHT

"MIKE!"

She was so startled by Mike's unexpected request to include her in their plans that his name was the only word of protest she could think to make.

Color rouged her cheeks for fear Wade might think she had previously hinted to Mike for the invitation. A sideways glance at Wade showed his curious frown.

Mike pursued his request, ignoring her outburst. "She's on vacation and she doesn't have anything to do, especially with me going places with you." He continued without giving Wade a chance to reply, "I know mom likes boats 'cause I've seen the pictures of the boat you two used to have."

"Mike," Maggie interrupted sharply, "your father wants to spend time alone with you. You and I will have time to do things together later."

"Yeah, but—" he was struggling for the words "—we've never done things together like a family. At least, I was too little to remember if we did. And—"

"But we aren't a family," Maggie protested.

"Yes, we are," Wade corrected her in a quiet but firm voice. "You are the mother, I am the father and Mike is the son. A divorce doesn't change that."

"No, but . . . ." She felt panic.

"Can she come along, dad?" Mike interrupted eagerly, his eyes alight with cautious hope.

"Of course she can come along," Wade agreed, and glanced at Maggie.

"Will you go boating with us?"

She was thrown into confusion. He couldn't really mean it, but there wasn't any reluctance in his voice or his expression.

"Oh, but I—" she began.

"Please, mom!" Mike inserted to ward off her refusal.

"Please, Maggie."

Wade lent his voice to Mike's. His expression was serious, not a hint of mockery to be seen.

She might have resisted Mike's plea, but to deny Wade's was impossible.

Her head was bobbing in agreement before she could get the words out.

"Very well, I'll come with you." Not without misgivings.

Her glance went down the crisp blue Levi's she wore and plain knit top. "I'll have to—"

Wade saw the direction her thoughts were taking and interrupted.

"There's nothing wrong with what you're wearing. A pair of tennis shoes and a Windbreaker are the only additions we'll need. Mike and I don't want to wait the time it would take you to change entirely."

This time there was a glint of mockery in his dark eyes.

"It doesn't take me that long," Maggie denied with a defiant tilt of her chin.

"Only forever," Mike exaggerated.

"That isn't true!" There was an indignant gleam in her look.

"The invitation was issued with the proviso to 'come as you are,' " Wade told her. "Mike, go and get her shoes and a Windbreaker."

"Right, dad."

And he put his agreement into action.

Common sense agreed that there was nothing wrong with what she was wearing. Her Levi's and top were neat and clean.

Vanity, however, insisted there were outfits in her wardrobe equally serviceable and much more fashionable. But between Wade and Mike, they had taken the choice out of her hands.

Wade added the last of the clothes to the basket and set it aside. Maggie watched him. He lifted the heavy basket so easily.

All thought of clothes was pushed from her mind, the void to be filled by recognition of his powerfully muscled frame and his innate virility.

She realized how dangerous it was to spend an afternoon or an hour with him.

"I don't think this is a good idea," she murmured aloud.

"What?" He cocked his head at an inquiring angle, a brow lifting slightly, a half smile touching his mouth. "Not changing clothes?" he mocked.

"No, my going with you." In self-defense, Maggie hastened to disguise the truth of her answer. "The idea is for Mike to adjust to your coming marriage. My coming along is just going to confuse the issue."

"I don't agree." He eyed her steadily. "Since Mike

has grown up, he's either been with you alone, or with me alone—never in the company of a couple where he isn't the sole object of attention. Today he's going to see what it's like when there are three people together. For the experiment, it's you instead of Belinda.''

''That's very logical,'' she murmured.

His motives for wanting her along became obvious. It wasn't a desire for her company, or for a last time to be together as a family.

No, Wade was sparing his darling Belinda from any outright rejection by his son. Some of the inner joy that Maggie had hardly dared to let herself feel faded at the discovery.

''What's very logical?''

Mike returned with her tennis shoes and yellow Windbreaker.

For a split second Maggie was at a loss for an answer. ''For your father to invite me along so he won't have to cook.''

''Yeah, that is pretty smart, dad,'' he agreed with a grin.

''I thought so.''

Stepping out of the casual leather loafers, Maggie put on the tennis shoes and tied the laces. The thin, slick jacket she let drape over one shoulder. When she was ready, Mike led the way outside.

If Maggie needed any further reminder that she was only a stand-in for Belinda, the silver Mercedes provided it. She began to wonder if the boat, too, belonged to his future bride.

For once, she didn't have the audacity to ask. Although there was ample room in the front seat for three, she chose to sit alone in the back. It saved making innocuous conversation.

"What do you think of the car, Mike? You never did comment on it yesterday."

Wade turned it onto a busy street, the luxury car accelerating into the flow of traffic.

"It's nice." Mike was obviously unimpressed by the plushness of the interior. "But I like that fourwheel-drive vehicle you have in Alaska a lot better. It can go anywhere!"

Wade chuckled and admitted, "There are times when you can't get around unless you have that kind of vehicle."

Personally Maggie thought Wade was more suited to the type of vehicle Mike had described. Not that he didn't look perfectly at home behind the wheel of this luxury model.

But the plush, elegant car seemed to shield its owner from the realities of life, whereas Wade was the kind of man who met life head-on, taking the knocks and driving forward, going anywhere he pleased.

But such admiration for the character of the man he was was not wise.

Maggie turned her attention to the city sprawling around them. Like the Eternal City of Rome, Seattle had originally been a city of seven hills. Shortly after the turn of the century, Denny Hill was leveled to permit the city to expand.

Water dominated the city, not just because it was a seaport, but because of the two lakes within its limits and a ship canal, as well as its being flanked by Lake Washington on the east and Puget Sound on the west.

Considering that fact, it wasn't surprising that there were more boats per capita than anywhere else in the country.

Maggie was positive they were all crowded into the marina where Wade stopped. Unerring, he led them past the rows of boats, all shapes, sizes, and kinds, to a sleek powerful cruiser.

It was larger and a later model than the one they owned when they were married. Maggie felt she was stepping back in time when she stepped aboard. As he helped her onto the deck, her flesh tingled at the impersonal grip of his hand.

"Where are we going? Just anywhere?"

Mike wanted to know their destination, at the same time not caring.

"We'll decide when we reach open water. How's that?" Wade loosed the mooring ropes. "Or maybe we won't go anywhere special."

"I suppose it's too far to go all the way to the ocean."

"No, it isn't too far, but I think we'll find enough to see and do without that."

The inboard motors roared to life and Wade began maneuvering the cruiser out of the crowded marina waters.

Mike was right at his side observing everything he did. There was a tightening in her throat as Maggie saw how strong the resemblance was between father and son, Mike a young miniature of Wade.

The breeze coming off the water was cool. Maggie started to slip her Windbreaker on, then decided, "I'll go below and start lunch now."

"Good idea," Wade agreed, and combed his fingers

through his wind-ruffled hair. "We're well stocked with food, so fix whatever you like." As she started down the open hatchway, he called after her, "Maggie? There's some bait shrimp in the refrigerator. I didn't want you to mistake it for the eating kind."

She heard the teasing laughter in his voice and retorted, "Are you sure you wouldn't like a shrimp cocktail?" reminding him of the time the first year they were married when she had unknowingly used bait shrimp for that purpose.

His rich laughter followed her below.

The private joke was beyond Mike, but he was more interested in the use of the shrimp. "Are we going to fish?"

"I thought we might. Fishing is supposed to be good."

"Hey, mom! Why don't you wait to fix lunch until after we catch some fish? Then you can cook what we catch."

"No, thanks. I might starve before then," Maggie called back.

"It doesn't sound as if she thinks too much of us as fishermen, does it?" she heard Wade say.

"That's because she's never been fishing with us," Mike replied.

"Didn't you tell her about any of the fish we caught?"

"Oh, sure."

Maggie walked from the galley to the bottom of the steps.

"Mike told me all those fish stories about the times he went with you in Alaska. You only brought back three fish apiece and each of the three fish weighed thirty pounds," she teased.

"It's the truth, mom, honest," Mike insisted.

"The next time we'll have to take a camera along, won't we?" said Wade.

"Then she'll have to believe me, huh?"

"Right."

Maggie went back to fixing lunch, listening to the bantering between father and son. It made her feel warm and secure inside, as if they were really a family. She wished it could always be this way . . . or that it had always been like this.

But it hadn't and it couldn't.

The lunch was simple fare, a mug of hot soup and a cold meat sandwich served on deck. Wade anchored the cruiser in a sheltered cover of Whidbey Island.

A beautiful wilderness beach stretched invitingly along the shore.

"Boy, this soup sure warms up your stomach," Mike declared.

"Tastes good, doesn't it?" Maggie sipped the hot liquid in her mug.

The breeze remained cool and a thickening layer of clouds shut out the warmth of the sun. She eyed the mat gray sky and glanced at Wade. Perceptively he read her thoughts.

"I checked the weather a few minutes ago. There's a front moving in—overcast skies, cooler temperatures, but very little rain is expected with it," he reported.

"That's pretty normal for the area, isn't it?" she smiled.

The Olympic Mountains to the west sheltered the islands in Puget Sound, as well as Seattle, from the brunt of weather fronts moving in from the Pacific.

The mountains divested the clouds of most of their moisture, keeping the rainfall inland to nominal amounts. Few storms of any intensity ever reached the protected sound.

CHAPTER NINE

AFTER LUNCH WAS OVER, Mike was designated cabin boy and ordered to clean the dishes. He grudgingly obeyed, after trying unsuccessfully to enlist help from either of them.

The boat remained anchored in the cove, with Maggie and Wade relaxing on the cushioned seats of the aft deck.

Her yellow Windbreaker was zipped to the throat, her hands stuffed in the front pocket. Thus protected, she leaned back to enjoy the brisk air, tangy with the scent of the sea.

All was quiet except for the lapping water against the boat's hull and the whispering breeze talking to the rustling leaves on the island's wooded interior. And, of course, there was the clatter of dishes in the cabin galley below.

"You've made a good job of raising Mike," Wade remarked quietly.

"I haven't done it alone. You've contributed, too." Maggie met his look, aware of its gentleness.

"The credit belongs to you. He's with you much more than he is with me. But thanks for making me feel I've had a hand in it."

Looking away from her, he took a deep breath and

let it out slowly, like a sigh. "Today you said you would want me to talk to Mike before you got married. Are you planning to marry again?"

"Someday, when I find the right man." The prospect looked dismal. "Like you, I don't want to make another mistake. The next time I want to be very, very sure."

"You don't have anyone in mind, then?" His gaze returned to her, dark and impenetrable.

"Not any one person. There are a few prospects on the horizon, but—" Maggie shrugged "—I'm not going to rush into anything."

"You said something the other day that's been bothering me."

His expression was thoughtful, slightly distant.

"What was that?"

"You said that after you'd wiggled out from under my thumb, you learned to value your freedom. What did you mean by that?"

Before she attempted an answer, Wade went on. "Granted, you said it in a moment of temper. But you rarely say things in the heat of anger that you don't mean.

"When we were married, you were always free to do as you pleased, within reason, of course."

"In theory, I was." At his gathering frown, Maggie tried to explain.

"All day long you gave orders to your employees. When you came home, you continued to give orders. You never seemed to *ask* me to do anything, you were always *telling* me.

"Instead of giving orders to the people who worked under you, you gave them to me—and I was much too independent to stand for that." A wry smile dimpled her cheeks.

"I never intended them to be orders."

"You probably didn't, but that's the way they came out."

"I'm . . . sorry." There was a certain grimness to his mouth.

"Don't be. It's in the past and forgotten." But Maggie guessed he was filing it away for future reference, something he didn't want to repeat in his new marriage to Belinda.

It hurt.

"I'm done!" Mike popped up the steps. "Can we fish now?"

The quiet interlude was over. Wade straightened from his comfortable position with obvious reluctance. "Get the bait out of the refrigerator while I find the rods and reels," he directed.

"Are we going to fish here?"

"Why not? If the fish aren't biting here, we'll move someplace else," Wade reasoned.

As far as Maggie was concerned, she found Mike's presence, his steady stream of chatter and expectant excitement, better than the confiding quietness when she and Wade had been alone.

He kept her mind from thinking intimate thoughts and envisioning hopeless dreams.

The fishing turned out to be not very good in that cove and Wade moved the boat to another. Early afternoon was not the best time of day for fishing, but at the second place they stopped, Mike did catch one that was big enough to keep.

They all threw several back. After they had moved again, Wade caught the next.

A fine mist began to fall, but despite their partial success, the weather didn't interfere with their sport. It dampened their clothes, but not their spirit. The water in the third cove was fairly deep.

A fish nibbled on Maggie's baited hook, then took it. She began reeling it in, feeling it fight and certain this time she had got a big one.

"Got a fish, mom?" Mike glanced over his shoulder from his position on the opposite side of the boat next to Wade.

"A fish or a baby." She had reeled in too many small ones that she thought would be large to brag about this one.

"At the rate your mother is going, you and I are going to be the only ones with food on our plates tonight, Mike," Wade teased.

"Yeah, and she's got to cook it for us."

Maggie kept her silence with an effort, ignoring the way they were ganging up on her. The fish broke surface and she had to swallow back her shout of glee. It looked big enough to keep. Now all she had to do was land it. A few minutes later she had it in her lap—literally, its tail flapping on her jeans while she tried to work the hook out of its mouth.

"What ya got there, mom? A goldfish?" Mike teased.

"No, I have a real fish." She struggled some more but couldn't work the hook free. "He's swallowed the hook."

"It's the only way she could have caught it," Wade laughed. "Watch my rod while I help your mother." He

107

walked over and Maggie surrendered her catch, a shade triumphantly, to him.

"You really hooked him. That's too bad." He crouched on the deck beside her and gently began working the hook in the gaping fish's mouth.

"Why is that too bad?" Maggie demanded to know.

"Because it isn't big enough to keep."

"It is, too!" she declared indignantly. "It's just as big as yours was."

"No, it's a couple of inches smaller," Wade replied.

"You have to throw it back, mom," Mike inserted.

"You just stay out of it," she told him, and turned angrily back to Wade. "You get out your fish and we'll see if mine is smaller."

He smiled. "I don't have to get out my fish. I already know yours is smaller—too small to keep." He freed the hook and tossed the fish over the side.

"My fish!"

Maggie wailed, and dived toward the rail, as if thinking she could catch it before it reached the water.

There was a splash before she even reached the side of the boat. Her hand went out for the railing to stop her progress.

The steady mist had coated the railing with slippery beads of moisture and her hand found nothing to grip on the wet surface of the rail and slid beyond it. The unchecked forward impetus carried her against the low rail, pitching her body over it.

Her startled shriek of fright and alarm was echoed by Mike's "Mom!"

Something grabbed at her foot and in the next second she was tumbling into the water. Immediately instinct

108

took over. Holding her breath, she turned and kicked toward the surface, taking care to avoid the hull of the boat.

She came up spluttering, gasping in air. She was shaking all over, more from cold than the initial fright. The first sound she heard was laughter, Wade's deep, chuckling laughter.

When he saw Maggie was safe and unharmed, Mike joined in.

"Have you found a new way to fish?" Wade mocked.

"You . . . ." In her surge of anger, Maggie forgot to tread water and ended up swallowing a mouthful of the salty stuff.

Coughing and choking, she resurfaced and struck out for the boat ladder. The weight of her saturated clothes pulled at her body.

His hand was there to help her aboard. With the fingers of one hand around the lowest rung, Maggie paused in the water to glare at him and the dancing light in his black eyes.

Ignoring his offer of his assistance, she pulled herself aboard unaided.

Standing on deck, a pool of sea water at her feet, water streaming from her sodden clothes, she looked first at Mike, who was giggling behind his hand. Her hair was plastered over her forehead, cheeks and neck. Water ran into her eyes and she wiped it away to glare again at Wade. A smile was playing with the corners of his mouth, regardless of his attempts to make it go away.

"You think it's all very funny, don't you?" she accused, her teeth chattering with an onsetting chill. "I could have drowned while the two of you were laughing!"

109

"That's hardly likely, Maggie. You're an excellent swimmer," Wade reminded her in a dry, mocking tone.

"I could have hit my head on the boat or a rock or something!" she sputtered.

"The water is fairly clear," Wade pointed out. "I could see you weren't in trouble. Here." He reached down and picked up a tennis shoe from the deck— Maggie's. "When I grabbed for you, all I got was your shoe. At least it's dry."

Maggie snatched it from his outstretched hand. "What good is one dry tennis shoe—" she waved it in front of his face "—when I have one wet one? Not to mention that my clothes are soaked! A dry tennis shoe just doesn't go with the rest of my outfit!" In a burst of temper, she hurled the lone, dry tennis shoe over the side, where it floated on the quiet surface.

Mike gasped in surprise, then broke out laughing, finding the scene uproariously funny.

It didn't help Maggie's growing sense of frustration one bit.

"You'd better practice your casting, Mike, and see if you can't hook that shoe before it sinks," Wade advised, keeping the amusement in his voice at a minimum. "As for you, Maggie, I think you'd better go below and get out of those wet clothes before you get chilled."

"Chilled! What do you think I am now?" she cried angrily. "My legs are shaking so badly now that I can hardly stand up."

"I'll help you."

Wade took a step toward her.

"No! I don't need any help from you. You take one more step and I'll push you over the side; then you can see

110

what it feels like to be drenched to the skin," she threatened, and not falsely.

"And stop giving me orders! I'm an adult. I know I have to get out of these wet clothes, you don't have to remind me of that."

The latter half of her statement wiped the gleam from his eyes. They were flat black as he stepped to the side, indicating by his action that he would make no move to help her.

Maggie swept by him to the steps with as much dignity as her dripping figure could muster, but her chattering teeth destroyed much of the effect.

Below, she tugged the saturated clothes from her body and piled them in the sink.

Taking a towel from the lavatory, she rubbed her skin dry until it burned. A second towel she wrapped around her straggly wet hair, securing it on top of her head with a tuck in front.

Then came the problem of something dry to wear. She opened a drawer, looking for a blanket. Inside were folded flannel shirts, men's shirts. A red and black plaid was on top.

At this point Maggie wasn't particular. Anything that was warm and dry and permitted movement would do.

The shirt engulfed her, the tails reaching to her knees, the sleeves almost as far. After a few awkward attempts she managed to roll the long sleeves up to her forearms and button the front.

With that accomplished, she began trying to towel her hair dry.

"How are you doing?" Wade called down.

"Fine," she snapped, and muttered to herself, "as a drowned rat."

She was still shivering.

After glancing around, she called, "Is there any cocoa?"

Instead of answering, Wade descended the steps as soundlessly as a cat. "If there isn't cocoa, there's instant coffee. With sugar, it will probably do you more good than cocoa."

"I know there's instant coffee. I would have made a cup if you'd told me there wasn't cocoa."

"Your temper still hasn't cooled off, has it?" he observed dryly, and walked to the cupboards above the galley sink.

"It's the only part of me that hasn't," Maggie muttered.

"I don't see any cocoa."

Wade moved items on the shelf around. "You'll have to settle for coffee."

"I can fix it myself," she insisted when he filled the kettle with water.

"Shut up, Maggie." It was said quietly but no less firmly. "Stop being so damned independent and go sit down." He saw the flashing green fire in her eyes and added, "Yes, it is an order. Because at the moment, you're so angry you'd cut off your nose to spite your face."

"Not mine," she retorted. "But I might cut off *your* nose!"

"I'll get the coffee, then give you the knife." He lit the gas burner and set the kettle over the flame. Shaking his dark head, he murmured, "Only you could get into these kinds of scrapes, Maggie."

Maggie didn't argue any more about making the coffee herself.

Neither did she go sit down as he had ordered. She resumed the brisk rubbing of her hair, deep red gold wavelets rippling over her head.

"I certainly didn't intend to fall overboard," she muttered.

"All because of a silly little fish." The corners of his mouth deepened.

"That you threw away," Maggie reminded him.

"It was too small."

"It was almost big enough to keep," she argued.

"There, you just admitted it yourself." Wade smiled, without triumph.

"Okay, so I admit it."

She tossed the towel aside.

"What are you doing in that shirt?"

The change of subject startled her. Her winged brows drew together in a frown and a short, disbelieving laugh came from her throat.

"I'm wearing it," she retorted.

A raking, impatient glance swept her from head to foot. "I suppose you think you look sexy wearing a man's shirt that comes to your knees, with shoulder seams that practically reach your elbows."

"It never occurred to me how I might look wearing it!" she answered defensively. "It was warm and I could move around freely while I was wearing it. If it reminded me of anything, it was a flannel nightgown. I wasn't even thinking about being sexy. The only male around here that I care about is Michael."

And she denied the thudding pulse racing in her slender neck.

"Believe me, you don't look a bit like my grandmother did in her flannel nightgown." Wade spooned coffee crystals into a mug and gave her a black, smoldering look. A muscle stood out along his jaw. "When a man sees you like that, dressed in a man's shirt without a stitch of clothing under it, looking lost and vulnerable, he wants to hold you in his arms and—" He snapped off the rest of that sentence. "As if you didn't know, you look damned cute!"

"I don't know if that's a compliment or a sin."

Confusion tempered her defensive anger as she turned aside.

His hand gripped her elbow to turn her back.

"The only place you have in my life is as the mother of my child."

The brutally frank statement stung.

"I know that," Maggie retorted, choking, unable to shrug out of his hold.

"Then explain to me why I can't forget that you're my wife?"

His grip shifted to clasp both her shoulders in hard demand.

CHAPTER TEN

HER LIPS PARTED to draw in a fearfully happy breath. As she gazed up at him, a fine mist of tears brought a jewel-like intensity to the green color of her eyes. She heard the groaning sound he made before his finger tightened to dig into her flesh and draw her to him.

The crush of his mouth ignited a sweet fire that raged through her veins.

Curving her arms around his neck, Maggie slid her fingers into his shaggy mane of black hair. The drifting mist of rain outside had left his hair damp and silken to the touch.

Behind the spinning wonder of his kiss, the recesses of her mind knew it couldn't last.

The knowledge that Wade belonged to someone else made her hungry response more desperate, savoring every fragment of the stolen embrace.

The driving possession of his mouth bent her backward while the large hand on her spine forced the lower half of her body against him. His muscled legs were hardwood columns, solid and unyielding.

The wideness of the shirt's collar made the neckline plunge to the valley between her breasts. With masterful ease he unfastened the single obstructing top button. His hand slid inside to mold itself to the mature curves of her breast, swallowing its fullness in the large cup of his hand.

Maggie shuddered with intense longing. His searing caress burned her already heated flesh.

The male smell of him was a stimulant more potent than any drug. Her heart was beating so wildly that she couldn't think.

Wade ended his imprisonment of her mouth, leaving her lips swollen with passion, and began a sensuous exploration of her curving neck. Desire quivered along her spine as he found the pleasure points that excited her, and Maggie couldn't stop the moan of delight from escaping her throat.

The fanning warmth of his disturbed breathing caressed her skin.

"God help me, Maggie, but I want you."

His husky, grudging admission sent tremors through her limbs.

She felt the pressure of his growing need for her. It was echoed by the empty ache in her loins. There was only here and now; nothing else existed, and this moment would never come again.

"Don't you think I feel the same, Wade?" she whispered.

With blazing sureness his mouth sought her lips. There was only one ultimate climax to the crushing embrace. But before a move could be made in that direction, a young voice jolted them back to reality.

"Mom! Dad! Look at the size of the fish I caught!" Mike's excited cry tore their kiss apart.

Almost immediately he came tumbling down the steps, holding the fish aloft.

There was no time for Wade to withdraw his arms from around her. A trembling Maggie was glad of their support.

Her head dipped to hide behind the protective shield of Wade's wide shoulders, concealing her love-drugged expression from her son.

She felt Wade take a deep, controlling breath before glancing over his shoulder.

"It's the biggest one yet!"

Instead of holding the fish by the gills, Mike was trying to hold it in his hands. It slipped through his grasp onto the cabin floor, giving both of them a momentary reprieve from his gaze.

"It is a big fish," Wade agreed.

"See it, mom?"

This time Mike picked it up correctly.

A supporting arm remained around her as Wade moved to one side.

"It's a beauty, Mike." Even to her own ears, her voice sounded strange.

It earned her a curious look from Mike. "Are you all right, mom?"

"I'm fine."

Maggie shivered in late reaction.

"She's just a bit chilled, that's all," Wade inserted.

Chilled. It was directly the opposite. Her whole body was suffused with heat, the heat of regret, of shame, and of love.

But Maggie didn't contradict his statement, letting it be an explanation of why Wade had been so obviously holding her.

Mike seemed satisfied with the answer and let his

attention return to the fish he held. "Actually I caught it on your pole, mom." He grinned at Wade. "I guess we'll have to say it's hers."

"I guess we will." Wade nodded in concession.

"I'd better go put this guy on the stringer and see if anything's biting on my line."

As quickly as he had come, Mike left, scurrying back on deck.

His departure left an uncomfortable void. Aware of Wade's piercing study, Maggie turned away from it. Her emotions were still too close to the surface. A bubbling sound provided the necessary distraction.

"The water's boiling," she said. "I'd better get that coffee before it boils away."

She turned her back on him as she shut off the gas to the burner.

"Maggie . . . ."

She could hear the beginnings of an apology in his voice.

No doubt it would be followed by a reminder that he was engaged to someone else and that the desire they had shared moments ago was all a mistake, and they were the very last things she wanted to hear. The tears weren't that far away.

Maggie sought refuge behind the excuse Wade had offered the last time.

"We were following the pattern of a memory, first arguing, then kissing. It didn't mean anything." *Not to you*, her heart qualified the last statement.

There was a long silence that left her with the uncanny feeling that Wade didn't believe she meant what she said. Then a drawer opened beneath one of the bunk beds.

"After you drink your coffee, it probably wouldn't hurt if you wrapped up in a blanket and stayed below."

"I think I will."

Maggie didn't fight his suggestion.

There was another pause before she heard Wade mounting the steps to the deck.

Her hand shook as she added the boiling water to the brown crystals in the mug. Now she did feel cold, and terribly lonely.

Carrying the mug to the bed, she wrapped herself in the blanket Wade had laid on the bunk.

Within minutes after she had curled herself into a ball of abject misery, Maggie heard the engines start. She knew Wade wasn't going to look for another fishing hole; he was returning to the marina. She closed her eyes and tried to forget.

Maggie didn't emerge from the cocoon of the blanket until the boat was docked, the mooring lines tied, and the engines silent.

She wadded her wet clothes into a bundle and started up the steps.

The instant she set foot on deck, Wade's voice barked, "Where do you think you're going?"

"I presume you're taking us home." His tone instantly put Maggie on the defensive. Poised short of the top step, she lifted her chin.

"Not dressed like that."

Wade softened his tone, but it was no less lacking in determination.

"I hope you don't think I'm going to wear these." She indicated the wet bundle of clothes in her hand. "They're wet. It may not bother you, but I'm not going to stain the upholstery in that expensive car by wearing these wet things."

He stood in her path, blocking it as effectively as a tall gate.

"You're not wearing that shirt."

"For heaven's sake, Wade—" his attitude rankled "—this shirt covers more than if I were wearing a bathing suit."

"I don't care how much it covers." There was a hardening set to his jaw. "No wife of mine is going to parade down these docks half-dressed."

His statement seared through her, but Maggie realized that Wade was unaware of what he had said. The swift rush of heat was quickly replaced by a chilling depression.

Avoiding his gaze, she made a bitterly mocking reply. "I'm not your wife anymore. Or had you forgotten?"

Out of the corner of her eye, she saw the startled jerk of his head. Taking advantage of the moment, she climbed the last step and brushed past him. Wade didn't try to stop her.

Mike was on the dock, standing by one of the mooring lines.

"Are you taking us straight home, dad? What about the fish?" He had seen them talking, but hadn't heard the substance of their conversation.

"Your mother needs some dry clothes," Wade answered. "As for the fish, we'll take them with us."

"You'll help me clean them, won't you? I'm still not very good at it." Mike scrambled back aboard to get the fish.

Maggie heard Wade agree as she stepped ashore. Within minutes the three of them were making their way to the silver Mercedes in the marina parking lot. Most of the looks that Maggie received focused on the bare length of her legs, rather than the oversized flannel shirt and what was, or wasn't, beneath it. Maggie ignored the mostly admiring glances, but it wasn't so easy to ignore Wade's growing aloofness.

At the house, Maggie carried her wet clothes to the utility room while Mike and Wade gathered what they needed from the kitchen to clean the fish. As they walked out the side door to the backyard, Maggie went to her bedroom to dress.

When they returned to the kitchen with the cleaned fish in a pan of water, they were laughing about something. A pain of loss and regret splintered through Maggie and she turned away to conceal it.

Mike came rushing forward. "Will you cook the fish tonight?"

"If you like," she agreed, taking the pan from him and setting it on the counter.

"Great!" With her agreement obtained, he turned back to his father. "Now we can eat what we caught, like real outdoorsmen."

"You can."

"Aren't you staying?" Mike was surprised, but Maggie wasn't.

"I can't. I have a date tonight." Wade's voice was smooth, his words cutting.

"But—" Mike searched for a protest "—this morning before mom agreed to come along, you said we might not get home until dark and we'd eat somewhere before you brought me home. Why can't you stay now?"

He was standing close to her. Maggie turned and

quickly but affectionately placed her hand across his mouth, silencing him before his innocent remarks made the situation more awkward than it already was.

"Your father said he had to leave, Mike. That's final." She took her hand away and saw the resigned droop of his mouth.

"I'm sorry, Mike. I'll be busy tomorrow, but I'll call you Thursday," Wade promised.

"I have baseball practice in the morning," Mike told him.

"I'll remember. Between now and Thursday afternoon, you can be thinking about what you'd like to do," Wade suggested.

"Okay," Mike agreed with halfhearted enthusiasm.

The exchange was prolonged for a few more minutes before Wade finally left.

Maggie's only acknowledgment from him was a curt nod of goodbye. She turned to the sink when the door closed and began rinsing the fish in cold water. Mike watched.

"You know where he's going, don't you?" Mike said glumly.

"Where?"

"He's got a date with *her*." The feminine pronoun was emphasized with scorn as Mike wandered away from the sink.

CHAPTER ELEVEN

MAGGIE WIPED THE PERSPIRATION from her forehead with the back of her gloved hand. She hadn't realized there were so many weeds in the flower bed when she'd started. The muscles in her back were beginning to cramp from constantly bending over. But she was almost done. Arching her shoulders briefly to ease the stiffness, she again stooped to her task.

A car turned into the driveway. Her backward glance recognized the station wagon as being familiar, but she couldn't immediately decide why.

Her brows drew together in a frown as she straightened up.

The passenger door opened and Mike scrambled out, baseball and glove in his hand. "You forgot to pick me up, didn't you?" he accused.

Her green eyes widened in disbelief. "Practice can't be over this soon?"

"Well, it is," he declared in disgust. "Coach gave me a ride home since you didn't show up."

Embarrassed, Maggie glanced at the bronzed man sliding out from behind the wheel of the car.

"I'm sorry, I honestly didn't realize it was so late. I started weeding the garden and lost all track of time, I guess."

"That's all right. Things like that happen." Smiling away her apology, Tom Darby walked around the hood of the car toward her.

"All the time," Mike mumbled, but thankfully not loud enough for Tom to hear.

Denny, the neighbor boy, called to Mike, wanting him to come over. With his coach there, Mike refused, shouting, "Later!"

"Denny has a new puppy he wants you to see," Maggie told him.

"Oh!" That changed things.

He shoved his baseball and glove into her hands and raced off.

Self-conscious about her oversight, Maggie tried to make amends.

"Thanks for bringing Mike home. I really appreciate it. I know it was out of your way."

"It was no trouble at all," Tom insisted. "In fact, it gave me the perfect excuse to see you again."

His boldness took her by surprise. It shouldn't have, she realized. Her actions in the past had encouraged him to show this interest.

It was just in the last few days all her thoughts had been concerned with Wade. Tom Darby had ceased to exist in her mind as anything but Mike's coach.

"Oh." It was a small sound, revealing Maggie's inner confusion.

The initial attraction she had felt toward Tom had faded into insignificance in the face of the overwhelming emotion that consumed her. How could she handle the change?

Tom appeared not to notice her hesitation. He contin-

124

ued with the confidence of a man whose suit had never been rejected. His hazel eyes looked steadily into her green ones.

"I would like you to have dinner with me one night this weekend. Friday or Saturday night, whichever is convenient for you?"

His technique was excellent, not giving her a chance to say no, only to choose which night to accept.

"I'm sorry, but I really can't say if I can come." Maggie stalled for a moment. "With Mike's father here, it's difficult for me to make plans until I know what his are. I'll have to take a raincheck on the invitation."

"Whatever you say." He wasn't happy with her answer, but he seemed resigned to it. Glancing up at the clear, blue sky overhead, he remarked, "It's going to be warm today."

Maggie sensed a hint behind the comment. Regardless of his motives, Tom had done her a favor by bringing Mike home.

The least she could do was repay him with some measure of hospitality.

"It's already warm. And you've been on the ball field with those boys all morning. Let me offer you something cold to drink since I can't accept your dinner invitation. Iced tea, beer, Coke?"

"A beer would taste good if it isn't too much trouble," Tom accepted with alacrity.

"It's no trouble. I'll get it."

Tom followed her into the house, something Maggie hadn't planned on, but she didn't object. She set Mike's ball and glove on the kitchen table and paused to remove her cotton work gloves.

Tom strolled along a few paces behind her, seeming to appear perfectly at home. She walked to the refrigerator.

"How is Mike doing?"

Maggie sought to establish a less personal topic of conversation, discuss Tom's work and steer away from his social life and whether it would or would not include her.

"He's doing fine, shows a real aptitude for the game."

As she opened the refrigerator door, she cast him a brief, smiling look.

"Except for his hitting, which is abominable. He was really upset that he didn't get a single hit in the game the other night."

"His hitting will improve before the summer is over," Tom replied with a certainty that revealed a firm belief in his teaching prowess. "Mike has to learn to keep his eye on the ball and stop swinging blindly at anything that comes over the plate."

"It must take a lot of patience to teach inexperienced boys how to play baseball."

Along with the can of beer, Maggie took the pitcher of iced tea from the refrigerator shelf. "Would you like a glass for your beer?"

"The can is fine."

He took it from her and pulled off the tab. "I suppose it does require patience, but the end results are rewarding. I enjoy sports and I enjoy working with kids. For me, it's natural to combine the two."

"That's good."

Taking a glass from the cupboard, Maggie filled it with tea from the pitcher for herself.

126

"Listen, Maggie . . . there isn't any reason why I can't bring Mike home after practice. You don't need to keep making special trips to pick him up."

He walked over to stand next to her, leaning a hip against the counter edge.

"It's very generous of you to offer, but I couldn't let you do it."

Maggie shook her head in refusal.

The sunshine streaming in through the window above the sink glinted on the fiery sheen of her hair.

It caught Tom's attention and he reached out to touch it as an innocent child would reach out for a dancing flame.

"Your hair is an extraordinary shade of red." A lock trailed across his finger. His voice was musing and absent. "Beautiful."

"Thank you." Maggie would have moved to the side to elude his involuntary caress, but the kitchen door leading outside opened.

She froze as Wade crossed the threshold and stopped, his gaze narrowing darkly, slashing from her to Tom. The curling strand of hair slid off Tom's finger. They were standing so close together at that moment that the scene didn't look as innocent as it had been: the hard glitter in Wade's eyes told Maggie that.

"Mike is at the neighbors'." Maggie took the step from Tom's side.

Her head assumed a defiant angle; she was irritated by the criticism and condemnation she saw written in Wade's features. She was single, thus free to have male friends.

"I know." Wade's attitude continued to be silently

127

intimidating. "I saw him when I drove in and he told me you were in the house. I wanted to speak to you."

Again, Maggie thought, and mentally braced herself. The last time he had wanted to speak to her privately it was to announce his marriage plans.

What was it about this time? Something equally shattering, she was sure.

Tom took the rather broad hint that his presence wasn't welcome and set his can of beer on the counter top.

"I'd better be moving along. Thanks for the beer, Maggie."

"I'll walk you to the door."

She had an unreasoning desire to postpone the inevitable conversation with Wade, if only for a few minutes. "Help yourself to something cold to drink, Wade. I'll be right back."

There was no response, but she hadn't expected there to be one.

Ignoring the side door Wade had entered, she led Tom through the living room to the front door.

"Thanks again for bringing Mike home."

"Maggie—" he paused at the door, his thoughtfully curious gaze resting on her face "—is there a reconciliation in the works between the two of you?"

"No, hardly," she answered with a bitterly rueful twist to her mouth.

"Are you sure? Because I had the distinct impression when he walked in that I was being confronted by an outraged husband." His head tipped skeptically at an angle.

"You must have been mistaken."

If Tom hadn't, it was probably a case that even if

128

Wade didn't want her anymore, he didn't want her to be with anyone else, either.

"I don't know . . . ." Tom was still hesitant.

"I do." Maggie smiled. "You see, Wade is engaged. The wedding is this month."

He seemed to digest the information before accepting it.

"I guess I did make a mistake, then." He shrugged the incident away. "I'll be seeing you, Maggie."

"Yes. Goodbye, Tom."

When he had left, Maggie returned to the kitchen. Wade had helped himself to a glass of tea and was putting the pitcher back in the refrigerator.

"Was he one of the marital prospects on your horizon?" Wade asked.

Pride made her answer, "He could be," although she seriously doubted it.

Maggie picked up her glass, glad to have something to do with her hands to hide her apprehension about this conversation.

"I'm sorry if I interrupted anything," he offered.

"No, you're not," she retorted. "If you were, you would have suggested that we talk another time and left." But she didn't confirm or deny his suspicions about the scene he had interrupted.

"What I came to discuss with you is important. I didn't think it was wise to put it off." Wade didn't defend his insincere apology.

"I'm sure it's important by *your* standards, but I might not think so."

"It's about Mike, and unless I'm greatly mistaken, he's always important to you."

129

It was almost a challenge.

The subject concerned Mike again, Maggie thought, the same as the last time. She didn't like the sound of it any more than the portentous feelings that made her so uneasy.

"Yes, Mike is important," she agreed warily. "What about him?"

"He hasn't met Belinda yet. Naturally she's very anxious to meet him," he said.

"Naturally."

Her voice was dry, tinged with cynicism, and it drew her a sharp look from Wade.

"I want to arrange something for this weekend."

"Fine," Maggie nodded. "Feel free to have Mike whichever day suits you best. You know I'm not going to make any objections."

"It isn't as simple as that." Wade sighed heavily in exasperation.

"Isn't it?" Mockery twisted her mouth.

"No. I want Mike to be on familiar ground when he meets her. I think it's going to be difficult enough for him without it occurring on alien ground."

"It won't be easy for Belinda, either," Maggie reminded him, not liking the direction his comments were pointing.

"She's an adult, more capable of handling a difficult situation than Mike is. It's more important for the boy to feel as comfortable as possible." He pushed aside her puny obstacle.

"What is your solution?" she challenged. "I'm sure you've already thought of one."

Wade breathed out a silent laugh, his mouth quirking cynically.

130

"Why do I have the feeling that the minute I answer that question this kitchen is going to turn into a battlefield?"

"Maybe because you already know I'm not going to like it."

Her nerves were tensing, her fingers tightening their grip on the moist glass, its coolness matching the temperature of her blood.

Wade held her gaze, refusing to let her look away.

"I want to bring Belinda over here to meet Mike. He would be here, in his own home, where he would be comfortable and relatively relaxed, and it would give you an opportunity to meet her at the same time. Your presence would also ease some of the pressure Mike might feel."

She didn't want that woman in her home. "You can't be serious?"

"I'm very serious."

"I can see it now, the four of us sitting around with our hands in our laps staring at each other." Maggie laughed aloud at the thought, but she didn't think it was funny, only preposterous.

"Granted, it may be awkward. It's bound to be no matter when or where it takes place," he argued, then suggested, "perhaps it would be better if we came for dinner."

"Dinner!"

"We could come in time to have a drink before we sit down to the table. There wouldn't be time for a lot of awkward silences before there'd be the distraction of the meal. Coffee afterward and then we'd leave."

"No!"

"Why?" Wade countered.

"Because . . . ."

Maggie sputtered helplessly, unable to think of an adequate reason.

"Mike has to meet her sooner or later. Why not when you're with him to lend moral support?" Wade drove home the logic of his suggestion.

But there was no one around to give her moral support, she argued silently. She sought refuge behind a weak protest.

"Mike has to meet her, but I don't!"

"Do you mean you would leave him in the care of a total stranger? Because that's exactly what you will be doing. Belinda is going to be my wife. When Mike visits me, he'll also be visiting her. Are you seriously trying to tell me you don't want to meet the woman who's going to be your son's stepmother, who'll take care of him when he's with me? I don't believe that, not for a minute."

Maggie turned away, because everything Wade had said was true.

For Mike's sake, she had to meet Wade's fiancée in order to have peace in her own mind when Mike visited Wade.

She was trapped in a corner and she resented Wade for maneuvering her there.

"Which night would you and your darling Belinda like to come for dinner?"

Cloying sarcasm rolled from her tongue, the only weapon she had left in her arsenal.

"Friday will be fine." His response was tautly controlled.

"What time?"

"Seven. There's no need to plan anything elaborate," he added.

"In other words, you don't want me to use our wedding china and crystal?" she asked sweetly.

"That attitude isn't going to make it easier," he warned.

"Easier? What do you know about making something easier?"

Her temper flared. "The only one who's finding any of this easy is you! It's going to be difficult for Mike, Belinda and myself. All you have to do is just sit back and wait for us to adjust!"

"What would you like me to do? Break the engagement?"

His look was cold, a dark brow arched in threatening challenge.

Yes! Instead Maggie cried, "No! I want you to stop telling me what my attitude should be!"

"For crissakes, I'm not telling you anything!" Wade snapped. "If you agree to my suggestion and want Belinda to dinner on Friday, then say so!"

"I do," she replied just as angrily.

"Good!"

In the next second Wade was slamming out the side door and Maggie was alone in the kitchen.

There was nothing to vent her anger on. It turned inward onto herself. Why had she baited him? What had she been trying to prove? That she was the shrew he had called her once? Why hadn't she been gracious about having Belinda to dinner? Because it hurt. The pain was agonizing.

Tension throbbed in her temples and she pressed her

fingers to them, their tips cool from holding the icy glass. The cool pressure brought temporary relief, but it came pounding back when she took her hands away. The side door opened and her head jerked up as she tried to regroup her defenses to face Wade. It was Mike who dashed in.

"Hi, mom. Dad said I was to come in and tell you I was going with him. I'll be home by five." He started back out, then paused. "Okay?"

"Yes, it's okay." She nodded with a stiff smile.

"Bye!"

CHAPTER TWELVE

MAGGIE GLANCED through the glass door of the oven to check the roast, something she had done half a dozen times in the last hour.

At the same time she checked her dim reflection in the door, an unconscious gesture to be sure her makeup didn't need retouching.

She rubbed her palms together, surprised to find them perspiring. She wiped them dry by smoothing the long black skirt over her hips.

She was nervous, her throat dry, her stomach churning. She felt like the harried image of a wife about to entertain her husband's boss—and the thought made her laugh aloud.

Mike walked into the kitchen. "What's so funny, mom?"

He wore a clean white shirt and dark blue pants. His face was scrubbed so clean that it practically shone.

"Nothing." She didn't attempt to explain the piece of irony that she had found amusing. Wade's boss was also his future father-in-law. Instead of his boss, she was about to entertain his future bride. The whole thing seemed ludicrous.

The doorbell rang. But for once Mike didn't race to answer it.

He gave her a sideways glance, and his dark eyes were filled with many of the apprehensions Maggie felt. She held out her hand to him.

"Come on, let's go and answer the door."

"I know I have to meet her," he mumbled, and moved reluctantly to walk with her, "but I wish she wasn't staying for dinner."

There wasn't any response she could make to that, so she just smiled her understanding. "Don't you feel kinda funny about meeting her?" Mike asked as they neared the front door. "I mean, because she's going to marry dad?"

"Yes, I do feel kinda funny," Maggie admitted, and that was putting it mildly.

They shared a quick smile before Maggie opened the door. She saw Wade first, standing tall and dark, dressed in a dark suit and tie, so casually elegant, and her pulse rocketed.

There was a breathless tightness in her chest. The two combined to make her feel weak at the knees.

"Hello, Maggie."

The gentle warmth in his gaze seemed to set her aglow.

"Hello, Wade." She returned the greeting with a slow smile.

Suddenly she realized this was the way she had visualized their first meeting, not the horrendous episode with hair curlers and old robe that had occurred. This was how she had imagined it—seeing each other and having the bitterness of their divorce fade under the mounting pleasure the reunion brought.

There was a movement by his side that compelled her

136

attention, and her gaze focused on a stunningly attractive blonde.

Belinda Hale was exactly as Maggie had pictured her to be, tall and willowy, her fairness a perfect complement to Wade's darkness.

Her hair was an unusual, and natural, shade of creamy toast, worn long and caught in a clasp at the back of her neck.

Every elegant bone reeked of smooth sophistication and poise. Her eyes were as blue as a clear Seattle sky, their color accentuated by the dress she wore in a subtle blue print.

There was only one thing about her that Maggie had not guessed—her age. *Woman* seemed a premature term. At the very most, Maggie suspected Belinda might be twenty-two.

It had never occurred to her that Wade might choose someone so much younger than himself for his future bride.

It was more disbelief than shock that kept her silent.

Belinda Hale had no such difficulty finding her voice. "Maggie, I've been looking forward to meeting you," she declared with husky sincerity and offered her hand.

Maggie managed the handshake. "How do you do, Miss Hale."

She knew she would never be able to carry off a first-name greeting, so she didn't try. In comparison to Belinda's friendliness, she knew she sounded stiff and polite. "Won't you come in?"

Moving out of the doorway, she nearly stepped into Mike, who had managed to stay well in the background and silently observe his future stepmother. Now it was his turn to be thrust into the limelight.

"You have to be Michael," Belinda deduced. "What does everyone call you? Mike or Mickey?"

He cringed at "Mickey" and quickly told her it was Mike.

Then he copied Maggie and greeted her. "How do you do, Miss Hale."

"Please call me Belinda."

She shook hands with him while Wade looked on. "You look so much like your father, Mike, I think I would have recognized you anywhere." Her gaze swung adoringly to Wade. "He's a handsome boy. No wonder you're so proud of him."

Mike shifted uncomfortably at this praise from a stranger. Maggie tried to rescue him and wondered why Wade hadn't. Was he going to leave all the conversation up to the three of them?

Of course, Belinda seemed to have enough poise to overcome any awkward silence.

"Please come into the living room and sit down." She moved toward the collection of sofas and chairs. "What can I get you to drink?" She threw a dagger at Wade for his silence. "You still drink Scotch and water, don't you?"

"Yes."

He inclined his head in agreement, nonplussed by her irritation.

"And you, Miss Hale?" Maggie inquired, and was stunned to hear herself add, "Mike is having a Coke. Would you like the same?" as if Belinda weren't old enough to drink.

138

The blonde seemed to miss the subtle insult, although Wade hadn't. His gaze narrowed dangerously, and Maggie knew it was a remark he wouldn't soon forget.

She bit down on her tongue and hoped she could control it.

"A glass of white wine would be nice, if you have it," Belinda answered.

"Of course."

This time Maggie was properly demure and didn't attach anything to her reply. "Make yourself at home. I'll be back in a moment."

As she started for the kitchen, Wade separated himself from Belinda's side.

"I'll help you. Mike can entertain Belinda for a few minutes."

Startled by his unexpected offer of assistance, Maggie stopped. Mike cast her a beseeching look, partly accusing her of deserting him in the face of the enemy.

But before Maggie could attempt to help him, Wade's hand was on her elbow, propelling her toward the kitchen. She didn't attempt to twist out of his hold until the door was swinging shut behind them and they were out of view.

"You left her slightly in the lurch out there," she accused.

"I think Belinda and Mike can survive for a few minutes on their own." He knew her concern wasn't for his fiancée.

Irritated, Maggie walked to the cupboard for the glasses. "The Scotch is—"

"I know where the Scotch is," he interrupted.

Pink warmed her cheeks as she remembered it hadn't

been very many days ago that he had drunk from the bottle.

She walked to the refrigerator and took out the chilling wine, as well as a Coke for Mike. Wade followed to get ice from the freezer compartment.

"Well?"

The cubes made a clinking sound as he dropped them in his glass.

"Well, what?" she retorted.

"Out with it."

"With what?" Maggie continued to be deliberately obtuse.

"It's tripping all over the tip of your tongue. You might as well say it and get it out of your system." Wade poured a shot of Scotch over the ice cubes while Maggie filled the wineglasses.

She debated silently with herself, then finally abandoned her pretended ignorance.

"When you were listing all of Belinda's virtues, you didn't mention her youth."

"She'll be twenty-two next month. It doesn't classify her as being fresh from the crib."

"But you have to admit, Wade, that Mike is closer to her age than you are."

It sounded so catty that Maggie wished she hadn't said it.

"It might make it easier for her to relate to him, and vice versa. Is her age the only objection you have to her?" he questioned.

"It wasn't an objection." She rushed to correct that assumption. "It just took me by surprise to discover she was so young. I expected her to be older, more mature. It

140

didn't occur to me you would be attracted to a . . . woman so young.''

"Why not? You were younger than Belinda is when we were married.''

Her fingers trembled as she recorked the wine bottle. She didn't want to be reminded of their marriage, since it also reminded her of their regrettable divorce. Without responding to his comment, she returned the wine bottle to the refrigerator, conscious of his hooded gaze watching her.

"In many ways Belinda is more mature than you are. Her head is squarely on her shoulders. She's practical and logical in her relationships with other people. I suppose you could describe her as sensible," he concluded.

"How very dull," was Maggie's first reaction, and naturally she said it.

"After our tumultuous years, I think it will be a refreshing change of pace to be married to Belinda." His retort was quick and intended to cut.

"I hope the two of you will be very comfortable together."

She arranged the glasses on a serving tray. "Now, Belinda may not need rescuing, but I think Mike does. Shall we go back to the living room?''

"After you. And, Maggie—" the hard line of his mouth was tempered by forced patience "—try to hold your tongue."

"I do try, Wade. Believe me, I do," she said, taking a deep breath and picking up the tray.

Maggie had expected their return would be met with a searching look. In Belinda's place, she would have been curious and a little jealous to have Wade alone in the

141

kitchen with his ex-wife. But there wasn't a trace of either emotion in the blonde's smiling look. Belinda was either very understanding or very confident that Wade loved only her.

"I hope we didn't take too long." Maggie felt their return demanded some remark from her as hostess, then immediately realized the words she had chosen might intimate that they had been doing more in the kitchen than fixing the drinks.

And after she had just promised Wade she would watch what she said!

She felt doomed.

"Not at all." Belinda seemed indifferent to their absence. She smiled at Wade as he sat on the sofa cushion beside her. "Mike and I have been talking about different things."

"Oh?"

Maggie glanced at Mike. He didn't look as if he'd been doing very much talking. But she felt a curiosity for their subject. "What about?"

Belinda answered, "He was telling me about the fishing trip the three of you took this week. He said each of you caught a fish."

"That isn't exactly true," Maggie corrected the impression, and wondered if Wade hadn't mentioned that she had accompanied him and Mike. "I didn't actually catch a fish. Mike caught one on my rod and gave me credit for it."

"You would have caught it," he came to her defense, "if you hadn't fallen overboard."

"You fell overboard?" The blonde's expression was all concern.

142

Maggie wished Mike hadn't offered that piece of information.

"Yes. It was really nothing."

"How did it happen?"

"Mom caught this fish," Mike started to explain, "and she couldn't get the hook out of its mouth, so dad had to do it for her. He said it was too small to keep and they started arguing."

Maggie wished he wouldn't go into such detail, but there didn't seem to be any way to stop him. "When dad tossed it back into the water, mom tried to catch it. She slipped and went headfirst over the side. Dad tried to grab her, but all he got was her shoe. It was the funniest thing you ever saw!"

Mike was beginning to smile at the memory.

In retrospect, Maggie could see the humor of the incident.

"Mom was soaking wet when she climbed back on the boat. She really got mad when she saw me and dad laughing at her," Mike confided. "When dad gave her the tennis shoe he'd grabbed off her foot, she threw it in the water. I hooked it with my line and got it back before it sank."

"You didn't laugh at her, did you, Wade?" Belinda glanced at him with reproach.

"I'm afraid I did," he admitted, a devilish, unapologetic light dancing in his dark eyes.

"That wasn't kind. No wonder you lost your temper, Maggie," Belinda sympathized.

"I imagine I looked pretty comical."

Maggie found herself defending their amusement at her expense.

"You looked even funnier in that shirt," Mike piped up.

"What shirt?" Belinda asked.

"All her clothes were wet, so mom had to wear this shirt. Only it was too big for her," Mike explained.

"How awful for you, Maggie! It must have been a trying experience."

Again Maggie dismissed the offer of sympathy. "Now that I'm warm and dry and on land, I've recovered my sense of humor. Looking back, it doesn't seem quite so bad."

"Do you like to fish, Miss Hale?" Mike wanted to know.

"Call me Belinda," she corrected him. "Yes, I do like to fish. Wade has taken me with him several times in Alaska. When you come to visit us, the three of us will have to go fishing together."

"It could be fun, huh?" Mike seemed to consider the possibility.

"Not the same kind of fun as you have with your mother." Belinda was making an attempt to show she didn't intend to try to take Maggie's place—a commendable gesture. "At least, I hope I don't fall into the river," she joked. "The water up there is very cold."

"I wouldn't worry about that." Wade's arm was draped over the back of the sofa, lightly brushing the girl's shoulders.

The affection in the implied caress sent a wave of jealousy through Maggie. "There's only one Maggie. The things that happen to her aren't likely to happen to anyone else."

"Thank heaven!" Her murmured response was dryly

144

sarcastic, directed at Wade. His barbed look made her cover it. "Do you ski, Miss Hale? With all that snow in Alaska, it would be a shame if you didn't."

"I love to ski. Of course, there are times when it's too bitterly cold to be out in it."

"I'm sure that's true, but what a perfect excuse to drape yourself in furs."

Maggie sipped at her wine, hating the image of the young blonde wrapped in sables.

"Oh, no, I never wear animal fur," Belinda denied that thought. "I can't stand the idea of an animal being killed just so its fur can be used for a coat."

Good heavens, doesn't she have any faults, Maggie wondered in irritation.

She didn't seem human. Even now, confronted by Wade's ex-wife, Belinda was gracious and charming and disgustingly friendly.

"Oh, dear," Maggie heard herself murmuring with false concern, "I do hope you're not a vegetarian. I have a beautiful rib roast cooking in the oven."

Belinda just laughed at the comment, a throaty, genuinely amused sound.

"No, I'm not a vegetarian. My concern for animal life doesn't seem to apply to my stomach. Or maybe it's the practical side of me that abhors waste. I've never been able to understand why people in India have to starve when there are all those sacred cattle roaming around. It's so senseless and tragic."

"Yes, I know what you mean." But Maggie had the feeling she had lost another round. She set her wineglass down. "Excuse me, I think I'd better check on the dinner."

145

"May I help?" Belinda offered.

"She's an excellent cook," Wade inserted, smiling when Belinda beamed at his compliment.

"I don't doubt it," was Maggie's slightly snappish reply of jealousy. Again she masked it with a quick smile. "Thank you, but I can manage. Excuse me."

CHAPTER THIRTEEN

IN THE KITCHEN she wanted to bang pots and pans, slam cupboard doors, release all this pent-up frustration. How could anyone possibly compete with a woman who was so perfect?

She forced herself to control the anger she felt, but it seethed inside her, bubbling like a volcano.

To make her feel worse, she didn't think there was a gram of jealousy in Belinda's body.

She herself was torn apart by the emotion, and it made her feel small and mean.

When she was satisfied that everything was in order in the kitchen, Maggie decided it was better to begin dinner now than wait and risk overcooking the meal. She carried the servings of spinach salad to the dining-room table before returning to the living room to suggest they come to the table.

"Spinach salad, one of my favorites," Belinda remarked as she sat in a chair opposite from Wade. "Did you tell her it was?" she asked him, and Maggie immediately wished she had chosen something else for the salad course.

"No, I didn't mention it to her."

"It's one of our favorites," Maggie explained grudgingly.

"Do you like spinach, Mike?"

Belinda smiled at the dark-haired boy sitting at the head of the table.

"I like it this way, but I don't like it when it's cooked."

"I don't think many children do," Belinda replied with understanding.

Maggie suspected she was a veritable paragon of understanding. "This is a beautiful set of china, Maggie."

"A wedding gift." Now why had she volunteered that information, Maggie wondered. Why hadn't she simply accepted the compliment with a thank-you? Her irritation increased.

"Are you and dad going to have kids?" Mike blurted out the question.

Maggie felt her cheeks flame in an attempt to match the color of her hair, but she was the only one who registered any embarrassment. Belinda seemed to find nothing wrong with it.

Wade shot Maggie a look that seemed to accuse her of somehow instigating the question.

"We want to have a family, yes," Belinda answered. "We both love children and hope to have several babies. What do you think about becoming a big brother?"

"I don't know."

Mike shrugged and attacked his salad.

Maggie's fork extracted vengeance from the innocent green leaves. Several babies. One big happy family. The only thing wrong with the picture was that Belinda would be in her place. The need to destroy the image consumed her.

"Are you sure you want to go through the two-o'clock

148

feedings, the croup and teething again, Wade?'' She hid her jealousy behind taut mockery. ''Don't you think you're getting a bit old for that? You should have children when you're young and your nerves are more capable of taking the strain. Of course, Belinda is still young and can handle it, but you . . . .'' Maggie let the sentence trail away unfinished, again drawing attention to their age difference.

There was a dangerous glitter in his dark eyes, but Wade responded with marked evenness. ''I'm certain I'll be able to cope, Maggie.''

''I think Wade will make an excellent father,'' Belinda remarked. ''But I suppose you've already had proof of that.''

Again, it was a calm statement of fact, with no envy.

''Wade was a very good father, and still is,'' Maggie agreed, mimicking the blonde's tone. ''I was only concerned that when your children are grown, Wade will practically be in his dotage.''

''What's dotage?'' Mike frowned.

''It's a diplomatic way of saying 'old age,' '' Wade explained, his mouth twisted wryly. ''Your mother is trying to point out that I'm getting older.''

''You are old, aren't you?'' Mike countered with perfect innocence.

It was all Maggie could do not to laugh.

Wade managed to maintain his composure, however tightly held. ''I prefer to believe that I'm just approaching my prime.''

''That's so very true in our society.'' Belinda expanded on his answer.

"A man's attraction increases when he's over thirty, but when a woman reaches that age, she's considered over the hill. I think it's terribly unfair. But haven't you found it to be true, Maggie?"

She was so outraged she couldn't speak.

It didn't matter that the remark hadn't been intended to be personal. It was an unnecessary reminder of her own age.

Wade recognized the danger signals flashing from her. "That opinion is changing. Women over thirty are still very desirable, and people are beginning to recognize that."

He salved her wounded ego.

Maggie had never been particularly sensitive about her age until that moment. Despite Wade's comment, she still felt slightly raw. She managed to bring her temper down to a low simmer. Maggie used the excuse that she had to bring the rest of the food from the kitchen in order to make a discreet exit and regain control of her turbulent emotions.

As she transferred the meat from its roasting pan onto a platter, she realized Wade hadn't said that for her sake. He had been protecting his fiancée from the scorching flash of her temper.

How stupid of her not to have guessed!

The heat of her anger increased a degree instead of lowering.

Maggie laid the carving knife and fork on the meat platter and carried it into the dining room, where she set it in front of Wade.

"Will you carve the meat?"

"Yes," he agreed, and eyed her with quiet speculation.

Gathering the salad plates, she carried them to the kitchen.

With an ominously steady hand she dished up the potatoes and vegetables to take them in.

Over and over in her mind she kept repeating that she wouldn't lose her temper no matter how sorely she was tried.

"Maggie, I think the relationship you have with Mike is quite remarkable," Belinda declared.

"Oh? Why is that?" She set the bowl of potatoes beside Mike's plate.

"I believe it's difficult to raise an only child, especially when the parents are divorced. The tendency for a single parent is to become overprotective. Yet Mike shows no signs of that, even though you are very close. I think it's marvelous that it's turned out that way, since you're nearing the age where it isn't wise to have more children."

There was absolutely nothing malicious in the comment, but it struck a nerve that had become touchy. It was sheer misfortune that Maggie was standing beside Belinda's chair when she made it.

And it was even worse that she had a bowl of cream peas and pearl onions in her hand.

With no conscious direction from her mind, her hand tipped the bowl and poured the creamy vegetables in Belinda's lap. The instant she heard the other girl's startled shriek and saw what she had done, Maggie was horrified.

"I'm so sorry! I don't know how it happened." She was grabbing for a napkin as Belinda pushed her chair away from the table.

151

"I'm sorry," she repeated, and dabbed ineffectually at the spreading stain of cream sauce and smashed peas.

"Damn you, Maggie!"

Wade was swearing under his breath and pushing her out of the way. "I should have known something like this would happen!"

While it hadn't been exactly deliberate, Maggie didn't try to protest her innocence. She wasn't entirely convinced herself that it had been an accident. She felt wretched.

Belinda recovered sufficiently from her stunned dismay to murmur, "It's all right. I'm sure it was an accident."

Maggie thought she would have felt better if the young woman had yelled abuse at her.

All this magnanimous forgiving and understanding was becoming too much.

Mike wasn't helping matters. Both hands were clamped over his mouth in an attempt to hold back his convulsing laughter.

One glance at Maggie and Mike turned away, his shoulders shaking all the harder.

"Come on, Belinda."

Wade was helping the girl to her feet. The worst of the cream sauce and peas were absorbed and blobbed on a once white napkin.

But they had left a large, ugly stain down the front of the blue dress. "I'll take you home," he told her.

"I'm sorry," Maggie repeated, helpless to undo what she had done.

"It will clean, don't worry," Belinda assured her, still slightly in a daze.

"Please send me the bill," Maggie insisted as she followed the couple to the front door. "I'll pay for it."

"You're damned right you will!" Wade snapped. And Maggie knew he wasn't talking about money.

"It was nice meeting you," Belinda called over her shoulder as Wade hustled her out the door.

That convinced Maggie the girl wasn't human. No ordinary mortal could have a bowl of peas spilled on her and still say with sincerity that it was nice to meet the person who did it.

Maggie walked numbly back into the dining room and stared at the peas and onions on the carpet beside Belinda's chair.

Mike no longer tried to contain his laughter as tears rolled from his eyes.

"Stop laughing, Mike! It isn't funny."

"Yes, it is. It's the funniest thing I ever saw!"

"Just shut up and help me clear up this mess before the peas get ground into the carpet."

Maggie bent down and began picking up the vegetables drenched in cream sauce.

Mike joined her, wiping the tears from his cheeks and trying to choke back the laughter. "Mom," he declared, "you're priceless!"

CHAPTER FOURTEEN

MAGGIE FOLDED the damp dish towel and hung it on its rack to dry.

Apart from the leftover roast and potatoes in the refrigerator, there was nothing about the house to suggest she had entertained guests that evening.

All the dishes were washed and put away. The carpet in the dining room had been spot-cleaned of its cream sauce.

The linen tablecloth was buried in the clothes hamper, along with the napkins.

This elimination of any hint of entertaining extended even to herself.

Her face was scrubbed clean of all makeup. The long black hostess skirt and silver lamé blouse were hanging in her closet once again. The onyx earrings were in her jewel box, and the black evening shoes were in her shoe bag.

In their place she wore her new forest green house robe. Barefoot, Maggie walked to the coffeepot and filled a cup with the fresh brew.

The doorbell rang and she didn't need a magic genie to tell her who it was. She had known all along that Wade would be coming back after he had seen Belinda safely home.

She walked into the dining room toward the living room.

Mike answered the door, as she had known he would. "Mom? Dad's here!"

Wade had not changed his clothes. But the knot of his tie was loosened and the top button of his shirt unfastened.

The small change seemed to remove the veneer of civilization to expose a ruthless quality.

As wrong as she was, Maggie wouldn't bow her head to him.

"Hello, Wade," Her voice was amazingly steady. "I've been expecting you. The coffee is fresh. Would you like a cup?"

"No."

Wade glanced at Mike, who was watching them both with silent expectancy.

"Go to your room, Mike. I want to speak to your mother in private."

"Okay."

Mike didn't argue. "Don't be too hard on her, dad. Mom feels pretty bad about what happened."

"On second thought, call your friend next door and see if you can spend the night with him," Wade told him.

Mike glanced hesitantly at Maggie. With a silent nod, she gave her permission. The strained silence over the next few minutes, during which Mike telephoned and got an invitation to spend the night with his friend, was an ordeal.

Maggie drank her coffee and tasted none of it. Both she and Wade were too tense to sit down. They wandered aimlessly around the living room like circling combatants until Mike left.

Then finally, when they were alone, they confronted each other.

Maggie took the initiative. ''There's no excuse for what I did tonight,'' she began.

''I'm glad you realize that.''

The fact that she took the blame didn't appease Wade's anger.

''I didn't do it intentionally, I swear,'' Maggie continued.

''It sure as hell wasn't an accident,'' he growled.

''It wasn't an accident, but it wasn't on purpose, either.''

She set her cup down and twisted her fingers together. ''I didn't even know what I was doing until it was too late.''

''Why, Maggie? Why?'' Wade raked his fingers through the side of his hair. ''Why did you do it?''

''How should I know?'' Maggie protested, angered by her helplessness to explain. ''It just happened.''

''Nothing 'just happens.' Not with you! You make things happen. You strike sparks, then fan them into flames. Before you know it, the fire sweeps through everything and you have a disaster on your hands.''

''If you feel that way, you never should have brought her over here in the first place!'' She struck back with equal vehemence.

''That's typical!'' Wade declared with an angry, exasperated sigh. ''Blame me because you can't control your temper.''

''I'm not blaming you—I blame myself. It was unforgivable and I know that! But I just couldn't take it anymore."

"Take what? Don't tell me you let all that talk about age get under your skin? Why should that bother you?"

"Oh, yes, I remember all you said about women over thirty still being desirable," Maggie said caustically. "It was nothing but talk.

"Look at you—you're marrying a twenty-year-old woman."

"Twenty-one."

"Twenty-one," she repeated. "Let's not forget that one year."

Sarcasm coated her tongue. "It makes all the difference, doesn't it?"

"For God's sake, Maggie, I meant every word I said!" He took her by the shoulders and shook her hard. "Haven't my actions since I came back proved that I find you a very desirable woman still?"

"I'm nothing but a habit to you!"

She flung back his words that had stung her before. "Like when a person quits smoking and keeps on wanting a cigarette."

"Yes," Wade agreed tightly, "even when he knows it's bad for him.

"The problem is when he lights up a cigarette again, all he remembers is how good it is. That's how it's been for me ever since I made the mistake of kissing you again. All I can think about is how good it is."

"Sure," she mocked. "That's why you're engaged to Belinda."

"It's confusing, isn't it?" One corner of his mouth curled in a cynical smile.

157

"You ought to be in my shoes if you want to know what real confusion is like. Belinda is a girl in a million, yet—"

"I don't care if she's a girl in ten million. I'm sick and tired of hearing about her!" Maggie was nearly in tears as she struggled futilely to break out of Wade's hold. "I don't want to hear about her virtues—or the children you're going to have!"

"Jealous?"

Maggie hesitated for only an instant before abandoning all pretense to the contrary. "Yes! Yes, I am jealous. I didn't want to be, I told myself I wouldn't be. But I am jealous of her!"

"Why?" His dark gaze seemed to bore deep into her very soul. "We're divorced. Remember?"

"I know that. And I know I should want you to be happy, but . . . . Why should both of us be alone and miserable?"

"Are you miserable, Maggie?" His hands tightened, drawing her a few inches closer.

Her fingers spread across his chest, slipping inside his jacket to cover the thinness of his shirt. She strained to keep him at a distance.

Conscious of the subtle change in the atmosphere, her pulse behaved erratically.

"Yes, I'm miserable," she admitted, and stared at the hairs curling near the hollow of his throat.

"Don't you like being alone?" Wade demanded.

"No."

"My independent, stubborn little Maggie doesn't like being alone?"

His faint skepticism made it a question. "That's a

change. Six years ago that was the one thing you wanted above all else."

"I know."

"Maggie—" his large hand curved around her throat and under her chin, lifting it up "—did we give up too soon? Could we have made our marriage work?"

A tear collected on the tip of her eyelash. "I don't know."

"What do you know?"

There was a mocking lilt to his low voice that was oddly pleasing.

"I . . . I know that I'm sorry for spilling those peas all over Belinda. I never meant to do it, honestly."

An attempt at a smile trembled over her lips. "There, you have your apology from me. Now you can go back to Belinda and tell her how very contrite I am. In a few days you'll both be laughing about what a termagant your ex-wife is."

"I never laugh about you, Maggie. I never have."

His hard features were composed in a serious expression.

"When we were divorced, I immediately asked my company to transfer me to Alaska because I knew I would never be able to stay away from you unless thousands of miles separated us. Each month, each year, the separation became easier to bear until finally I met Belinda.

"Then I came back here." Wade took a deep breath and released it in a long sigh. "And I find I still can't stay away from you."

"It hasn't been easy to get you out of my system, either."

159

Maggie was moved by his words into admitting her own impossible position.

His hands relaxed on her shoulders and slid around to cross her back. It happened so gently and without force that she barely realized she was being enfolded in his arms.

Her head rested against his shoulder. She felt the feather-light brush of his mouth against her hair, but she didn't object.

"What are we going to do about us?" he mused.

"There isn't any us."

She slid her hands the rest of the way inside his jacket to wind her arms around his middle, unconsciously hugging closer.

"Isn't there, Maggie?"

He kissed the corner of her eye.

She lifted her head and his mouth found her lips.

It was a warm, drugging kiss, slow to passion, allowing Maggie to enjoy the sensation as she moved toward the heights.

Wade was content to make the climb at a leisurely pace.

"Legally we may not be bound to each other," he murmured against the sensitive cord along her neck. "But we haven't broken that one tie that keeps pulling us back together."

"Not Mike?"

"No, not Mike."

His hands roamed with indolent ease over her slim figure, slowly but surely molding her to his granite length.

"We're like two pieces of flint, Maggie. Every time

160

we rub up against each other, we strike sparks. We keep forgetting to put the fire out.''

''It's just physical.''

Her lips began to intimately trace the outline of his jaw, so strong and firm.

''That's what I keep telling myself.'' Wade nibbled at the lobe of her ear. ''That you just know how to please me.''

''That was a long time ago.''

Maggie felt her heart hammering in response to the rapid beat of his.

Her legs felt shaky and weak.

''Was it?'' He moved back to nuzzle her lips. ''Or was it only last night in my dreams?''

His fingers located the zipper latch in the front of her robe.

It slid slowly down to her waist, the hair-roughened back of his hand tickling her bare skin. She seemed to lose her breath as his hand slid inside.

''This is crazy, Wade. We argue all the time.'' But even as she made the protest, her lips were parting in anticipation of his kiss.

''We aren't having an argument now, unless you intend to start one.'' His mouth hovered close to hers, without taking it.

''I should.'' But Maggie hadn't the strength to resist, only to press her mouth to his and accept its hard possession.

Flames leaped and soared around them. Their desire melted them together.

His hands burned over her skin, arousing her flesh to the demands of his.

They were reaching the corner where there would be no turning back.

To her surprise, Maggie found herself breaking away from his kiss. She was trembling, weak with her hunger for him.

Yet she was resisting. It confused her.

"Maggie?"

His fingers sought her chin, trying to twist her head back to him.

"I can't," she answered his unspoken question.

"Why?" His bewildered demand echoed what she was feeling.

"I do want you to make love to me." Maggie looked at him at last, her heart in her eyes.

"But I can't let you. I don't understand it myself, so don't ask me to explain."

"Is it because of Belinda?"

His hand continued its caressing massage of her lower back, an unconscious motion that was sensually disturbing.

"Maybe," she conceded without knowing if it were true.

"It's just . . . that I don't want this to happen for old times' sake. I don't want tonight to be one last fling before you marry Belinda."

Although Wade didn't move, Maggie felt him withdrawing behind a wall of reserve. He was taking control of his emotions and his desires. She wasn't sure if she was glad about that or not.

"I understand," he murmured.

"Do you?" Maggie hoped he did. "We've always done things so impulsively, made decisions in the heat of

162

the moment. Getting married, *and* getting divorced. Before we make another foolish decision, I—"

His forefinger pressed itself against her lips for silence. "Don't say any more." He smiled tightly. "I couldn't stand the shock of hearing practical, sensible statements coming from you."

With a reluctance that thrilled her, he withdrew his arms from around her and zipped the front of her robe shut all the way to her neck. Maggie stood there uncertainly, regretting that she had stopped him even though she knew she was right.

"I don't want you to go," she sighed.

His mouth crooked into a wry smile. "Don't ask me to stay and sleep on the couch."

"Okay, I won't."

She copied his smile. "You sleep in the bed and I'll take the couch."

She was joking and Wade knew it, but he answered seriously.

"I need to think, Maggie, and I can do a better job of it if I don't have the distraction of knowing you are in another room."

"You're leaving, then?"

Maggie said it almost as if she were repeating a verdict.

"Yes."

"Tomorrow . . ." she began.

Wade bent and kissed her lightly on the lips. "We'll see what tomorrow brings.

"By then we'll both have time to be sure our decision is right."

Maggie could have told him that her decision was

163

already made, but pride demanded that she remain silent.

A shiver of apprehension chilled her skin. What if she had missed her chance for happiness?

He walked to the door and paused, not looking back. "Good night, Maggie."

At least it hadn't been goodbye. Not yet, anyway. "Good night, Wade."

WHAT WAS SHE DOING, Maggie wondered as he opened the door and walked out into the night.

Was she sending him back into Belinda's waiting arms?

She hadn't told him that she loved him. Maybe it was better that way.

If his decision went against her, at least she could save face.

She had to accept the probability that Wade wouldn't choose her. He had to care a great deal for Belinda or he would never have asked her to marry him in the first place.

Maggie had no such choice to make. There was only Wade.

A car door slammed. Shortly afterward she heard the engine start and the car reversed out of the driveway. It was going to be a long night, the waiting turning it into an eternity.

She picked up her coffee cup and carried it to the kitchen.

She refilled it and sat down at the chrome table.

It was three in the morning before she turned off the lights and went to bed.

She lay there for a long time, staring at the pattern the moonlight made on the ceiling. At some point in the aching loneliness of time, Maggie drifted off to sleep.

CHAPTER FIFTEEN

A BELL RANG. At first Maggie thought it was her alarm clock and swung her hand to the bedside table to shut it off.

But it wasn't the alarm clock. She fumbled for the telephone, but there was a dial tone on the other end. The bell sounded again as she was about to decide she had dreamed it.

"Mike! Answer the door!" she called, and tried to bury her head under the pillow.

At this hour of the morning any visitor had to be one of Mike's friends.

Then she realized that Mike wasn't home. He had spent the night with Denny next door. And there was only one possible person who might be coming at this hour to see her.

Maggie shot out of the bed like a loaded cannon. She pulled on her robe as she raced down the hall.

"I'm coming!" she called as the doorbell rang again.

Breathless, her face aglow with excitement and hope, she pulled back the bolt and unhooked the safety chain. She jerked the door open, beaming a smile of welcome. But it wasn't Wade standing outside.

It was Belinda Hale.

Maggie stared.

The blonde looked immaculate, not a hair out of place, a sparing but efficient use of makeup. In comparison Maggie felt tousled and sleep-worn, her eyes puffy, her hair a tangle of red silk, too pale without makeup.

"May I come in?" Belinda asked.

Too startled to do anything else, Maggie stepped to one side to admit her.

"I'm a mess, I'm afraid," she apologized for her appearance. "I've just got out of bed."

"That's all right, I understand. I'm never at my best until I've had my orange juice and a morning cup of coffee." Again, there was that smooth, understanding smile.

"About last night and your dress . . ." Maggie began.

"I think we would both feel better if we just forgot about last night and that little incident," Belinda suggested. "I'm convinced you didn't do it intentionally."

"I didn't," Maggie assured her.

"You must be dying for some juice and a cup of coffee. Why don't we go into the kitchen?

"I wouldn't mind another cup myself, if it isn't too much trouble." There was nothing pushy in her manner.

On the contrary, the young woman was being very thoughtful.

"The kitchen is through here."

Maggie led the way. Her mind raced to find a reason for Belinda's arrival here this morning, but she was hesitant to ask.

"This is nice." Belinda glanced around the kitchen in

approval. "Very efficient. It must be a pleasure to cook here."

"It is, when I have the time."

Maggie quickly made a pot of coffee and plugged it in before walking to the refrigerator for the orange juice.

"Where's Mike this morning?"

Was that the reason for Belinda's visit? To renew her acquaintance with Mike? "He's next door at the neighbors'." It was logical since he hadn't yet returned home.

"That's good. It will give us a chance to have a private talk."

"Talk?"

Her hand halted in midair, the orange juice glass poised short of her mouth.

"Yes. I made sure Wade's car wasn't here before I stopped. I knew he wouldn't like me coming to talk to you."

Belinda smiled with faint conspiracy and sat down at the chrome table.

"Wade's car?" Maggie repeated.

"Please don't try to spare me. And please don't be embarrassed," the other girl insisted. "I know Wade spent the night with you last night. I'm not upset. In fact, I think it might be a good thing in the long run."

"You know Wade spent the night here with me?" Maggie repeated the statement to be certain she had heard it correctly.

"Yes. It was fairly obvious. When he took me home, I knew he was coming back here. He came back because he was upset and angry about what had happened to my

168

dress. You're a strikingly beautiful woman, Maggie. When Wade didn't come home, I knew that whatever sparks had flown between you hadn't all been from anger," Belinda explained.

Maggie couldn't believe what she was hearing. "You know he made love to me and you don't mind?" She found that impossible.

"No, I don't mind." Belinda shook her blond head, her expression indulgently gentle. "You see, I think I understand what happened. When a man sees his ex-wife again, it's natural for him to wonder if that old feeling is still around."

"And last night Wade satisfied his curiosity?" Maggie was incredulous that Belinda could take the supposed defection of her fiancé so calmly.

"It's better than having him marry me and wonder about you," Belinda answered.

"Don't you think so?"

"Oh, yes, much better, I'm sure," Maggie agreed dryly, and walked to the cupboard to take out two clean mugs.

"Do you take cream or sugar?"

"Both, please."

"Have you talked to Wade this morning?" She took the sugar bowl out of the cupboard and walked to the refrigerator for the cream.

"No, he wasn't back yet when I left the house. Naturally I'm not going to tell him that I know all about last night. He may volunteer the information on his own, but I won't admit that I know. I think it's the wisest thing. I don't want him to think that I'm the possessive type and will check up on him all the time."

169

"You are definitely not the possessive type," Maggie agreed with the faintest trace of sarcasm.

"It's a waste of emotion. A man is either going to be faithful or he's not. A woman can do all the worrying in the world about where he is or who he's with, but it won't change anything. It can make your life miserable," Belinda declared. "And I'm not going to let my life become miserable."

"It's a commendable philosophy, but difficult to live by, I would think."

The coffeepot stopped perking and Maggie filled the cups.

"Not if you set your mind to it. It becomes amazingly easy."

There was an expressive lift to her shoulders. "It's a matter of not being distracted by harmful emotions."

"I see."

Maggie didn't see at all. By nature she was an emotional person. Belinda seemed the complete opposite. "What is it you wanted to talk to me about?" She carried the mugs to the table, set one in front of Belinda along with the cream and sugar, and carried the second to her chair.

"About Wade."

Mentally Maggie braced herself.

This was the part she understood, where Belinda would ask her to stay away from him, that he no longer belonged to her.

"What about Wade?" Maggie sipped the steaming coffee.

"I want to know all about him—the things that irritate him, the things he likes. There are so many pitfalls in a

170

marriage. I thought if I talked to you first, I could avoid some of the major ones.''

Maggie set the cup down with a jerk, brown liquid slopping over the rim.

There would be no ultimatum for her to leave Wade alone, she realized.

''You can't be serious!''

She choked on her disbelief.

''Oh, but I am. Don't you see how sensible it is?'' the other girl reasoned.

''Sensible? You just accused me of having slept with your fiancé last night. Don't you realize that?'' Maggie asked incredulously. ''Now you're asking me to tell you all the do's and don'ts so your marriage to him can survive. I could tell you all the wrong things, deliberately.''

''But you wouldn't do that, Maggie.'' Belinda laughed away the suggestion.

''Wade has always said that one of your greatest faults was your honesty. If anything, you have proved that to me this minute.''

''Did it ever occur to you that I might want Wade back?'' Maggie argued.

''Of course it occurred to me. But if there'd been any chance of a reconciliation between you, it would have happened before now.''

The woman's confidence was unshakable. Belinda's total lack of jealousy put Maggie at a loss. It was impossible to be angry, or even irritated, in the face of this insanely sensible girl.

That left bewilderment.

''What if I told you Wade and I discovered that old

special feeling was still there? What would you say?"
Maggie wanted to know.

"That it's a good thing Wade found out before he
married me."

Belinda's tone indicated that that was the only logical
reaction.

Logic had never ruled Maggie's heart. She leaned back
in her chair, completely baffled.

"I give up," she sighed in helpless confusion. "You
can't be real!"

Belinda laughed, that throaty, practiced sound.

CHAPTER SIXTEEN

THE SIDE DOOR OPENED and Wade walked in.

He let the door close behind him as he stopped and a puzzling frown of disbelief spread across his male features.

His jacket and tie had been discarded, but otherwise he was wearing the same clothes he had had on last night.

There was a shadowy growth of beard on his cheeks to indicate that he hadn't shaved yet this morning. His black hair was rumpled as if he'd run his fingers through it many times.

His dark gaze narrowed on Belinda.

"I saw your car in the driveway."

His voice indicated that he hadn't believed what he'd seen.

"Our little triangle is complete now," Maggie quipped. "Sit down, Wade. Join us for a cup of coffee, although you might feel the need for something stronger."

He slid a questioning glance at her before sharply returning his attention to Belinda. "What are you doing here?"

If Belinda found the situation awkward, she didn't show it.

"I was in the neighborhood so I thought I'd stop by and assure Maggie that there was no permanent damage to my dress. I had no idea you were coming."

"When you weren't home, I had no idea you would be here, either."

His attitude was wary and suspicious, not completely accepting the surface explanation.

Maggie rose from her chair, a false smile, tinged with cynicism, curving her mouth. "I'm afraid the cat is out of the bag, darling." She walked past him to the kitchen cupboard.

"What cat? What are you talking about?" His frown darkened in confused anger.

Lack of sleep had deepened the lines in his face, high-lighting his male attraction.

"Belinda knows you spent the night with me," she told him sweetly, and poured a third cup of coffee.

"She knows *what!*" Wade roared after a stunned second.

"Don't raise your voice, darling," Maggie chided him with mock reproof. "I said Belinda knows you and I were together all night. Don't worry, dear, she doesn't mind."

"Wade, I don't want you to think I was checking up on you," Belinda inserted as he was momentarily at a loss for words. "Believe me, that's the last thing I would do."

"You see?" Maggie's green eyes rounded with inno-cent serenity. "She does understand."

She started to hand Wade the cup of coffee and paused. "Would you like it plain, or shall I lace it with a little Scotch?"

"I'll take it plain," he snapped, and reached for the

cup. His accusing dark eyes impaled Maggie. "Perhaps you'd better explain to me what's going on? What have you been telling Belinda?"

"Me? I haven't told her anything." Mockingly Maggie placed one hand on her heart and lifted the other as if taking an oath.

Wade gritted his teeth, anger seething through. "You—"

"Don't be angry with Maggie," Belinda broke in. "She didn't tell me anything until she found out that I already knew."

"Knew what?" Wade turned roundly on the girl at the table.

"Darling, you aren't listening," Maggie taunted, and brushed past him to take her chair at the table.

He flashed her an impatient look and demanded of Belinda, "What makes you think I spent the night here?"

"It's fairly obvious, I think." Belinda shrugged. "After you left me, you came back here. And you never came home last night."

"Naturally, she reached the logical conclusion that—"

"Stay out of this, Maggie." Wade cut her short and glowered at Belinda.

"So you assumed I spent the night with Maggie. I admit I was tempted. With the right encouragement, I probably would have!"

"Oh."

For the first time, Belinda looked to be in water out of her depth.

"Then where were you?" Immediately her hand waved aside the question, indicating Wade should ignore it.

175

"No. No, you don't have to answer that. I don't expect you to report your every move to me. I have no intention of tying you down, or interfering in any way with the freedom of your movements."

"You certainly can't accuse Belinda of being possessive, Wade."

"Maggie!"

Wade warned her to keep silent.

"Sorry," she said with false innocence laughing in her green eyes.

"If you like, I can leave you two to thrash this out on your own."

"If there's anything that needs thrashing, it's you," he retorted.

"I feel so awful, Maggie. I owe you an apology for what I was thinking," Belinda insisted.

"No, you don't." Maggie's natural candor surfaced. "If I could live last night over again, it would probably turn out to be just the way you thought it had. Your assumption was wrong, but not because I didn't want Wade to stay.

"I did, but I was afraid one of us, or both of us, might regret it in the morning. So don't apologize. If anyone is sorry, it's me," Maggie concluded and stared into her coffee cup, all her cynical humor at the situation gone.

"Now that you have that confession out of your system," Wade declared, "I think it's time Belinda was leaving.

"Come on," he told his fiancée and helped pull her chair away from the table. "You and I have some things to discuss."

176

"Of course, Wade," Belinda agreed. But he wasn't giving her a chance to disagree as he took hold of her arm and forced her to walk to the side door.

Over her shoulder, she managed, "Goodbye, Maggie. I'm sorry. Maybe we can have our talk another time."

Maggie nodded and suppressed a shudder of dread. "Another time," she agreed. "Goodbye," and hoped she never saw her again. But of course she would; Maggie was convinced of that.

As the door closed she heard Wade demand, "What were you going to talk to Maggie about?"

She didn't hear Belinda's reply, but she knew the answer. Their little tiff would work itself out; Belinda would see to it.

There was no doubt in Maggie's mind that Wade had chosen his fiancée.

A remark he had made when he first walked in had given his decision away.

He had said that when he hadn't found Belinda at home, he had wondered where she was. So he had obviously been returning to her.

A broken sigh came from her heart, and her fingers raked into her tousled red hair to support her lowered head.

Being prepared for his decision didn't make the wrenching pain any easier to accept. The rest of her life yawned emptily before her and Maggie wondered how she would make it alone.

She squeezed her eyes tightly shut and bit into her lower lip.

Car doors slammed and engines started. Sniffing back a

sob, Maggie tossed her head to shake away the throes of self-pity.

Mike could walk in at any minute and she didn't want him to find her crying. There would be plenty of lonely hours to indulge in that.

CHAPTER SEVENTEEN

BRISKLY SHE ROSE to clear the coffee cups and juice glass from the table.

Returning the sugar bowl and cream to their respective places, she wiped the table and refilled her cup with coffee.

As she was walking back to the table, the side door opened.

When she saw Wade enter the kitchen, Maggie dropped the cup in her hand. It shattered on impact, spilling its hot contents on the floor amid the fragments of broken pottery.

"Damn, look what you made me do!" she cried angrily to hide the leaping joy of hope in her heart. "Do you have to burst in on people all the time? Why can't you ever knock?"

As she stooped to pick up the broken pieces, Wade was there to help.

"Be careful or you'll cut yourself," he muttered impatiently. "Let me do it. You get a rag to mop up the coffee."

Finding his closeness too disturbing, Maggie obeyed.

She took a rag from under the sink and began mopping up the floor, careful to avoid the fragments Wade hadn't collected yet.

"I thought you'd left with Belinda," she murmured to explain her shock when he had returned to the house. "I heard your car."

"I was parked behind her. I had to move my car so she could get out."

He put the broken pieces of the coffee cup in the waste bin.

"You could have gone with her. You didn't have to come back."

Maggie wished he hadn't.

"I didn't?"

A dark eyebrow lifted quizzically.

"No."

She refused to meet his look. "I realized that you'd made your decision. You didn't have to come back to tell me or explain."

"You're as bad as Belinda about jumping to conclusions," he said.

There was an underlying grimness to his voice.

Maggie thought she understood the reason for it. "Look, I know you're upset with Belinda right now. But she's young and she's trying very hard to behave the way she thinks best."

"You think I've decided to go ahead with my plans to marry Belinda?"

"Yes—you said . . . ."

Maggie made the mistake of glancing at him, and the look in his eyes confused her.

"What did I say?" Wade prompted, still watching her in that bemused way.

"Where were you last night?" she asked instead of answering.

Belinda might have been reluctant to ask him, but Maggie wasn't.

"Driving. Thinking. I drank a lot of coffee at a lot of different restaurants—I don't remember which ones."

"This morning you went to Belinda's home to see her. You said so," she reminded him.

"So you assumed that meant I was returning to her." Wade followed her comment to the conclusion Maggie had reached.

"Weren't you?" she asked, suddenly breathless.

"No, I was trying to do the proper thing. I wanted to break my engagement to her before coming to you."

He took the wet rag from her hand and tossed it in the sink.

"I never dreamed she was here."

"Are you sure?"

Maggie hardly dared to believe him. "What happened this morning didn't have anything to do with your decision?"

"It eliminated any doubts that might have been lingering."

His hands gently settled on her shoulders.

"Belinda is very understanding. I doubt if she ever loses her temper or starts arguments."

Maggie felt bound to point out the sharp contrast between them.

"Milk toast can make one feel better for a while, but a steady diet of it would soon make life very bland. Life with you was never dull, Maggie.

"I much prefer the road ahead of me to be filled with challenge. How about you?"

"Yes."

Maggie gravitated toward him. In the next second she was wrapped in the hard circle of his arms, his mouth crushing down on hers.

Joy burst from her like an eternal fountain, her happiness spilling over in the wild rush to give him all of her love. It was impossible. It would take a lifetime to do that.

Wade seemed to recognize that, too. He broke off the kiss to bury his face in the lustrous thickness of her red gold hair.

His arms remained locked around her, and she felt the powerful tremors that shuddered through him.

"I love you, Maggie." The deep intensity of his emotion couldn't be muffled.

"I pretended I didn't, even to myself. But I never stopped loving you."

"And I never stopped loving you, but I was too scared to admit it," she responded.

"You? Scared?" Wade laughed softly at the thought. "My tigress has never been afraid to tackle anything."

"That isn't true, because I was always afraid of you. I realized that last night after you'd left." Her fingers outlined the angle of his jaw, free at last to caress him as much as she wanted.

Wade lifted his head to look at her, a frown creasing his forehead.

"Why should you be afraid of me?"

Her dimples came into play for a moment. "Whether you're aware of it or not, there's a certain quality about you that's dominating. But I don't think I was so much afraid of that.

"Subconsciously I realized that I loved you so much

nothing else mattered. I was in danger of becoming totally absorbed in your personality, losing my own identity.

"I was constantly fighting that, which meant always arguing with you."

"Now?"

"Now I'm going to stop fighting the fact that I love you," Maggie promised, rising on tiptoe to kiss him.

His gaze roamed possessively over her face, the hands on her back keeping her close.

Faint, loving amusement glittered in the jet blackness of his eyes.

"Does that mean no more arguments?" he mocked.

"I doubt it," she laughed. "I'd hate to start boring you."

"I'd probably start picking fights if you did." His mouth teased the edges of her lips. "If only to have the fun of making up afterward."

CHAPTER EIGHTEEN

WHEN MAGGIE COULD no longer stand the tantalizing brush of his mouth, she sought the heady excitement of his kiss.

Wade let her take the initiative for a few breathless moments before taking over with a mastery that left her weak at the knees.

She clung to him, her heart beating wildly, as Wade forced her head back to explore the hollow at the base of her throat.

"Poor Belinda," murmured Maggie. "She's going to feel so badly when you tell her."

"I already have," he said against her skin.

"You have?"

"Yes, when I walked her to her car."

In the unending circle of his love, Maggie was generous enough to feel sympathy.

"Was she very upset?"

"Belinda?" said Wade as if it were impossible. "She took the news with her usual calmness."

"Don't tell me!" Maggie swallowed back a disbelieving laugh. "She didn't recite some platitude that it was better you found out before you married her, did she?"

"You took the words right out of her mouth," he admitted.

"She should be on exhibit in some museum. Sometimes I can't believe she's for real," she sighed.

"Belinda has a lot to learn about life and people. It's easy to think you have all the answers when you're young."

"Yes," Maggie agreed. "I'm just glad, though, that we have a second chance."

"Our marriage will be better this time," Wade promised her.

"Our heads may be in the clouds, but our feet are solidly on the ground.

"Speaking of marriage, when do you want the wedding? Is next week too soon?"

"Tomorrow couldn't be too soon," she declared.

"For me, either."

His arms tightened to crush her ribs.

"Dad?"

Mike's voice called from the living room.

The front door was closed and the sound of running feet approached the kitchen.

Maggie and Wade exchanged a smile as he burst in on them.

"I didn't know you were here, dad, until I saw the car in the driveway." His dark eyes rounded as he took in the fact that his mother was firmly enwrapped in his father's arms.

He seemed hesitant to draw any conclusion. "You aren't mad at mom anymore, are you?" was the closest he would come.

"No, I'm not mad at her anymore." Wade smiled down on Maggie, then bent his head to kiss the tip of her nose.

"By the way, Mike, I've decided I'm not going to marry Belinda."

"You're not?" he repeated uncertainly.

"No, I'm not. I've decided your mother is much more in need of a man to look after her and keep her out of trouble. I've volunteered for the job, having had past experience. And she's accepted."

"Does that mean . . ." Mike began. "Are you and mom going to get married again?"

"Yes, we are," Maggie answered.

"For good?" Mike asked.

Wade answered, "For good . . . and bad, fighting and arguing and loving for the rest of our life." He looked at Maggie as he spoke, warming every inch of her with the love that shone in his eyes. "I hope you're as happy about it as we are, Mike."

"You bet I am!" he exclaimed now that he was fully convinced that they meant it.

"Oh, wow! I hoped—does this mean we're going to live in Alaska?"

"Yes. Would like that?" Wade watched closely for Mike's reaction.

"Would I? You could teach me how to ski! And maybe we could buy a sled and some dogs? And mom could go fishing with us and catch one of those big fish like we did!"

Mike began making plans.

"With our luck, the fish will probably pull her into the water," Wade laughed.

"Wow! I gotta go tell Denny we're moving to Alaska!" Mike exclaimed, and shot out of the kitchen for the neighbor's house.

186

As the door banged shut behind him, Wade curved a finger under Maggie's chin and turned her head to look at him.

There was a shimmer of tears in her eyes.

"What's the matter, honey?"

"Mike was so happy." She smiled at being so silly as to cry over that.

"I know."

He gently wiped the glistening tears from her lashes. "I never did ask you whether you wanted to live in Alaska."

"You know I don't care where I live so long as it's with you," Maggie told him.

"Careful! You're beginning to sound corny," Wade teased her.

"I don't care," she sighed, and rested her head against his shoulder.

She had never known such contentment.

"We'll call the real estate company on Monday and put the house up for sale. What about the furniture? Do you want to store it or take it with us?"

"We can take some of it and store the rest," Maggie decided, and sighed.

"What's that for?"

"I was just thinking about all the packing and sorting that has to be done. I have to give notice at my job. There's the utilities to call—there's so much to do."

"Would you rather not move?" Wade asked.

"No, it's not that. I just wished I had a genie who would do it all for me."

She laughed at her laziness. "How soon will we be going?"

"After our honeymoon."

"Are we going to have a honeymoon?"

"Don't all newlyweds?" he teased.

"Where are we going?"

Maggie was curious.

"I thought we'd take the boat and go up to the San Juan Islands in the sound, maybe all the way to Vancouver," Wade told her.

"What boat? You don't mean Belinda's?"

Maggie pulled away from his arms, astounded by his suggestion. "Isn't that expecting rather a lot from her?"

"That wasn't Belinda's boat. Did you think it belonged to her family?" he queried in amusement.

"Yes. Whose else would it be? I mean, you'd borrowed her car, so I naturally assumed you'd borrowed her boat."

"Well, I didn't. It belongs to one of the men who works with me.

"He gave me the keys and told me to use it while I was here," Wade explained.

"Oh."

"Do you feel better now?" He gently drew her back into his arms.

"Much better. I'm not as open-minded as Belinda," Maggie warned him.

"The thought of spending my second honeymoon in her family's boat—"

"—touched a spark to your temper?" Wade finished the sentence for her.

"Something like that," she admitted.

"It's fitting, isn't it?"

"What?"

188

"For us to be leaving Seattle for Alaska, the same way the prospectors did, using this place as the jumping-off point on their way to the goldfields."

"I suppose so, except we aren't going to find gold."

"No. The only gold I'm interested in is a plain hollow circle to go around your finger." Wade found her left hand carried it up to kiss her ring finger. Then he glanced at the bareness of it. "What did you do with your rings?"

"Don't ask." Maggie shook her head and tried to withdraw her hand from his hold. "It's better if you don't know."

"Why? What *did* you do with them?" Her answer had fully aroused his curiosity.

Maggie knew he wouldn't leave the subject alone until she answered him. "I threw them in the river."

CHAPTER NINETEEN

"YOU DID *WHAT?*" Disbelieving anger darkened his eyes.

"You threw your wedding band *and* your diamond ring in the river?"

"I told you it would be better if you didn't know," she reminded him of her warning.

"Why on earth would you do that?" he demanded.

"I was mad. That day you left for Alaska, you brought Mike home, but you never came in to say goodbye to me.

"The next day I was at my lunch break. There was the river and there were the rings on my fingers. I decided if you didn't think enough of me to say goodbye, I didn't think enough of you to wear your rings. So I took them off and threw them in the river."

"Oh, Maggie!"

His anger dissipated into a rueful smile. "I didn't come in to say goodbye because I knew I'd never be able to go if I did. It wasn't because I didn't want to see you. I couldn't."

"We must be the most stubborn people in the world. Neither one of us wanted to be the first to admit we'd made a mistake about the divorce."

"It's a communication problem that isn't going to happen again. I love you, Maggie. Whatever else I say, for whatever reason, always remember that,'' he ordered.

"Yes, sir," she agreed with mock obedience.

"You're being impertinent!"

"You'd better do something about it," she suggested. "Try a little communication."

"We're going to have a lot of communication, but first there's a problem that needs immediate attention."

"Oh? What is that?"

Maggie challenged the thought that anything could be important.

"A place to stay. I can't very well stay at Belinda's home now that I've broken the engagement."

"That is a problem," Maggie agreed. "I guess you could always move in here. You can always sleep on the couch."

"The couch, hell!" he growled against her lips.

WITH A LITTLE LUCK

BEING ALONE WITH HIM
MADE HER FEEL UNEASY

When Luck crouched beside her, Eve found it difficult to breathe normally. His warm scent was all around her.

"Thanks for the picnic, Eve." His hand reached out to cup the back of her head and pull her forward.

Lifting her gaze, Eve watched the sensual line of his mouth coming closer. She couldn't have resisted him if she wanted to. The kiss started her trembling all the way to her toes. But much too soon Luck was lifting his head, leaving her lips aching for the warm pressure of his mouth.

The very brevity of his kiss reminded Eve that it was a gesture of gratitude. Lowering her head, she struggled to appear as unmoved by the experience as he seemed to be.

CHAPTER ONE

"ARE YOU SURE you wouldn't like a ride home?" the Reverend Mr. Johnson inquired. "If you don't mind waiting a few minutes, I would be happy to drive you."

Mr. Johnson didn't look like a minister in his plaid shirt and khaki-colored pants. In his mid-forties, he resembled a fisherman who had strayed into church by mistake. In fact, he was an ardent angler, overjoyed that his Wisconsin parish was situated in an area with so many lakes, streams and rivers. He loved to state that while he was a "fisher of men" like the Lord, he was also a fisherman, an occupation and an avocation that he felt were ideally suited to one another.

"No, thank you, Reverend. It's a lovely evening and I'll enjoy the walk," Eve Rowland insisted as she slipped on her summer-weight coat of brown. "Besides, it isn't that far, really."

"Yes, but I don't like the idea of your walking alone after dark."

"Cable isn't Minneapolis or Milwaukee," she laughed. There were times when she even forgot to lock the front door of her parents' house, but she didn't worry unduly on those occasions.

"My city background is showing, isn't it?" he smiled at himself. "Thanks for filling in for Mrs. Alstrom at the organ tonight." She was the regular church organist. A minor crisis at home had kept her from attending choir practice and Eve had been asked to substitute for her. "I hope it didn't upset any of your plans for the evening."

"I didn't have any plans," she said, and didn't go any further in her reply. It was rare for her ever to have plans for an evening—social plans, that is.

"That's a pity." The minister's eyes darkened with sympathy, even as he changed his expression to give her an encouraging smile. "You are a warm and generous woman. Maybe I should whisper in the ears of the eligible male members of my congregation."

He meant to be kind but his offer had a demoralizing effect. Eve fixed a quick smile in place to hide her reaction. "That's a nice thought, but most of them are already semiattached to someone else. You might as well save your matchmaking talents for another time." She started to leave. "Good night. And I'm glad I could help out."

"I'll see you in church on Sunday." Mr. Johnson lifted his hand in a saluting wave.

"Not this Sunday," she said. "We're opening

the summer cottage on the lake, so neither my parents nor I will be in church.''

"Oh? Which lake?" His fishing curiosity was awakened.

"Namekagon." Which was only a few miles east of town.

"Marvelous fishing there," he stated.

"I know. It's dad's favorite." She glanced at her wristwatch, a utilitarian piece with a plain leather band that made no pretense of being decorative. "I'd better be going. Good night, Reverend Johnson."

"Good night."

Leaving the church, Eve buttoned her coat against the invading night air. Although it was officially summer, the temperature in the Northwoods dipped to the cool range in the evening hours. The sky was crystal bright with stars, hundreds of thousands of them lighting the heavens. A moon, big and fat, competed with the stars; its silver globe was nearly a spotlight shining down on the earth. The streetlights along the main thoroughfare were almost unneeded.

As she walked along the sidewalk, her mind kept echoing the matchmaking offer the minister had made. Having lived in Cable for all of her twenty-six years—with the exception of four years spent at college in Madison—Eve knew virtually every single man in the area. Those she might have been interested in never noticed her;

and those that noticed her she wasn't interested in. She was almost convinced she was too particular.

Her mother despaired that Eve would ever find a man who could satisfy her, and kept reminding her that with each passing year she was becoming more set in her ways. Eve had given up hope long ago that Prince Charming would ever come this far north, but she wasn't going to get married just for the sake of being married, no matter how nice and respectable a suitor might be. She didn't intend to marry unless she had, at least, a deep affection for the man. So far, no one had aroused even that. There had been boyfriends now and then. Most of them she genuinely liked, but not with any depth. It seemed she was always attracted to men who weren't attracted to her.

It wasn't because she was homely. She was attractive, in a plain sort of way. With brown hair and eyes, she had a flawless complexion, but her features were unassuming. Her figure was average, neither thin nor plump. She wasn't too tall or too short. She simply didn't stand out in a crowd. In a sea of pretty faces, hers would be the last to be noticed.

Eve was just as realistic in her assessment of her personality traits. She was intelligent, basically good-natured and possessed a good sense of humor. As a music teacher, she appreciated music and the arts. But she tended to be quiet and not quick to make friends. Her early years as a wallflower had lessened her inclination for parties. She preferred celebrating with a few close friends to attending a large social function. By nature she wasn't aggressive, although she wouldn't allow herself to be walked on.

There were some who suggested that, at twenty-six, she was too old to be living at home. When Eve considered the cost of living alone versus her salary, it became a matter of sheer practicality. Besides, she and her parents were good friends. She was just as independent as she would have been living in an apartment.

With all her thoughts focused inward, Eve didn't notice the tavern she was approaching. A window was open to let out the smoke and let in fresh air. Inside, a jukebox was loudly playing a popular song. Eve didn't hear it or the laughter and spirited voices. Her gaze was on the sidewalk in front of her feet.

Suddenly a man stepped directly in front of her. Eve didn't have time to stop or step aside. Her hands came up to absorb the shock of the collision. He evidently didn't see her, either, as he took a step forward and collided head-on. In a reflex action his arms went around to catch her, while his forward progress carried her backward two steps.

Dazed by the total unexpectedness of the accident, Eve lifted her head. She wasn't certain that the fault belonged entirely to either one of them. Too stunned yet to speak, she stared at the stranger she'd bumped into—or vice versa.

The light from the neon tavern sign fully illuminated his face. Nearly a head taller than she was, he had dark hair that waved in thick strands to fall at a rakish angle across his forehead. His eyes were blue, with a perpetual glint of humor in them. Tanned skin was stretched across very masculine features. He was handsome in a tough rakehell sort of way. A reckless smile showed the white of his teeth.

"What's this I've caught?" His mocking voice was matched by the laughing glint in his eyes as they traveled over her, taking in the brown of her hair and eyes and the brown coat. "I believe it's a brown mouse."

The teasing remark did not go down well, considering the earlier demoralizing remark by the minister. Her gaze dropped to the cream-colored pullover and the thin-striped blue-and-cream color of his shirt collar. Since he had obviously just left the tavern, Eve wasn't surprised that there was liquor on his breath. He'd been drinking, but he wasn't drunk. He was steady on his feet, and there was no glaze of alcohol in the rich blue of his eyes.

"I'm sorry," Eve apologized stiffly. "I wasn't paying attention to where I was going." Then she realized his arms were still holding her and her hands were flattened against his chest—a very solid chest. Her heart began to beat unevenly.

"I wasn't looking where *I* was going, so it seems we were both to blame, brown mouse. Did I hurt you?" It was more disturbing to listen to the low pitch of his voice without seeing his face, so Eve looked up. His half-closed eyes were difficult to meet squarely.

"No, you didn't." When he showed no inclination to release her, she stated, "I'm all right. You can let go of me now."

"Must I?" he sighed deeply. His hands moved, but not away from her. Instead they began roaming over her shoulders and spine in an exploring fashion, as if testing the way she felt in his arms. "Do you know how long it's been since I held a woman in my arms?"

The well-shaped line of his mouth held a latent sensuality as his question confirmed the direction that Eve had suspected his thoughts were taking. His hands were exerting a slight pressure to inch her closer to him. They were standing on the sidewalk of a main street a few feet away from a tavern full of people.

Surely he wouldn't try to accost her in such a place? She wanted to struggle, but she was afraid he might view it as provocation rather than resistance. Yet she recognized the inherent danger in the situation. She kept her body rigid.

"Would you please let me go?" she requested.

"I'm frightening you, aren't I?" He tipped his head to one side, regarding her lazily, while his hands stopped their movement.

201

"Yes," Eve admitted, because her heart was beating a mile a minute and there was a choked sensation in her throat.

He let his hands slide away to let her stand free. She had expected an argument. It was a full second before she realized he was no longer holding her. She brushed past him and was a step beyond him when his hand snaked out to catch her arm.

"Don't scurry off into the dark, brown mouse." His voice chided her for running. "Stay a minute."

"No." His hand forced her to stop, but she lifted her arm in protest of his grip, straining against the unyielding strength of his fingers.

"What's your hurry? Are you meeting someone?"

The questions were curious, interested.

"No." Eve was confused and wary. He wouldn't release her, but he was making no move to do more than keep her there.

"Where are you going in such a rush?" Shadows fell across his face to throw the angles and planes of his features into harsh relief. They enhanced his rough virility, adding to the aura of dangerous attraction.

"I'm going home," she stated.

"I don't have any place to go but home, either," he said. "So why don't we go some place together? Then we won't have to go home."

"I want to go home," Eve insisted firmly, despite the faint quiver that was spreading up her arm from the restraining touch of his hand.

"Why? It's lonely there."

She had difficulty imagining a man like him ever being lonely. It was obviously a line. She wasn't going to be strung along by it.

"Let me put it another way: I don't want to go with you."

"I think I'm giving you the wrong impression." A half smile slanted his mouth, casually disarming. "I want to go someplace where we can talk."

Another line, Eve guessed. "I doubt that you're interested in talking," she returned with a tinge of sarcasm.

"It's true," he insisted, and moved to stand more to the front of her, without letting go of her arm.

Eve stared straight ahead in an effort to ignore him and the strange leaping of her pulse. His other hand moved to touch the side of her silky brown hair. Instinctively she jerked away from the soft caress, preferring force to his present means of intimidating her. She turned her head to stare at him.

When she met his gaze, Eve realized he was a man who communicated by touching—with his hands or his gaze. . . or his mouth and his body. Unbidden, her mind had added the last. She didn't doubt his expertise in any area. Her composure began to splinter a little, undermined by her unexpectedly wayward imagination.

"It is true," he repeated. "Don't you know that a man can talk to a brown mouse?"

Which was hardly flattering in the light of her own low opinion of her sex appeal.

"Would you please not call me that?" Irritation flashed through her as she refused to comment on his observation.

"I always wondered if a brown mouse would retaliate when it was backed into a corner. There is some spirit there, behind that apparent timidity." It was obvious by the look of satisfaction on his face that she had heightened his interest. Eve wished she had kept her mouth shut. "A brown mouse. That's what you are, you know. With your brown hair and your brown eyes and your brown coat."

He was baiting her, but this time she ignored him. "I am a brown mouse who is anxious to go home, so would you let me go?" She injected a weary note in her voice, as if she were finding him quite tiresome. Fleetingly it occurred to her that she wouldn't be in this situation if she had accepted the Reverend Mr. Johnson's offer of a ride home.

"If you insist that's what you want to do, I'll walk with you to make sure you arrive safely and no cat pounces on you on the way home."

"I can think of only one 'cat' that might pounce on me and that's you," Eve retorted.

"Touché!" he laughed, and she was upset with herself for liking the sound of it.

She faced him directly. "If you don't leave me alone, I'm going to have to scream."

"Mice squeak," he corrected, but his gaze had narrowed on her, judging to see how serious she was about her threat.

"This brown mouse screams," she insisted.

She could, and if she felt sufficiently threatened, she would. It hadn't reached that point yet, but this conversation had gone on long enough.

"I believe she does," he agreed after a second had passed. He released her arm and lifted his hands in a mocking indication that he wouldn't touch her again.

"Thank you." Eve wasn't sure why she said that. Immediately she began walking away, trying not to walk too fast. She could feel him watching her with those magnetic blue eyes. It was an unnerving sensation.

"Good night, brown mouse." His low voice called after her, a hint of regret in its tone.

She didn't answer him. For another ten feet, Eve wondered if he would start following her. She forced herself not to look back. A few seconds later she heard the tavern door open and close. She glanced over her shoulder, but he wasn't in sight. Since no customer had come out, he had obviously gone back inside. She didn't have to wonder anymore whether he would come after her. Instead Eve found herself wondering who he was.

It was after ten when she reached her home. Both her parents were in the living room when she walked in. Neither of them was particularly striking in his appearance. Her father was a tall spare man with hazel eyes and thinning brown hair, while her mother was petitely built, with graying brown hair and brown eyes. It was a toss-up from whom Eve had inherited her common looks.

"Choir practice must have run late," her mother observed. It was a statement of conversation, not a remark about Eve's lateness in getting home.

"A little." She shrugged out of her brown coat and wondered if she would ever wear it again without thinking of herself as a brown mouse. "Mr. Johnson offered me a ride home, but it was such a lovely evening I decided to walk. So it took a little longer."

She didn't mention the stranger outside the tavern. They were still her parents. Eve didn't want to cause them needless concern. It had been a harmless incident anyway, not worth recounting.

IN THE MIDDLE OF THE NIGHT Toby McClure rolled onto his side. His long, little boy lashes fluttered, his sleep disturbed by a faint sound. He slowly let them come open, his sleepy blue eyes focusing on the door to his bedroom, which stood ajar. Listening, he heard hushed movement in another part of the house. A smile touched the corners of his mouth and deepened when he heard the person bump into a chair and curse beneath his breath.

Throwing back the covers, Toby slipped out of his single bed and walked to the hall door. His bare feet made no sound on the carpeted floor. He opened the door wide and waited until he saw the towering frame of his father separate from the darkness. He was walking unsteadily, trying so hard to be quiet.

The light from the full moon streamed through the window at the end of the hallway where Toby stood, including him in its path. The instant he saw the boy, his father, Luck McClure, stopped abruptly and swayed, bracing a hand against the wall to steady himself. A frown gathered on his forehead as he eyed the boy.

"What are you doing out of bed? You're supposed to be asleep," he accused in a growling voice that had a trace of a slur.

"You woke me up," Toby replied. "You always do when you try to sneak in."

"I wasn't sneaking." He emphatically denied that suggestion and glanced around. "Where's Mrs. Jackson, the lady who is supposed to be sitting with you?"

"She was going to charge double after midnight, so I paid her off and sent her home. You owe me twelve dollars."

"You—" Luck McClure clamped his mouth shut on the explosion of anger and carefully raised a hand to cradle his forehead. "We'll talk about this in the morning, Toby," he declared in heavy warning.

"Yes, sir. I'll remind you if you forget," he promised. A mischievous light danced in his eyes. "You owe me twelve dollars."

"That's another thing we'll discuss in the morning." But it was a weak facsimile of his previous warning, as a wave of tiredness washed over him. "Right now, I'm going to bed."

Luck pushed away from the wall and used that impetus to carry him to the bedroom door opposite his son's. Toby watched him open the door to the darkened room and head in the general direction of the bed. Without a light to see the exact location of his destination, Luck stubbed his toe on an end post. He started to swear and stopped sharply when Toby crossed the hall to flip the switch, turning on the overhead light.

"Why aren't you back in bed where you belong?" Luck hobbled around to the side of the bed and half sat, half fell onto the mattress.

"I figured you'd need help getting ready for bed." Toby walked to the bed with all the weary patience of an adult and helped finish tugging the pullover sweater over his father's head.

"For an eight-year-old kid, you figure a lot of things," Luck observed with a wry sort of affection. While he unbuttoned the cuffs of his shirt, Toby unfastened the buttons on his shirtfront.

"You've gotta admit, dad, I did you a favor tonight," Toby said as he helped pull his arms free of the shirt. "How would it have looked if Mrs. Jackson had seen you come home drunk?"

"I'm not drunk," Luck protested, unfastening his pants and standing long enough to slip them down his hips. Toby pulled them the rest of the way off. "I just had a few drinks, that's all."

"Sure, dad." He reached over and pulled down the bedcovers. It didn't take much persuasion to get his father under them.

"It feels so good to lie down," Luck groaned, and started to shut his eyes when Toby tucked the covers around him. He opened them to give his son a bleary-eyed look. "Did I tell you I talked to a brown mouse?" The question was barely out before he rolled onto his side, burrowing into the pillow. "You'd better get some sleep, son," he mumbled.

Shaking his head, Toby walked to the door and paused to look at his already snoring father. He reached up to flip off the light.

"A brown mouse," he repeated. "That's another thing we'll discuss in the morning."

Back in his moonlit room, Toby crawled into bed. He glanced at the framed photograph on the table beside his bed. The picture was a twin to the one on his father's bureau. From it, a tawny-haired blonde with green eyes smiled back at him—his mother, and easily the most beautiful woman Toby had ever seen. Not that he remembered her. He had been a baby when she died—six years ago today. His gaze strayed in the direction of his father's bedroom. Sighing, he closed his eyes.

SHORTLY AFTER EIGHT the next morning, Toby woke up. He lay there for several minutes before he finally yawned and climbed out of bed to stretch. Twenty minutes later he had brushed his teeth and washed, combed his hair and found a clean pair of jeans and a yellow T-shirt to wear.

Leaving his bedroom, he paused in the hallway to look in on his father. Luck McClure was sprawled across the bed, the spare pillow clutched by an encircling arm. Toby quietly closed the door, although he doubted his father would be disturbed by any noise he made.

In the kitchen, he put a fresh pot of coffee on to perk, then pushed the step stool to the counter and climbed it to reach the juice glasses and a cereal bowl in the cupboard. Positioning the stool in front of another cupboard, he mounted it to take down a box of cornflakes. With orange juice and milk from the refrigerator, Toby sat down to the kitchen table to eat his breakfast of cereal and orange juice.

By the time he'd finished, the coffee was done. He glanced from it to the pitcher of orange juice, hesitated, and walked to the refrigerator to take out a pitcher of tomato juice. Climbing back up the step stool, he took down a tall glass and filled it three-quarters full with tomato juice. When he returned the pitcher to the refrigerator, he took out an egg, cracked it, and added it to the tomato juice. He stirred that mixture hard, then added garlic and Tabasco to it. Sniffing the end result, he wrinkled his nose in distaste.

Taking the glass, he left the kitchen and walked down the hallway to his father's room. He hadn't changed position in bed. Toby leaned over, taking great care not to spill the contents of the glass, and shook his father's shoulder with his free hand.

"It's nine o'clock, dad. Time to get up." His statement drew a groan of protest. "Come on, dad."

With great reluctance, Luck rolled onto his back, flinging an arm across his eyes to shield them from the brightness of the sunlight shining in his window. Toby waited in patient silence until he sat up.

"Oh, my head," Luck mumbled, and held it in both his hands, the bedcovers falling around his waist to leave his torso bare.

Toby climbed onto the bed, balancing on his knees while he offered his father the concoction he'd made. "Drink this. It'll make you feel better."

Lowering his hands part way from his head, Luck looked at it skeptically. "What is it?"

"Don't ask," Toby advised, and reached out to pinch his father's nose closed while he tipped the glass to his lips. He managed to pour a mouthful down before his father choked and took the glass out of his hand.

"What is this?" Luck coughed and frowned as he studied the glass.

"It's a hangover remedy." And Toby became the recipient of the glowering frown and a raised eyebrow.

"And when did you become an expert on hangover remedies?" Luck challenged.

"I saw it on television once," Toby shrugged.

Luck shook his head in quiet exasperation. "I should make you drink this, you know that, don't you?" he sighed.

"There's fresh coffee in the kitchen." Toby hopped off the bed, just in case his father intended to carry out that threat.

"Go pour me a cup. And take this with you." A smile curved slowly, forming attractive grooves on either side of his mouth—male dimples—as he handed the glass back to Toby. "I'll be there as soon as I get some clothes on."

"I'll pour you some orange juice, too," Toby volunteered.

"Just straight orange juice. Don't put anything else in it."

"I won't." A wide grin split Toby's face before he turned to walk swiftly from the room.

With a wry shake of his head, Luck threw back the covers and climbed slowly out of bed. He paused beside the bureau to glance at the photograph. *Well, pretty lady, do you see what kind of boy your son has grown into?* The blue of his eyes had a pensive look as he walked to the bathroom.

CHAPTER TWO

"YOUR COFFEE IS COLD," Toby accused when his father finally appeared in the kitchen.

Dressed in worn blue jeans and a gray sweat shirt, Luck had taken the time to shower and shave. His dark brown hair gleamed almost black, combed into a careless kind of order. He smiled at the reproval from his son.

"I had to get cleaned up," he defended himself, and sipped at the lukewarm coffee before adding some hot liquid from the coffeepot. He sat down in a chair opposite from his son and rested his forearms on the table. "Do you want to explain to me what happened to Mrs. Jackson last night?"

"She was going to charge you double for staying after midnight, so I paid her and sent her home," Toby said, repeating his previous night's explanation.

"And she went—just like that," Luck replied with a wave of his hand to indicate how easy it had been. "She just went and left you here alone?"

"Well. . . ." Toby hedged, and squirmed in his chair.

"Why did she leave?"

"She got the impression we were broke, I think. She got a little upset thinking that you'd asked her to stay when you knew all you could afford to pay was twelve dollars."

"Why did you do it?"

"I'm too old to have a sitter, dad," Toby protested. "I can take care of myself."

"Maybe you can, but what about my peace of mind? I'm an adult. You're a child. When I leave, I want to know there's an adult with you—looking after you—yes. But mostly in case there's an emergency—if you should get sick or hurt. I'd like to know there is someone here with you to help," he explained firmly. "Do you understand?"

"Yes." It was a low admission.

"From now on, when I go out for the evening, you will have a sitter and she will stay here until I come back. Is that understood?"

"Yes."

"Good." With the discussion concluded, Luck raised the coffee cup to his mouth.

"What about the twelve dollars?" As far as Toby was concerned, the discussion wasn't over. "It's from the money I've been saving to buy a minibike."

"You should have considered that before you spent it."

"But that's what you would have had to pay her if I hadn't," Toby reasoned with the utmost logic. "You would have had to pay her that and more."

"I'll give you the twelve dollars back on one condition," Luck replied. "You call Mrs. Jackson, tell her what you did, and apologize."

There was a long sigh before Toby nodded his agreement. "Okay."

"Have you had breakfast?" Luck changed the subject.

"Cornflakes."

"Would you like some bacon and eggs?"

"Sure," Toby agreed. "I'll help."

While he set the table, Luck put the bacon in the skillet and broke eggs in a bowl to scramble them. Finished with his task before his father, Toby walked over to the stove to watch.

"Dad?" He tipped his head back to look up to his tall parent. "Do you want to explain about the brown mouse?"

"The brown mouse?" Luck frowned at him, his expression blank.

"Yeah. Last night when you came home, you said you had talked to a brown mouse," Toby explained. "I thought people only saw pink elephants when they were drinking."

"People can have all kinds of illusions when they are drinking. Evidently mine was a brown mouse," Luck murmured. "I must have had a few more drinks than I realized."

"It was because of mom, wasn't it?" Toby asked quietly.

There was a moment of silence. Then Luck gave him a smiling glance. "What do you want to do today? Do you want to go fishing? Boating? Just name it." He deliberately avoided his son's question, and Toby knew there was no need to repeat it.

"Let's go fishing," Toby decided.

"Fishing it is," Luck agreed, and smiled as he rumpled the top of his son's brown hair.

TWO HOURS LATER the dishes were washed and the beds were made and they were sitting in the boat, anchored in a cove of Lake Namekagon. A thick forest crowded the meandering shoreline, occasionally leaving room for a sandy stretch of beach. A mixture of hardwood and conifers, with extensive stands of pine and spruce, provided a blend of the green shades of summer. The unruffled calm of the lake reflected the edging wall of forest, home for the black bear, deer, beaver and other wildlife.

Their fishing lines were in the water, their rods resting against the sides of the boat in their stands. Toby was leaning back in his seat, his little-boy legs stretched out in front of him and his hands clasped behind his head for a pillow. He stared at the puffy cloud formations in the blue sky with a frown of concentration.

Luck was equally relaxed, yet suspicious of

the long silence that was only broken by the infrequent lapping of water against the boat or the cry of a bird. His sidelong glance studied the intent expression of his son.

"You seem to be doing some pretty heavy thinking, Toby," he observed, and let his gaze slide skyward when his son glanced at him. "What's on your mind?"

"I've been trying to figure something out." Toby turned his head in the pillow of his hands. The frowning concentration remained fixed in his expression. "What exactly does a mother do?"

The question widened Luck's eyes slightly. The question caused him to recognize that his son had never been exposed to the life of a family unit—father, mother and children. There was only one grandparent living, and no aunts or uncles. During the school year, the weekends were the times they had to share together. Luck had often permitted his son to invite a friend over, sometimes to stay overnight, but mostly to accompany them on an afternoon outing; but Toby had never stayed overnight with any of his friends.

The question was a general one—and a serious one. He couldn't avoid answering it. "Mothers do all sorts of things. They cook, wash dishes, clean the house, take care of you when you're sick, do the laundry, all sorts of things like that. Sometimes they work at a job during the day, too. Mothers remember birthdays without being reminded, make special treats for no reason, and think up games to play when you're bored." He knew it was an inadequate answer because he'd left out the love and the caring that he didn't know how to describe.

When Luck finished, he glanced at his son. Toby was staring at the sky, the frown of concentration replaced with a thoughtful look. "I think we need a mother," he announced after several seconds.

"Why?" The statement touched off a defensive mechanism that made Luck challenge it. "Since when have you and I not been able to manage on our own? I thought we had a pretty good system worked out."

"We do, dad," Toby assured him, then sighed. "I'm just tired of always having to wash dishes and make my bed."

The edges of his mouth deepened in a lazy smile. "Having a mother wouldn't mean you'd get out of doing your share of the daily chores."

Unclasping his hands from behind his head, Toby sat upright. "How do you go about finding a mother?"

"That's my problem." Luck made that point very clear. "In order for you to have a mother, I would have to get married again."

"Do you think you'd *like* to get married again?"

"Don't you think your questions are getting a

little bit personal?" *And a little bit awkward to handle,* Luck thought as he sat up, a tiny crease running across his forehead.

"I'm your son. If you can't talk to me about it, who can you?" Toby reasoned.

"You are much too old for your age." His blue eyes glinted with dry humor when he met the earnest gaze of his son.

"If you got married again, you could have more children," Toby pointed out. "Have you thought about that?"

"Yes, and I don't know if I could handle another one of you," Luck teased.

With a sigh of exasperation, Toby protested. "Dad, will you please be serious? I am trying to discuss this intelligently with you. You wouldn't necessarily have another boy. You could have a little girl."

"Is that what this is about? Do you want brothers and sisters?" There was something at the bottom of all this interest in a mother. Sooner or later, Luck felt he would uncover the reason.

"Do you know that it's really impossible to have a father-son conversation with you?" Toby declared with adult irritation. "You never answer my questions. You just ask me another. How am I ever going to learn anything?"

"All right." Luck crossed his arms in front of him and adopted a serious look. "What do you want to know?"

"If you met the right girl, would you get married again?"

"Yes, if I met the right girl," he conceded with a slow nod.

With a satisfied smile, Toby resumed his former position stretched out in the seat, his head pillowed in his hands, and stared at the sky. "I'll help you look."

Luck took a deep breath, started to say something, then decided it was wiser to let the subject drop.

THE LAKE COTTAGE was built of logs, complete with a front porch that overlooked the lake across the road. The rustic, yet modern structure was tucked in a forest clearing, a dense stand of pines forming a semicircle around it.

Over the weekend, Eve Rowland and her parents had moved in lock, stock and barrel for the summer. It had been a labor of fun opening up their vacation home again and reawakening happy memories of previous summers.

Standing on the porch, Eve gazed at the azure waters of Namekagon Lake. Here in the northwoods of Wisconsin and Minnesota was where the legend of Paul Bunyan and his blue ox, Babe, was born. According to the tales, Paul and Babe stomped around a little in Namekagon, just one of the many lakes in Wisconsin. Eve could remember looking at a map of the area as a child and believing the tale. The mythical figure of Paul Bunyan had been as real to her as the Easter Bunny and Santa Claus, even if he didn't pass out presents.

Eve lifted her head to the clear blue sky and breathed in the clean pine-scented air. On a sigh of contentment, Eve turned and walked into the cottage. It was small, just two bedrooms, the kitchen separated from the living room by a table nook. She let the screen door bang shut. Her father had his fishing gear spread over the table and was working on one of his reels. Her mother was in the kitchen, fixing some potato salad to chill for the evening meal.

"Is it all right if I use the car?" Eve asked. "I want to go to the store down the road. I'm out of shampoo and I'm going to need some suntan lotion."

"Sure." Her father reached in his pants' pocket and tossed her the car keys.

"Was there anything you needed?" Eve reached to pick up her canvas purse where she'd left it on a sofa cushion.

"Maybe some milk," her mother answered, "but other than that, I can't think of anything."

"Okay. I'll be back later," she called over her shoulder as she pushed open the door to the porch.

Sliding into the driver's seat of the sedan, Eve felt as bright and sunny as the summer afternoon. She had dressed to match her mood that day. The terry-cloth material of her short-sleeved top and slacks was a cheerful canary yellow, trimmed with white. A white hairband kept her brown hair away from her face, framing its oval shape.

It was a short drive to the combination grocery and general store that served the resort community. The Rowland family had traded there many times in past summers, so Eve was a familiar face to the owners. She chatted with them a few minutes as she paid for her purchases.

When she started to leave, she heard a man's voice ask to speak to the owner. It sounded vaguely familar, but when she turned to see if it was anyone she knew, the man was hidden from her view by an aisle. Since the man had business with the owner, and since it was possible she didn't even know him, Eve continued out of the store, dismissing the incident from her mind.

She'd left the car in the store's parking area. She walked toward it, but it was only when she got closer that she began to realize something was wrong. Her steps slowed and her eyes widened in disbelief at the sight of the shattered windshield and the three-inch-diameter hole in the glass.

Stunned, Eve absently glanced in the side window and saw the baseball lying on the front seat. Reacting mechanically, she opened the door and reached to pick up the ball amid the splintered chips of glass on the car seat.

"That's my ball." A young boy's voice claimed ownership of the object in her hand.

Still too stunned to be angry or upset, Eve turned to look at him. A baseball cap was perched atop a mass of dark brown hair, while a pair of unblinking innocent blue eyes stared back at her. Eve judged the boy to be eight, no older than nine. She had the feeling that she had seen him somewhere before, possibly at school.

"Did you do this?" She gestured toward the broken windshield, using the same hand that held the baseball.

"Not exactly. You see, my dad just bought me this new baseball glove." He glanced at the oversized leather mitt on his left hand. "We were trying it out to see how it worked. I asked dad to throw me a hard one so I could tell whether there was enough padding to keep my hand from stinging. Only when he did, it was too high and the ball hit the tip of my glove and bounced off, then smashed your windshield. It must have hit it just right," he declared with a rueful grimace. "So it was really my dad who threw the ball. I just didn't catch it."

"A parking lot isn't the place to play catch." At the moment, that was the only thing Eve could think of to say. It was a helpless kind of protest, lacking the strength to change a deed that was already done.

"We know that now," the boy agreed.

"Where's your father?"

"He went into the store to see if they knew who the car belonged to," he explained. "He told me to stay here in case you came back while he was gone."

The comment jogged her memory of the man who had been in the store asking to speak to the owner. She started to turn when she heard the same voice ask, "Is this your car?"

"It's my father's." Eve completed the turn to face the boy's father.

Cold shock froze her limbs into immobility. It was the stranger she'd met outside the tavern last week. The rumpled darkness of his hair grew in thick waves, a few strands straying onto his forehead. The same magnetic blue eyes were looking at her with warm interest. The sunlight added a rough vitality to the handsomely masculine features.

Eve waited, unconsciously holding her breath, for the recognition to show in his eyes as she mentally braced herself to watch that mouth with its ready smile form the words "brown mouse." But it didn't happen. He didn't recognize her. Evidently the combination of liquor and the night's shadows had made her image hazy in his mind. Eve just hoped it stayed that way, as feeling began to steal back into her limbs.

He glanced at the baseball in her hand. "I hope Toby explained what happened." His expression was pleasant, yet serious.

"Yes, he did." She was conscious of how loudly her heart was pounding. "At least he said you threw the ball and he missed it."

"I'm afraid that's what happened," he admitted with a faintly rueful lift of his mouth. "Naturally I'll pay the cost of having the windshield replaced on your father's car, Miss—"

"Rowland. Eve Rowland." She introduced herself and was glad that between the sack of groceries in one arm and the ball in the other hand, she wasn't able to shake hands.

"My name is Luck McClure, and this is my son, Toby." He laid a hand on the boy's shoulder with a trace of parental pride. "We're spending the summer at a lake house a few miles from here."

Eve was certain she had misunderstood his name. "Did you say Luke McClure?"

"No." He smiled, as if it were a common mistake. "It's Luck—as in good luck. Although in actual fact the proper name of Luck has its derivations in the name of Luke or Lucias. It's one of those family names that somehow manages to get passed along to future generations."

"I see," she murmured, and glanced at Toby, who had obviously not been named after his father. She wondered if there were another little Luck somewhere at home. At least now she understood why the boy had seemed familiar at first. There was a definite resemblance between him and his father.

"With that windshield smashed, you aren't going to be able to see to drive home," Luck stated. "I would appreciate it if you would let us give you a ride."

Under the circumstances, Eve didn't know any other way that she could get back to the cottage if she didn't accept his offer. "Yes, thank you," she nodded.

"May I have my baseball back?" the boy spoke up.

"Of course." She handed it to him.

"Our car is parked over here." Luck McClure reclaimed her attention, directing her toward a late-model Jaguar. "Did you say the car was your father's?"

"Yes. He's at the cottage."

"Is that where you would like me to drive you?" He walked around to open the passenger door for her, while his son climbed in the back seat.

"Yes. My parents and I are spending the summer there." Eve waited until he was behind the wheel to give him directions.

"That isn't far from our house," he commented, and Eve wished it was in the opposite direction. Any minute now she just knew he was going to recognize her, which would make things uncomfortable, if not embarrassing. "I'll make arrangements with your father about paying for the windshield."

Briefly Eve wondered if that was a slur at her

sex, insinuating that she wasn't capable of making adequate arrangements because she was a woman. She doubted it, though. Luck McClure was definitely all man, but he didn't strike her as the chauvinistic type. More than likely he simply wanted to deal directly with the owner of the car. Which suited her fine. The less she saw of him, the less chance there would be that he'd remember her.

The rounded bill of a baseball cap entered her side vision as the boy leaned over the seat. "I really thought you'd be mad when you saw what we did to your car. How come you weren't?"

The question made her smile. "I was too stunned. I couldn't believe what I saw."

"I couldn't, either, when it happened," Luck admitted with a low chuckle. It reached out to share the moment of amusement with her and pulled her gaze in his direction.

With less wariness, Eve let herself forget their first meeting outside the tavern. There was an easy charm about Luck McClure that she found attractive, in addition to his looks. It had a quality of bold friendliness to it.

"Flirting" was a word that had a female connotation, but this was one time when Eve felt it could apply to a man without diminishing his virility. In fact, the gleam lurking in his blue eyes and the ready smile enhanced it. Part of her wished this was their first meeting, because she knew sooner or later he would recognize his "brown mouse." And a man like Luck McClure would never be attracted to a brown mouse.

His gaze slid from the road long enough to meet her eyes. There was warm male interest in the look that ran over her face, a look that probably had its basis in a curiosity similar to the one Eve had just experienced. She was briefly stimulated by it until she remembered how futile it was to be attracted to him. Eve glanced at the road a second before his attention returned to it.

"Our place is just ahead on the left," Eve stated.

As Luck slowed the car to make the turn into the short driveway, the boy, Toby, announced, "We go by here all the time. I didn't think anybody lived in that house. When did you move in?"

"This past weekend," she replied, then wondered if that would jog Luck's memory of the tavern incident. A quick glance didn't find any reaction. "We spend the summers here. We sometimes come here during the winter holidays to snowmobile or ice-fish and do some cross-country skiing."

"Do you like to ski?" Toby's questions continued even after the car stopped.

"With Mt. Telemark practically in our backyard, it would be a shame if I didn't." A faint smile touched her mouth as she shifted the sack of groceries to open the door. "As it happens, I enjoy it."

"Me, too. Dad took me skiing last Christmas." The boy scrambled out of the back seat to join his father. "Next year I'll be good enough to ski with him." He tipped his head back to look up at his father for confirmation. "Won't I, dad?"

"By the end of next winter, you'll be a veteran of the slopes," Luck agreed with a lazy smile, and waited until Eve had walked around the front of the car before starting toward the log cottage.

With this tall, good-looking man beside her, she felt oddly self-conscious—a sensation that had nothing to do with their previous encounter. It was more an awareness of physical attraction than an uneasiness. She failed to notice that Toby wasn't with them until the car door slammed again and the boy came running after them. Simultaneously she paused with Luck McClure to see what had delayed Toby.

"You left the keys in the ignition again, dad," the boy declared with an adult reprimand in his expression, and handed the car keys to his father. "That's how cars get stolen."

"Yes, Toby." Luck accepted the admonishment with lazy indulgence and slipped the keys into his pocket.

When they started toward the porch again, Toby tagged along.

Her parents recovered quickly from their initial surprise at the strange man and boy accompanying Eve into the house. She introduced them, then Luck took over the explanation of the shattered windshield. Exhibiting his typical understanding, her father was not angered by the accident. . . more amused than anything.

While they discussed particulars, Eve went into the kitchen to put away the milk she'd got. She remained in the alcove, satisfied to just observe the easy way Luck McClure related to her parents. It was a knack few people had. It came naturally to him, part of his relaxed, easygoing style.

With all his apparent friendliness, Eve didn't doubt that he could handle authority equally well. There was something in his presence that commanded respect. It was an understated quality, but that didn't lessen its strength.

Her gaze strayed to the boy standing beside Luck. He was listening attentively to all that was being said, possessing an oddly mature sense of responsibility for a boy of his age. His only motion was tossing the ball into his glove and retrieving it to toss it methodically again.

With the milk put away, Eve was running out of reasons to dawdle in the kitchen. Since she didn't want to take part in the conversation between her parents and Luck McClure, she took her suntan lotion and shampoo and slipped away to her bedroom. She paused in front of the vanity mirror above her dresser and studied her reflection.

The white band sleeked her brown hair away from her face, emphasizing features that were not so serene as they normally were. Eve touched the mouth that looked softer and fuller, fingertips brushing the curve. There was an added glow of suppressed excitement in the luminous brown of her eyes. The cause of it was Luck McClure and that never ending question of when he would recognize her.

With all the cheery yellow of her pants and top, Eve admitted to herself that she didn't look like a brown mouse. If anything, a sunflower was more apt—with its bright yellow petals and brown center.

"You really are a 'vanity' mirror," Eve murmured, and turned away from the reflecting glass before she became too wrapped up in her appearance.

But her subconscious made a silent resolution not to wear brown again. From now on, only bright colors would be added to her wardrobe. Drab clothing did nothing to improve her looks. "Brown mouse"—the phrase mocked her with its recollections of that night.

Eve dreaded the time when she would meet his wife, but in this small resort community it would be impossible for their paths not to cross sometime during the course of the summer. It would be foolish to try to avoid it. But what do you say to a woman whose husband tried to pick you up?

What kind of marriage did he have? He had said it was lonely at home and he wanted to talk to someone. He and his wife were obviously having trouble, Eve concluded. Or maybe he was just the type that stepped out anyway. No, she shook that thought away. Indulging in an idle flirtation would come naturally to him, but Luck McClure wasn't the type to let it go beyond the bantering of words. There was too much depth to him for that.

What did it matter? He was married. Regardless of the problems he was having, Luck was the kind who would persist until he solved them. It was ridiculous to waste her time thinking about a married man, no matter how interesting and compelling he might be.

The closing of the screen door and the cessation of voices from the front room turned Eve to face her bedroom door. She listened and heard the opening of car doors outside. The tall arresting man and his son were leaving.

It was just as well. Now she could come out of hiding—the realization stopped her short of the door. She had been hiding. Hiding because he had looked at her with a man's interest in the opposite sex and her ego hadn't wanted him to remember that she was a plain brown mouse. So what had she done? Scurried off into her hole, just like a brown mouse.

Never again, Eve resolved, and left her "hole" to return to the front room. The only occupant was her mother. Eve glanced around, noticing the Jaguar was gone from the driveway.

"Where's dad?"

"Mr. McClure drove him back to the car. They called a garage. A man's coming over to pick up our car and replace the broken windshield," her mother explained. "He should be back shortly."

An hour later her father returned, but it was the mechanic who brought him back—not Luck McClure.

CHAPTER THREE

THE ROWLANDS were without transportation for two days. On the morning of the third day, the garage owner delivered the car, complete with a new windshield. The day had started out with gray and threatening skies. By the time the car was returned it began drizzling. And by noon it was raining steadily, confining Eve indoors.

With the car returned, her parents decided to restock their grocery supplies that afternoon. They invited Eve to come with them, but since they planned to visit some of their friends while they were out, she declined.

On rainy days she usually enjoyed curling up with a book, but on this occasion she was too restless to read. Since she had the entire afternoon on her hands, she decided to do some baking and went into the kitchen to stir up a batch of chocolate chip cookies, her father's favorite.

Soon the delicious smell of cookies baking in the oven filled the small cottage and chased away the gloom of the gray rainy day. Cookies from two sheet trays were cooling on the kitchen counter, atop an opened newspaper. Eve glanced through the glass door of the oven at the third sheet. Its cookies were just beginning to brown, a mere minute away from being done.

The thud of footsteps on the wooden porch floor reached her hearing, straightening Eve from the oven. An instant after they stopped, there was a knock on the door. She cast a glance at the oven, then went to answer the door. A splash of flour had left a white streak on the burgundy velour of her top. She brushed at it but only succeeded in spreading the white patch across her stomach. Eve was still brushing at it when she opened the door.

The slick material of a dark blue Windbreaker glistened with rain across a set of wide shoulders that turned at the sound of the opening door. Her hand stopped its motion when Eve looked into a pair of arresting blue eyes.

A tiny electric shock quivered through her nerve ends at the sight of Luck McClure on the other side of the wire mesh screen. Dampness gave a black sheen to his dark brown hair. Toby was beside him, his face almost lost under the hooded sweat shirt pulled over his head and tied under his chin. Beyond the shelter of the porch roof, rain fell in an obscuring gray curtain.

"Hello, Mr. McClure," Eve recovered her voice to greet him calmly.

An easy casual smile touched his mouth, so absently charming. "I stopped to—"

His explanation was interrupted by the oven timer dinging its bell to signal Eve the cookies should be done. "Excuse me. I have something in the oven." Manners dictated that she couldn't leave them standing on the porch, so she quickly unhooked the screen door. "Come in," she invited hurriedly, and retraced her path to the kitchen to remove the cookies before they burned.

Behind her she heard the screen door open and the shuffle of incoming footsteps. "Don't forget to wipe your feet, dad," Toby murmured the conscientious reminder.

Opening the oven door, Eve took a pot holder and used it to absorb the heat of the metal cookie sheet while she lifted it out of the oven. Another tray of individually spooned cookie dough was sitting on the counter, ready to be put in to bake. She slipped it on the rack with her free hand and closed the oven door.

"My parents are gone this afternoon." She said, carrying the sheet of baked cookies to the counter where the others were cooling, conscious that Luck McClure and his son had followed her to the kitchen. "Was there something I could help you with?" she offered, and began removing the cookies from the sheet with a metal spatula.

"I told your father he could use my car if he had any errands to run while his was in the shop," he explained. "I stopped to see if he needed it."

"The garage delivered our car this morning." Eve half turned to answer him and felt the slow inspection of his look.

Her cheeks were flushed from the heat of the oven. The sweep of his glance left behind an odd licking sensation that heightened her already high color. It was a look he would give to any semiattractive woman—a man's assessment of her looks—but that didn't alter its effect on her.

Toby appeared at her elbow, offering her a distraction. He peered over the top of the counter to see what she was doing. Untying his hood, he pushed it off his head, tousling his brown hair in the process.

"What are you making?" he said curiously.

"Chocolate-chip cookies." She smiled briefly at him and continued to slide the cookies off the flat spatula onto the newspaper with the rest.

He breathed in deeply, his blue eyes rounded as if drinking in the sight. "They smell good."

"Would you like one?" Eve offered. As an afterthought, she glanced at Luck, who had moved into her side vision. "Is it all right if he has a cookie?"

"Sure." Permission was granted with a faint nod of his head.

Toby reached for one that she had just set on the paper. "Careful," she warned, but it came too late. Toby was already jerking his hand away, nursing burned fingers.

"They're hot," he stated.

238

"Naturally. They just came out of the oven. Try one of those at the back." She pointed with the spatula. "They've had a chance to cool."

He took one of the cookies she'd indicated and bit into it. As he chewed it, he studied the cookie. "These are really good," he declared.

"You'll have to help your mother make some for you." Eve flashed him a smile at the compliment.

"I don't have a mother anymore," Toby replied absently, and took another bite of the cookie.

His statement sent invisible shock waves through her. She darted a troubled glance at Luck. Had his problems at home ended in divorce? Except for a certain blandness in his gaze, he didn't appear bothered by the topic his son had introduced.

"My wife died when Toby was small," he explained, and glanced at his son. The corners of his mouth were pulled upward in a smile. "Toby and I have been baching it for several years now, but I'm afraid our domestic talents don't stretch to baking cookies."

"I see," she murmured because she didn't know what else to say.

The knowledge that he was married, and therefore out of circulation, had made her feel safe from his obvious male attraction. The discovery that he was a widower caught her off guard, leaving her shaken.

"May I have another cookie?" Toby asked after he'd licked the melted chocolate of a chip from his finger.

"Of course." She'd made a large batch, so there was plenty to spare. Homemade cookies were obviously a special treat for the boy.

As he took another one, Toby glanced at his father. "Why don't you try one, dad? You don't know what you're missing."

"Go ahead." Eve added her permission and moved aside as she laid the last cookie down.

While Luck took her up on the offer and helped himself to a cookie, Eve carried the empty sheet to the adjoining counter and began spooning cookie dough onto it from the mixing bowl. The ever curious Toby followed her.

"What's that?"

"This is the cookie batter. When you bake it in the oven, it turns into a cookie." It was becoming obvious to her that this was all new to him. If he'd seen it before, it had been too long ago for him to remember clearly.

"How do you make it?" He looked up at her with a thoughtful frown.

"There's a recipe on the back of the chocolate-chip package." The teaching habit was too firmly ingrained for Eve to overlook the chance to impart knowledge when interest was aroused. She paused in her task to pick up the empty chip package and show it to him. "It's right there. It tells you all the ingredients and how to do it."

With the cookie in one hand and the package with its recipe in the other, Toby wandered to the opposite side of the kitchen and studied the printing with frowning concentration. The kitchen was a small alcove off the front room. When Luck moved to lean a hip against the counter near Eve, she began to realize how limited the walk space was.

"There is something very comfortable about a kitchen filled with the smell of fresh baking on a rainy day. It really feels like a home then," Luck remarked.

"Yes, it does," Eve agreed, and knew it was that casual intimacy that was disturbing her.

"Have you eaten one of your cookies? They *are* good," Luck said, confirming his son's opinion.

"Not yet," she admitted, and turned to tell him there was coffee in the electric pot if he wanted a cup. But when she opened her mouth to speak, he slipped the rounded edge of a warm cookie inside.

"A cook should sample her wares," he insisted with lazy inoffensive mockery.

There was an instant of surprised delay as her eyes met the glinting humor of his. Then her teeth instinctively sank into the sweet morsel to take a bite. Luck held onto the cookie until she did, then surrendered it to the hand that reached for it.

With food in her mouth, good manners dictated that she not speak until it was chewed and swallowed. It wasn't easy under his lazily watchful eyes, especially when he took due note of the tongue that darted out to lick the melted chocolate from her lips. Her heart began thumping against her ribs like a locomotive climbing a steep incline.

"I'll finish it later with some coffee." Eve set the half-eaten cookie on the counter, unwilling to go through the unnerving experience of Luck watching her eat again. She picked up the spoon and worked at concentrating on filling the cookie sheet with drops of dough.

"And I thought all along that Eve tempted Adam with an apple," Luck drawled softly. "When did you discover a cookie worked better?"

Again her gaze raced to him, surprised that he remembered her name and stunned by the implication of his words. No matter how she tried, Eve couldn't react casually to this sexual bantering of words the way he did. He was much more adept at the game than she was.

"What does 'tempted' mean?" Toby eyed his father curiously.

Luck turned to look at his son, not upset by the question nor the fact that Toby had been listening. "It's like putting a worm on a hook. The fish can't resist taking a nibble."

"Oh." With his curiosity satisfied, Toby's attention moved on to other things. He set the empty chocolate-chip package on the counter where Eve had left it before. "This doesn't look hard to do, dad. Do you think we could make some cookies sometime?"

"On the next rainy day we'll give it a try," he promised, and sent a twinkling look at Eve. "If we have trouble, we can give Eve a call."

"Yeah," Toby agreed with a wide grin.

Unexpectedly, just when Eve had decided Luck was going to become a fixture in the kitchen for what was left of the afternoon, he straightened from the counter. "Toby and I have taken advantage of your hospitality long enough. We'd better be leaving."

The timer went off to signal the other sheet of cookies was ready to come out of the oven. Its intrusive sound allowed her to turn away and hide the sudden rush of keen disappointment that he was leaving. It also permitted her to remember the reason for his visit.

"It was thoughtful of you to stop," Eve replied, taking the cookie sheet from the oven.

"It was the least I could do," Luck insisted, and paused in her path to the counter. She was compelled to look into the deep indigo color of his eyes. A half smile slanted his mouth. "I hope you have forgiven me for what happened the other time we met."

She went white with shock. "Then you do remember."

Although the smile remained, an attractive

243

frown was added to his expression. "I was talking about the broken windshield. Was there something else I was supposed to remember?"

She felt the curious intensity of his gaze probe for an answer, one that she had very nearly given away. "No. Of course not." She rushed a nervous smile onto her face and stepped around him to the counter, her pulse racing a thousand miles an hour.

For an uneasy moment, Eve thought he was going to question her answer, then she heard him take a step toward the front room and the door. "Tell your parents I said hello."

"I will," she promised, and turned when the pair were nearly to the door.

"Goodbye, Eve." Toby waved.

"Goodbye," she echoed his farewell.

The cottage seemed terribly quiet and empty after they'd gone. The gray rain outside the windows seemed to close in, its loneliness seeping in through the walls. Eve poured a cup of coffee and sat at the table to finish the cookie Luck had given her. It had lost some of its flavor.

THE FOLLOWING WEEK Eve volunteered to make the short trip to the store to buy bread, milk and the other essential items that always needed replenishing, so her parents could go boating with friends that had stopped by. When she arrived at the store, she was quick to notice the sleek Jaguar sedan parked in front of it. She wasn't aware of the glow of anticipation that came to her eyes.

Luck and Toby were on their way out of the store with an armful of groceries when she walked in. "Hello." Her bright greeting was a shade breathless.

The wide lazy smile that Luck gave her quickened her pulse. "You are safe today. Toby left his baseball and glove at the house," he said.

"Good. I was wondering whether I should stop here or not." Eve laughed as she lied, because she hadn't given the broken windshield incident another thought.

"Look what we bought." Toby reached into the smaller sack he carried and pulled out a package of chocolate chips. "We're going to make some the next time it rains."

"I hope they turn out," she smiled.

"So do I," Luck murmured dryly, and touched the boy's shoulder. "Let's go, Toby. We'll see you, Eve," he nodded, using that indefinite phrase that committed nothing.

"Bye, Eve."

The smile faded from her expression as she watched them go. Turning away from the door, she went to do her shopping.

"WHEN DO YOU SUPPOSE it's going to rain again?" Toby searched the blue sky for a glimpse of dark clouds, but there wasn't a sign of even a puffy white one. He sank to his knees

245

on the beach towel that Luck was stretched out on. Grains of sand clung to his bare feet, wet like the rest of him from swimming in the lake. "It's been almost a week."

"Maybe we're in for a drought," Luck suggested with dry humor at his son's impatience.

"Very funny." Toby made a face at him and turned to squint into the sunlight reflected off the lake's surface. "The water is pretty warm. Are you going to come in for a swim now?"

"In a little bit." The heat of the sun burning into his exposed flesh made him lazy.

A red beach ball bounced on the sand near him and rolled onto his towel. Luck started to sit up and made it halfway before the ball's owner arrived.

"Sorry," a breathless female voice apologized.

Turning, he leaned on an elbow as a shapely blonde in a very brief bikini knelt on the sand beside him and reached for the ball. Her smile was wide and totally beguiling.

"No harm done," he assured her, and noticed the amount of cleavage that was revealed when she bent to pick up the ball.

His gaze lifted to her face and observed the knowing sparkle in her eyes. Wisely he guessed that it had all been a ploy to attract his attention. It was an old game. Despite the beautiful packaging, he discovered he wasn't interested in playing.

The blonde waited for several seconds, but he didn't make the expected gambit. Disappointment flickered in her expression, then was quickly veiled by a coy smile. Rising in a graceful turning motion, she ran back to her friends.

"That blonde was really a knockout, huh, dad?"

Amused, Luck cast a glance over his shoulder at his son, who was still staring after the shapely girl. "Yes, I guess she was," he agreed blandly, and looked back to the trio playing keep-away. Then he pushed himself into a full sitting position, his attention leaving the scantily clad blonde.

"She thought you were pretty neat, too," Toby observed, a hint of devilry in his smile. "I saw the sexy look she gave you."

"You see too much." Luck gave him a playful push backward, plopping him down on the sand.

Toby just laughed. "Why don't you marry someone like her?"

Luck sighed. He'd thought that subject had been forgotten. He shook his head in a mild form of exasperation. "Looks aren't everything, son." Rolling to his feet, he reached down to pull Toby up. "Let's go for that swim of yours."

"Race ya!" Toby challenged, and took off at a dead run.

He loped after him, his long strides keeping

the distance between them short. Wading into the lake until he was up to his knees, he then dived in. Powerful reaching strokes soon carried Luck into deeper water, where he waited for Toby to catch up with him.

"What do you think, pretty lady?" Luck murmured in a voice that was audible only to himself. "Have you ruined me for anyone else?"

The image of his wife swirled through the mists of his mind, her face laughing up at him as she pulled him to their bed. Her features were soft, like a fading edge of a dream, her likeness no longer bringing him the sharp stabbing pain. Time had reduced it to a beautiful memory that came back to haunt him at odd times.

Although he still possessed a man's sexual appetite, emotional desire seemed to have left him. Except for Toby, it seemed that all the good things in life were behind him. Tomorrow seemed empty, without promise.

A squeal of female laughter from the lake-shore pulled his gaze to the beach and the cavorting blonde. Her bold bid for his attention had left him cold, even though he had liked what he had seen. He found the subtle approach much sexier—like the time Eve had licked the chocolate from her lips. Strange that he had thought of her instead of the way his wife, Lisa, used to run her finger around the rim of a glass.

A hand sprayed water on his face. Luck

blinked and wiped the droplets from his eyes as Toby laughed and struck out, swimming away from him. The moment of curious reflection was gone as he took up the challenge of his son.

THUNDER CRASHED AND ROLLED across the sky, unleashing a torrent of rain to hammer on the roof of the cottage. A rain-cool breeze rushed in through a window above the kitchen sink, stirring the brown silk of Eve's hair as she washed the luncheon dishes.

Lightning cracked outside the window. "My, that looked close," her mother murmured, always a little nervous about violent storms.

"The baseball game in Milwaukee has just been postponed because of the rain," her father sighed in disappointment and switched off the radio atop the refrigerator. "And they always have doubleheaders on Saturday, too." If her father had one passion besides fishing, it was baseball. "Maybe it will clear off later this afternoon and—" He was interrupted by the ring of the telephone in the front room. "I'll get it."

"If it's Mabel and Frank, tell them to come over," her mother called. "It's a good day to play cards."

On the third ring, he answered it. "It's for you, Eve." He had to raise his voice to make himself heard above the storm.

Grabbing a towel, Eve wiped the dishwater

from her hands as she walked to the phone. "Hello?"

"Hello, Eve. This is Toby. Toby McClure."

A vague surprise widened her eyes. "Hello, Toby." Warm pleasure ran through her voice and expression.

"I'm trying to make some chocolate-chip cookies," he said, and she smiled when she remembered this was the first rainy day since he and Luck had been over. "But I can't figure out how to get cream from shortening and sugar."

"What?" A puzzled frown creased her forehead as she tried to fathom his problem.

"The directions say to 'cream' the sugar and shortening," Toby explained patiently.

Eve swallowed the laugh that bubbled in her throat. The directions probably didn't make sense to him. "That means you should blend them together until they make a thick 'creamy' mixture."

A heavy sigh came over the phone. "I thought this was going to be easy, but it isn't." There was a pause, followed by a reluctant request, "Eve, I don't suppose you could maybe come over and show me how to make them?" There was so much pride in his voice, and a grudging admission of defeat.

"Where's your father? He should be able to help you," she suggested.

"He didn't get home until real late last night,

so he's lying down, taking a nap," Toby explained. "Can you come?"

It was impossible to turn him down, especially when she didn't want to. "Yes, I'll come. Where exactly do you live?" Eve knew it was somewhere close from other comments that had been made. Toby gave her precise directions. After she had promised to be there within a few minutes, she hung up the phone. "Dad, were you or mom planning to use the car this afternoon?"

"No. Did you want to use it?" He was already reaching in his pocket for the keys.

"I'm off to the McClures to give Toby his first lesson in baking cookies," Eve explained with a soft laugh, and told them the boy's problem understanding the directions. Their amusement blended with hers.

"Never mind the dishes. I'll finish them," her mother volunteered. "You'd better take an umbrella, too, and wear a coat."

In her bedroom, Eve brushed her hair and freshened her lipstick. She didn't allow herself to wonder why she was taking so much trouble with her appearance when she was going to see an eight-year-old. It would have started her thinking about his father, something she was trying to pretend not to do at this point. She hesitated before taking the brown coat out of her closet, but it was the only one she had that repelled water.

The sheeting rain was almost more than the windshield wipers could handle. It obscured her vision so that, despite Toby's excellent directions, she nearly missed the turn into the driveway. The lake house was set back in the trees, out of sight of the road. Eve parked her car behind the Jaguar.

The umbrella afforded her little protection from the driving rain. Her coat was stained wet by the time she walked the short distance from the car to the front door. Toby must have been watching for her, because he opened the door a second before she reached it. He pressed a forefinger to his lips and motioned her inside. She hurried in, unable to do anything about the rainwater dripping from her and the umbrella.

"Dad's still sleeping," Toby whispered, and explained, "He needs the rest."

The entry hall skirted the living room, paneled in cedar with a heavy beamed slanted ceiling and a natural stone fireplace. Toby's glance in that direction indicated it was where Luck was sleeping. Eve looked in when Toby led her past. There, sprawled on a geometric-patterned couch, was Luck, naked from the waist up, an arm flung over his head in sleep. It was the first time Eve had ever seen anyone frowning in his sleep.

In the kitchen, Toby led her to the table where he had all the ingredients set out. "Will you show me how to make cookies?" he asked, repeating the request he'd made over the phone.

"No, I won't show you," Eve said, taking off her wet coat and draping it over a chair back. "I'll tell you how to do it. The best way to learn is by doing."

Step by step, she directed him through the mixing process. When the first sheet came out of the oven, Toby was all eyes. He could hardly wait until the cookies were cool enough to taste and, thus, assure himself that they were as good as they looked.

"They taste just like yours," he declared on a triumphant note after he'd taken the first bite.

"Of course," Eve laughed, but kept it low so she wouldn't waken Luck in the next room.

"I couldn't have done it if you hadn't helped me," Toby added, all honesty. "You're a good teacher."

"That's what I am. Really," she emphasized when he failed to understand. "I *am* a teacher."

"What subject?"

"Music."

"Too bad it isn't English. That's my worst subject," he grimaced. "Dad isn't very good at it, either."

"We all have subjects that we don't do as well in as others," Eve shrugged lightly. "Mine is math."

"Dad is really good at that, and science, but he has to use it all the time in his work."

"What does he do?"

253

"He works for my grandpa." Then realizing that didn't answer her question, Toby elaborated, "My grandpa owns North Lakes Lumber. Mostly my dad works on the logging side. That way we can spend more time together in the summer when I'm out of school. He had a meeting with grandpa last night. That's why he was so late coming home."

"I thought he had a date." The words were out before Eve realized she had spoken.

"Sometimes he goes out on dates," Toby admitted, finding nothing wrong with her comment. "We like going places and doing things together, but sometimes dad is like me. I like to play with kids my own age once in a while; so does he. I imagine you do, too."

"Yes, that's true." She silently marveled at his logical reasoning. He was quite a remarkable boy.

Without being reminded, he checked on the cookies in the oven and concluded they were done. He took the cookie sheet out with a pot holder and rested it on the tabletop while he scooped the cookies off.

"We've been talking about dad getting married again," he announced, and didn't see the surprised arch of her eyebrow. "Dad gets pretty lonely sometimes. It's been rough on him since my mother died six years ago. Three weeks ago it was six years *exactly*," he stressed, and shook his head in a rueful fashion when he looked at her. "Boy, did he ever go on a binge that night!" He rolled his eyes to emphasize the point.

Three weeks ago. Eve did a fast mental calculation, her mind whirling. "Was...that on a Thursday?"

"I think so. Why?" Toby eyed her with an unblinking look.

The night she'd bumped into him outside the tavern. He had wanted someone to talk to, Eve remembered. A man can talk to a brown mouse, Luck had said. But she had refused, and he had gone back inside the tavern.

"No reason." She shook her head absently. "It was nothing important." But she couldn't resist going back to the subject. "You said he got drunk that night." She tried to sound mildly interested.

"I guess," Toby agreed emphatically. "He even had hallucinations."

"He did?"

"After I helped him into bed, he claimed that he had talked to a brown mouse." He looked at her, laughter suddenly dancing in his eyes. "Can you imagine that?"

"Yes." Eve swallowed and tried to smile. "Yes, I can." Her suspicions were confirmed beyond question. Now she wanted off the subject. "I'll help you spoon the cookie dough on the tray," she volunteered, letting action take the place of words.

When the last sheet of cookies came out of the oven, Eve washed the baking dishes while Toby wiped them and put them away. He leaned an elbow on the counter and watched her scrub at the baked-on crumbs on the cookie sheet.

"I don't really mind helping with dishes, or even making my bed," Toby said, and propped his head up with his hand. "But I'm going to like having a mother."

She didn't see the connection between the two statements. "Why is that?"

"Because sometimes my friends tease me when I have to dust furniture or fold clothes," he explained. "Dad told me that mothers clean and cook and do all those kinds of things."

"That's true." Eve tried very hard not to smile. It had to be rough to have your manhood questioned by your peers when you were only eight years old. Reading between the lines, she could see where Toby had acquired his air of maturity. Responsibility had been given to him at an early age, so he didn't possess that carefree attitude typical of most children his age.

She rinsed the last cookie sheet and handed it to Toby to dry. Draining the dishwater from the sink, she wiped off the counter, then dried her hands. She glanced at the wall clock and wondered where the afternoon had gone.

"Now that we have everything cleaned up, it's time I was leaving," she declared.

"Can't you stay a little while longer?"

"No, it's late." She removed her brown coat from the chair back and slipped it on.

Toby brought her the umbrella. "Thanks for coming, Eve." He stopped for an instant as a thought occurred to him. "Maybe I should call you Miss Rowland, since you're a teacher."

"I'd like it better if you called me Eve," she replied, and started toward the entry hall.

"Okay, Eve," he grinned, and walked with her.

As she passed the living room, her gaze was automatically drawn inside. Luck was sitting up, rubbing his hands over his face as though he had just wakened. The movement in front of him attracted his attention. He glanced up and became motionless for an instant when he saw Eve.

Because of the clouds blocking out the sun, there was little light in the entry way. Eve didn't think about the dimness as she started to speak, smiling at the grogginess that was evident in his expression.

But Luck spoke before she did. "Don't scurry off into the darkness...brown mouse." There was a trancelike quality to his voice.

Her steps faltered. She had escaped recognition for so long that she had stopped dreading it. Now that he remembered her, she felt sick. Tearing her gaze from him, she hurried toward the front door. As she jerked it open, she heard him call her name.

"Eve!"

She didn't stop. She didn't even remember to open the umbrella until the slow rain drenched her face. There was water on the ground. It splashed beneath her running feet as she hurried toward her car.

CHAPTER FOUR

A STARTLED OUTCRY was torn from her throat by the hand that caught her arm and spun her around. Eve hadn't thought Luck would come after her—not out in the rain. But there he was, standing before her with his naked chest glistening a hard bronze from the rain, the sprinkling of chest hairs curling tightly in the wetness. The steady rain beat at his dark hair, driving it onto his forehead. Reluctantly, Eve lifted her gaze to the blue of his eyes, drowning in the full recognition of his look.

"You *are* the girl I bumped into outside the tavern that night," Luck stated in final acceptance of the fact.

"Yes." The hand holding the umbrella wavered, causing Luck to dodge his head and duck under the wire spines stretching the material.

His gaze swept her face, hair and eyes. "I thought I'd conjured you out of a whiskey bottle. I don't know why nothing clicked when I met you." A frown flickered between his brows, then vanished when his gaze slid to her coat. "It must have been the combination of the shadows and the brown coat...and the fogginess of sleep. Why didn't you say anything before?"

"And remind you that I was the brown mouse?" There was bitterness in the laughing breath she released.

"What's wrong with being a brown mouse?" The corners of his mouth deepened in an attractive smile. "I recall that I happened to like the brown mouse I met."

"A brown mouse is just a small rat. It's hardly a name that someone wants to be called." This time Eve worked to keep the bitterness out of her voice and turn the comment into a joke for her pride's sake. She succeeded to a large degree. "You certainly don't want to remind someone of it if they've forgotten."

"It's all in the eye of the beholder, Eve," Luck corrected with a rueful twist of his mouth. "You see a rat, and I see a soft furry creature. You are a strong sensitive woman, but you aren't very sure of yourself. I wish you had stayed that night. It all might have turned out differently."

How could she say that she wished she had, too, knowing what she knew now. Hindsight always altered a person's perspective.

"Dad!" Toby shouted from the opened front door. "You'd better come inside! You're getting soaking wet out there!"

"Toby's right." Her gaze fell to the rivulets of rainwater running down the muscled contours of his bare chest, all hard sinew and taut sun-browned skin. His blatant maleness spun a whole new set of evocative sensations. "You're getting drenched. You should go in the house."

"Come in with me." Luck didn't let go of her arms, holding her as he issued the invitation.

"No. I have to go home." She resisted the temptation to accept, listening to the steady drip of rain off her umbrella, its swift fall in the same rhythm as her pulse.

His mouth quirked. "That's what you said then, too."

"It's late. I—" The sentence went no farther as the wetness of his palm cupped her cheek. Eve completely forgot what she was going to say, her thoughts scattered by the disturbing caress of his touch.

"Dad!" Toby sounded impatient and irritated. "You're going to catch your death of pneumonia!"

It was the diversion Eve needed to collect her senses before she did something foolish. "You'd better go." She turned away, breaking contact with his hand and lifting the umbrella high enough to clear his head. There was no resistance as she slipped out of his grasp to walk the last few steps to the car.

"We'll see you again, Eve." It was a definite statement.

But she wasn't certain what promise it contained. "Yes." She opened the car door and slipped inside, struggling to close the wet umbrella. Luck continued to stand in the rain, watching her.

"Do you think it will be sunny tomorrow?" he asked unexpectedly.

"I haven't been paying any attention to the weather forecast," Eve replied.

"Neither have I," Luck admitted.

HE WAS INDIFFERENT to the slow rain falling on him as he watched Eve reverse the car at a right angle to turn around in the drive. The incident had not been a figment of an alcoholic imagination. The woman he'd thought he had only dreamed about had actually been under his nose all this time.

The one good feeling he'd experienced in six years had happened when he had held her in his arms, but he hadn't believed it was real. Even now Luck wasn't sure that part hadn't been imagined. Comfortable didn't describe the feeling it had aroused. It was something more basic than that. It had been right and natural with his arms around her, feeling the softness of her body against his.

The woman had been Eve. It was strange he hadn't realized it before. She was quiet and warm, with an inner resiliency and a gentle humor that he liked. A smile twitched his mouth as Luck remembered she had a definite will of her own, as well. She wasn't easily intimidated.

"Dad!"

He turned, letting his gaze leave the red tail-lights of her car, and walked to the house, wet feet squishing in wet shoes. A smile curved his mouth at the disapproving expression on his son's face when he reached the door.

"You're sopping wet," Toby accused. "You wouldn't let me run out there like that with no coat or anything. You tell me I'll catch cold. How come you can do it?"

"Because I'm stupid," Luck replied, because he couldn't argue with the point his son had raised.

"You'd better get out of those wet clothes," Toby advised.

"I intend to." He left a watery trail behind him as he walked to the private bath off his bedroom where he stripped and put on the toweling robe Toby brought him. "Why was Eve here?" he asked, vigorously rubbing his wet hair with a bath towel.

"She came over to help me make cookies. They're good, too." A sharp questioning glance from Luck prompted Toby to explain. "I called and asked her to come over 'cause I was having trouble with the directions and you were asleep." Then it was his turn to tip his head to one side and send a questioning look at his father. "How come you called her a brown mouse?"

"It turns out Eve was the one I talked to that

night and referred to as a brown mouse," he shrugged, and tossed the towel over a rack.

"I thought you were drunk that night."

"I had a few drinks, more after I met her than before. Which probably explains why I wasn't sure whether it had happened or I had imagined it."

"But why did you call her a brown mouse?" Toby didn't understand that yet.

"It's a long story," Luck began.

"I know," Toby inserted with a resigned sigh. "You'll tell me all about it some other time."

"That's right." A smile played with the corners of his mouth as he turned his son around and pushed him in front of him out of the bathroom. "Is there any coffee made?"

"Yeah." Toby tilted his head way back to frown at him. "I just hope you remember all the things you're going to tell me 'some other time.'"

In the kitchen, Luck filled a mug with coffee and helped himself to a handful of the cookies stacked on the table. "What did you and Eve talk about?" Settling onto a chair, he bit into one of the cookies and eyed Toby skeptically. "Did you really make these?"

"Yeah," was the defensive retort. "Eve told me how. She says you learn best by doing. She's a teacher. Did you know that? I mean a for-real teacher. She teaches music."

"No, I didn't know that," Luck admitted.

"We talked about that some and a bunch of other things." Toby frowned in an attempt to recall the subjects he'd discussed with Eve. "I told her you were thinking about getting married again."

Luck choked on the drink of coffee he'd taken and coughed, "You did what?!!" He set the mug down to stare at his son, controlling the anger that trembled beneath his disbelieving look.

"I mentioned that you were talking about getting married again," he repeated with all the round-eyed innocence of an eight-year-old. "Well, it's true."

"No, *you've* been talking about it." Luck pointed a finger at his son, shaking it slightly in his direction. "Why on earth did you mention it to Eve? I thought it was a private discussion between you and me."

"Gosh, dad, I didn't know you wanted to keep it a secret," Toby blinked.

"Toby, you don't go around discussing personal matters with strangers." He ran his fingers through his damp hair in a gesture of exasperation. "My God, you'll be blabbing it to the whole neighborhood next. Why don't you just take an ad out in the paper? Wanted: A wife for a widower with an eight-year-old blabbermouth."

"Do you think anyone would apply?" Behind

the thoughtful frown, there was the beginnings of a plan.

"No!" Luck slammed his hand on the table. "If I find out that you've put an advertisement in any paper, I swear you won't be able to sit down for a week! This marriage business has gone far enough!"

"But you said—" Toby started to protest.

"I don't care what I said," Luck interrupted with a slicing wave of his hand to dismiss that argument. "I've played along with this marriage idea of yours, but it's got to stop. I'll decide *when* and *if* I'm getting married again without any prompting from you!"

"But face it, dad, you should get married," Toby patiently insisted. "You need somebody to keep you company and to look after you. I'm getting too old to be doing all this woman's work around the house."

"You don't get married just for companionship and someone to keep house." Luck regretted his earlier, imprecise explanation of a mother's role. It had started this whole mess. "There is more involved than that. A man is supposed to love the woman he marries."

"You're talking about hugging and kissing and that stuff," Toby nodded in understanding.

"That and...other things," Luck conceded with marked impatience.

"You mean sex, like in that book you and I read together when you explained to me how babies were made," his son replied quite calm-ly.

Luck shook his head and scratched his fore-head. "Yes, I mean sex and the feelings you have toward the woman you marry."

"Would you consider marrying someone like Eve?" Toby cocked his head at a wondering angle. "You said looks weren't everything."

"Why did you say a thing like that?" he challenged with irritation. "Don't you think Eve is an attractive woman?"

"Eve is all right, I like her, but—"

"No buts!" Luck flashed. "Eve is a lovely young woman and I don't want you implying otherwise with comments like 'looks aren't everything.' It's thoughtless remarks like that that hurt people's feelings." He should know. He had already wounded Eve when he called her a brown mouse, even though he hadn't meant it to be unkind. "Don't ever say anything to slight her!"

"Gee, dad, you don't have to get so hostile," Toby admonished, and defended his position. "Eve just doesn't look anything at all like the blonde we saw on the beach the other day. That blonde could have been the centerfold in *Playboy* magazine."

Luck started to ask where Toby had gotten his hands on a magazine like that, but he remembered his own curiosity at that age and decided not to pursue the issue at this time. Instead he just sighed, "I'm not interested in marrying a woman who has staples in her stomach."

Toby jerked his head and frowned. "Why would she have staples in her stomach?"

"Never mind." He lifted his hands in defeat. "The whole subject of women and marriage is closed. But you remember what I said about Eve," he warned. "I don't want to hear you making any disparaging remarks about her."

"I wouldn't, dad." Toby looked offended. "She's nice."

"Don't forget it, then," he replied less forcefully, and stood up. "I'm going to get out of this robe and put some clothes on. You'd better find something to put these cookies in."

"Yes, sir," Toby agreed in a dispirited tone.

Luck hesitated. "I didn't mean to be rough on you, Toby. I know you mean well. It's just that sometimes you make situations very awkward without realizing it."

"How?"

"I can't explain." He shook his head, then reached out to rumple his son's hair in a show of affection. "Don't let it worry you."

THE RAIN had washed the land clean. The sky was a fresh clear blue while the green pine needles had lost their coat of dust to contrast sharply with the blue horizon. After a day's worth of summer sunshine, the ground was dry-ing out, with only water standing in the low spots as a reminder it had rained.

Sitting on the seat in front of the upright piano, Eve let her fingers glide over the keys, seeking out the Mozart melody without conscious direction. She played from memory, eyes closed, listening to the individual notes flowing from one to another. The beauty of the song was an indirect therapy for the vague dejection that had haunted her since Luck had recognized her as his brown mouse less than two days ago.

When the last note faded into the emptiness of the cottage, Eve reluctantly let her fingers slide from the keys to her lap. The applause from a single person sounded behind her. Startled, Eve swung around on the piano seat to discover the identity of her audience of one.

The wire mesh of the screen door darkened the form of the man standing on the porch, but Eve recognized Luck instantly. An alternating pleasure and uncertainty ran through her system, setting her nerves on edge while quickening her pulse.

"I didn't hear you come." She rose quickly to cross the room and unhook the door. "Mom and dad went fishing this morning." As she pushed open the door to let him in, she noticed the only car in the driveway belonged to her parents. "Where's your car?"

"I came by boat." He stepped inside, so tall and so vigorously manly. Eve kept a safe distance between them to elude the raw force of his attraction that seemed to grow stronger with each meeting. "I tied it up at the shore. Toby's watching it."

"Oh." The knack of idle conversation deserted her. It was foolish to let that brown-mouse episode tie her tongue, but it had. She should never have allowed herself to become so sensitive about it. She should have accepted Luck's explanation the other day and let it die.

"Toby and I decided to take a ride around the lake this morning and thought you might like to come along." That lazy half smile that Eve found so disturbing accompanied his invitation.

Her delight was short-lived as she read between the lines. "It's thoughtful of you to ask, but I don't want you to feel that you're obligated to do so because you think you should make up for what happened outside the tavern that night." There was a trace of pride in the way she held her head, tipped higher than normal.

His smile grew more pronounced, bringing a gentleness to his hard-hewn features. "I'm not going to apologize for anything I said or did then," Luck informed her. "I regret that you felt slighted by the phrase of brown mouse, but I meant it in the kindest possible way. I'm asking you to come with us because we'd like your company. If you feel that I need an excuse to ask, then let's say that it is my way of thanking you for showing Toby how to make cookies." Glinting blue eyes gently mocked her as he paused. "Will you come with us?"

Eve smiled in a self-mocking way that etched attractive dimples in her cheeks. "I'd like to, yes," she accepted. "Just give me a couple of minutes to change." It would be too awkward climbing in and out of a boat in the wraparound denim skirt she was wearing.

"Sure." He reached for the screen door to open it. "We'll be stopping for lunch, probably at one of the resorts along the lake."

Eve hesitated, wondering if she was being too presumptuous, then threw caution to the wind to suggest, "If you'll give me another fifteen minutes, I can fix some sandwiches and stuff for a picnic lunch. Toby would like that."

"Toby would love it," Luck agreed. "We'll meet you at the boat in fifteen minutes."

"I'll be there," she promised as he pushed the door open and walked out.

Lingering near the door, Eve watched him descend the steps and strike out across the road toward the lakeshore, a warm feeling of pleasure running swiftly through her veins. Before he had disappeared from view, she retreated to the kitchen to take the picnic basket out of the pantry cupboard and raid the refrigerator. To go with the ham sandwiches she fixed, Eve added a wedge of Wisconsin Cheddar cheese along with some milder Colby, plus crackers and red

Delicious apples. She filled a thermos cooler with lemonade and packed it in the basket, then laid a bag of potato chips on top.

Most of the allotted time was gone when she entered her bedroom. She quickly changed out of the skirt and blouse into a pair of white shorts and a flame-red halter top. At the last minute, she slipped on a pair of white canvas shoes with rubber soles and grabbed a long-sleeved blouse from the closet, in case she wanted protection from the sun.

With her arm hooked through the handle of the picnic basket, Eve crossed the road to the lake. Toby was skipping stones across the flat surface of the lake, a picture of intensity. A cigarette dangled from Luck's mouth, his eyes squinting against the curling smoke as he stood in a relaxed stance beside his son. At the sound of Eve's approach, the upper half of his body swiveled toward her. His gaze swept her in slow appreciation, setting her aglow with pleasure.

"Hi, Eve!" Toby greeted her with an exuberant welcome, the handful of stones falling from his hands so he could brush the dust from them.

"You still have two minutes to go." Luck dropped the cigarette to the ground, grinding it dead under his heel.

"Maybe I should go back to the cottage," Eve laughed in a suddenly buoyant mood.

"Oh, no, you don't," Luck denied the suggestion, a matching humor shining in his look.

She surrendered the picnic basket to his reaching hand. A line tied around a tree moored the pleasure cruiser close to the shore. Luck swung the basket onto the bow, then turned to help Eve aboard. Previously she had only guessed at the strength in the sinewed muscles of his shoulders and arms. But when his hands spanned the bareness of her rib cage and lifted her with muscles rippling to swing her up onto the bow as easily as he had the basket, she had her belief confirmed.

The imprint of his firm hands stayed with her, warming her flesh and letting her relive the sensation of his touch as she carried the basket to the stern of the boat and stowed it under one of the cushioned seats. Toby was tossed aboard with equal ease and came scrambling back to where Eve was. After untying the mooring line, Luck pushed the boat into deeper water and heaved himself on board.

"All set?" Luck cast them each a glance as his hand paused on the ignition key.

At their nods, he turned the key. The powerful engine of the cruise boat sputtered, then roared smoothly to life, the blades churning water. Turning the wheel, Luck maneuvered the boat around to point toward the open water before opening the throttle to send it shooting forward.

The speed generated a wind that lifted the swath of brown hair from Eve's neck, blowing and swirling it behind her. A little late she realized she hadn't brought a scarf. There was nothing to be done about it now, so she turned her face to the wind, letting it race over her and whip the hair off her shoulders.

Resting her arm on the side of the boat, Eve had a clear view of all that was in front of her, including Luck. He stood behind the wheel, his feet braced apart. The sun-bronzed angles of his jutting profile were carved against a blue sky as vividly blue as his eyes. The wind ruffled the virile thickness of his dark hair and flattened his shirt against his hard flesh, revealing the play of muscles beneath it. Snug Levi's outlined the slimness of his hips and the corded muscles of his thighs, reinforcing an aura of rough sexiness. Something stirred deep within her.

The instant Eve realized how openly she was staring, she shifted her gaze to the boy at his side, a youthful replica of his father. This day Toby had left behind his mask of maturity to adopt the carefree attitude that was usually so evident in Luck with that dancing glint in his eyes and easy smile.

The loud throb of the engine made conversation impossible, but Eve heard Toby urge his father to go faster. She saw the smile Luck flashed him and knew he laughed, even though the wind stole the sound from her. The throttle was pushed wide open until the powerboat was skimming over the surface of the water and bouncing over the wakes of other boats as the churning blades sent out their own fantail.

Luck glanced over at her and smiled, and Eve smiled back. For a brief moment, she allowed herself to consider the intimate picture they made—man, woman and child. For an even briefer minute, she let herself pretend that that's the way it was, until realism caught her up sharply and made her shake the image away.

After a while, Luck eased the throttle back and turned the wheel over to his son. Toby swelled with importance, his oversized sense of responsibility surfacing to turn his expression serious. Luck stayed beside him the first few minutes until Toby got the feel of operating the boat. Then he moved to the opposite side of the boat to lean a hip against the rail and keep an unobtrusive vigil for traffic that his son might not see. The position put him almost directly in front of Eve.

His sweeping side-glance caught her looking at him and Luck raised his voice to comment, "It's a beautiful day."

"Lovely," Eve shouted the agreement, because it did seem perfect to her. The wind made an unexpected change of direction and blew the hair across her face. Turning her head, she pushed it away. When she looked back, Luck was facing the front.

A quarter of an hour later or more, he straightened and motioned to her. "It's your turn to be skipper!" Luck called.

"Aye, aye, sir," she grinned, and moved to relieve Toby at the wheel.

She was quick to notice that the small boy was just beginning to show the tension of operating the boat. Wisely Luck had seen it and had Eve take over before it ceased to be fun for Toby and became onerous instead. Out of the corner of her eye, Eve saw Toby dart over to receive praise from his father for a job well done. Then her attention was centered on guiding the boat.

Luck said something to her, but the wind and the engine noise tore it away. She shook her head and frowned that she didn't hear him. He crossed over to stand in a small space behind her.

"Let's go to the northern side of the lake," he leaned forward to repeat his suggestion.

"I'm not familiar with that area. We don't usually go up that far." Eve half turned her head to answer him and discovered he had bent closer to hear her, which brought his face inches from hers. Her gaze touched briefly on his mouth, then darted swiftly to his eyes to be captured by their vivid blueness.

"Neither am I. Let's explore strange waters together," Luck replied, his eyes crinkling at the corners.

"Okay." But there was a breathless quality to her voice.

It was some minutes after she turned the boat north before Luck abandoned his post behind her. It was only when he was gone that Eve realized how overly conscious she had been of his closeness, every nerve end tingling, although no contact had been made.

Familiar territory was left behind as they ventured into unknown waters. When a cluster of islands appeared, Eve reduced the boat's speed to find the channel through them. She hesitated over the choice.

"Want me to take over?" Luck asked.

"Yes." She relinquished the wheel to him with a quick smile. "That way if you run into a submerged log, it will be your fault instead of mine."

"Wise thinking," he grinned.

"Look!" Toby shouted, and pointed toward the waters ahead of them. "It's a deer swimming across the lake."

In the lake waters off their port side, there was the antlered head of a young buck swimming across the span of water between two islands. Luck throttled the engine to a slow idle, so they could watch him. When the deer reached the opposite island, it scrambled onto shore and disappeared within seconds in the thick stand of trees and underbrush.

"Boy, that was really something, huh, dad?" Toby exclaimed.

"It sure was," was the indulgent agreement.

With a child's lightning change of subject, Toby asked, "When are we going to have our picnic?"

"When we get hungry," Luck replied.

"I'm hungry," Toby stated.

Luck glanced at his watch. "I guess we can start looking for a place to go ashore. Or would you rather drop anchor and eat on the boat?" He included Eve in the question.

"It doesn't matter to me," she shrugged.

"Maybe we can land on one of the islands," Toby suggested.

"I don't know why not," Luck smiled down at the boy, then began surveying the cluster of islands for a likely picnic spot.

"Who knows? Maybe we'll find Chief Name-kagon's lost silver mine," Eve remarked.

Toby turned to her. "What lost silver mine?"

"The one that belonged to the Indian chief the lake was named after. Legend has it that it's on one of the islands on the lake," she explained.

"Is it true?" Toby frowned.

"No one knows for sure," she admitted. "But he paid for all his purchases at the trading post in Ashland with pure silver ore. Supposedly the old chief was going to show the location of his mine to a friend, but he saw a bad omen and postponed the trip. Then he died without ever telling anyone where it was."

"Wow!" Toby declared with round-eyed excitement. "Wouldn't it be something if we found it?"

"A lot of people have looked over the years," Eve cautioned. "No one has found it yet."

"How about having our picnic there?" Luck pointed to an island with a wide crescent of sand stretching in front of its pine trees.

"It looks perfect." Eve approved the choice, and Luck nosed the boat toward the spot.

CHAPTER FIVE

THE THREE OF THEM sat cross-legged on a blanket Luck had brought from the boat while Eve unpacked the picnic basket. "Cheese, fruit, crackers," Luck said, observing the items she removed. "All that's missing is a bottle of wine. You should have said something."

There were too many romantic overtones in that remark. Eve wasn't sure how to interpret it, so she tried the casual approach and reached in the basket for the cold thermos.

"I guess we'll have to make do with lemonade," she shrugged brightly.

"I like lemonade," Toby inserted as she set the thermos aside to arrange a sandwich and a portion of chips on a paper plate and handed it to him. "This looks good, Eve."

"I hope you like it." She fixed a plate for Luck, then one for herself, leaving the cheese, fruit and crackers on top of the basket for dessert.

"Have you ever looked for the lost mine, Eve?" Toby munched thoughtfully on his sandwich while he studied her.

"Not really. Just a few times when I was your age."

The subject continued to fascinate him. Throughout the meal, he pumped her for information, dredging up tidbits of knowledge Eve had forgotten she knew. Toby refused the slice of cheese she offered him when his sandwich was gone but took the shiny apple.

Luck ate his. When it was gone, he used the knife to slice off another chunk. "This is good cheese."

"Wisconsin cheese, of course," she smiled. "Anything else would be unpatriotic."

"Did Chief Namekagon really have seven wives?" Toby returned to his favorite subject.

"Yes, but I guess he must have kept the location of the mine a secret from them, too," Eve replied.

"Seven wives," Toby sighed, and glanced at his father. "Gee, dad, all you need is one."

"Or none," Luck murmured softly, and sent a look of silencing sharpness at his son. "More lemonade, Toby?"

"No, thanks." He tossed his apple core into the small sack Eve had brought along for their wastepaper. Rising, Toby dusted the sandwich crumbs from his legs. "Is it okay if I do a little exploring?"

At Luck's nod of permission, Toby took off. Within minutes, he had disappeared along a faint animal path that led into the island's thick forest. For the first few minutes, they could hear him rustling through the underbrush. When that stopped, Eve became conscious of the silence and that she was alone with Luck. Her gaze strayed to him, drawn by an irrepressible compulsion, only to have her heart knock against her ribs when she found him watching her.

"More cheese?" She spoke quickly to cover the sudden disturbance that seethed through her. In the far distance, there was the sound of a boat traversing the lake, reminding her they weren't the only ones in the vicinity, no matter how isolated they seemed.

"No. I'm full." Luck shook his dark head in refusal.

Inactivity didn't suit her at the moment because she knew it would take her thoughts in a direction that wasn't wise. "I'd better pack all this away before it attracts all the insects on the island."

Eve tightly wrapped the cheese that was left and stowed it in the basket with the thermos of lemonade and the few potato chips that were left. As she added the paper sack with their litter to the basket, she was conscious that Luck had risen. When he crouched beside her, balanced on the balls of his feet, she found it diffcult to breathe normally. His warm scent was all around her, heightened by the heat of the sun. She was kneeling on the blanket, sitting on her heels, aware of him with a fine-tuned radar.

"The food was very good. Thanks for the picnic, Eve." His hand reached out to cup the back of her head and pull her forward.

Lifting her gaze, she watched the sensual line of his mouth coming closer. She couldn't have resisted him if she wanted to, which she didn't. Her eyes closed an instant before his mouth touched her lips, then moved onto them to linger an instant. The kiss started her trembling all the way to her toes. Much too soon he was lifting his head, leaving her lips aching for the warm pressure of his mouth.

The very brevity of the kiss reminded her that it was a gesture of gratitude. It had meant no more than a peck on the cheek. She would be foolish to read more into it than that. Lowering her head, she struggled to appear unmoved by the experience, as casual about it as he seemed to be. Her fingers fastened on the wicker handle of the picnic basket.

"Do you want to put this in the boat now?" She picked it up to hand it to him, her gaze slanting upward.

For an instant Eve was subjected to the probing search of his narrowed eyes. Then his smooth smile erased the sensation as he took the picnic basket from her.

"Might as well," Luck agreed idly, and pushed to his feet.

Standing up, Eve resisted the impulse to

watch him walk to the boat. Instead she shook the crumbs and grains of sand off the blanket and folded it into a square. Feeling the isolation again, she turned her gaze to the treed interior of the island. The blanket was clutched in front of her, pressed protectively to her fluttering stomach. Behind her Eve heard the approach of Luck's footsteps in the sand.

"Where do you suppose Toby has gone?" she wondered.

"Leave the blanket here. We'll see if we can find him," Luck suggested, and took her hand after she'd laid the blanket down.

His easy possession sent a warm thrill over her skin. Eve liked the sensation of her slender hand being lost in the largeness of his. Together they walked to the narrow trail Toby had taken, where they would have to proceed single file.

"I'll go first, in case we run into some briers. I wouldn't want your legs to be scratched up." The downward sweep of his gaze took note of the bareness of her legs below the white shorts.

Instead of releasing her hand to start up the path, as Eve had expected he would, Luck curved his arm behind his back and shifted his grip to lead her. The forest shadows swallowed them up, the ground spongy beneath the faintly marked earth, the smell of pine resin heavy in the air.

Out of sight of their picnic site, a fallen timber blocked the trail, its huge trunk denoting the forest giant it had once been. Luck released her hand to climb over it and waited on the other side to help her. The rubber sole of her shoe found a foothold on the broken nub of a limb, providing her a step to the top of the trunk. All around them was dense foliage, with only a vague glitter of the lake's surface shining through the leaves.

"I'm glad this is a small island," Eve re-marked. "A person could get lost in this."

"It's practically a jungle," Luck agreed.

His hands gripped the curves of her waist, spanning her hipbones to help her down. Eve steadied herself by placing her hands on his shoulders while he lifted her off the trunk to the ground. When it was solidly beneath her, she discovered the toes of her shoes were touching his, a hand's length separating them.

Beneath her hands she felt his flexed muscles go taut, his hands retaining their hold on her waist. Looking up, Eve saw his keen gaze going over every facet of her appearance. She became conscious of the lack of lipstick and the wind-ratted hair. It caused a tension that forced her to speak so it would be broken.

"I should have brought a comb. My hair is a mess," she remarked tightly.

Luck's gaze wandered slowly over it and back to her face, the color of his eyes changing, deepening. "It looks like a man mussed it while he was making love to you."

His hand reached to smooth the hair away from her face and cup the back of her head. The idle caress parted Eve's lips in a silent breath, fastening his attention on them. While his mouth began moving inexorably closer, his other hand shifted to her lower spine and applied pressure to gather her in.

The tension flowed out of her with a piercing sweetness as his mouth finally reached its destination. It rocked slowly over her lips, tasting and testing first this curve, then another. The trip-hammer beat of her heart revealed the havoc he was raising with her senses.

This intimate investigation didn't stop there. His hard warm lips continued their foray, grazing over her cheek to the sensitive area around her ear. Growing weaker, her hands inched to his shoulders, clinging to him for support and balance in this dizzying embrace.

"Do you have any idea how good this feels, Eve?" he murmured in a rough disturbed tone.

She felt the shuddering breath he took and moaned softly in an aching reply. It turned his head, bringing it to a different angle as he took firm possession of her lips, the territory already familiar to him from the last exploration. Now Luck staked his claim to it and made a driving search into the dark recesses of her mouth.

Eve curved her arms around his neck, seeking the springing thickness of his hair. His hands began roaming restlessly over her shoulders and back, left bare by the red halter top she wore. The softness of her curves were pressed and shaped to his hard bone and taut muscle. The kiss deepened until Eve was raw with the hot ache that burned within her.

Gradually she felt the passion withdrawing from his kiss. It ended before his mouth reluctantly ended the contact. Breathless and dazed, she slowly lowered her chin until it was level. She was conscious that Luck was trying to force his lungs to breathe normally. She tried to get a hold of her own emotions, but without his success. His head continued to be bent toward her, his chin and mouth at a level with her eyes.

"We'll never find Toby this way," he said finally.

"No, we won't," Eve agreed, and self-consciously brought her hands down from around his neck.

He loosened his hold, stepping back to create room between them. She slid a glance at him, trying to obtain a clue as to how she was expected to treat this kiss. Luck was half-turned, looking down the trail. Something was troubling his expression, but it smoothed into a smile when he glanced at her. Yet Eve was conscious that a faint puzzled light shaded his eyes.

"Toby can't be far. The island is too small," he said, and reached for her hand again before starting up the trail.

Twenty yards farther, they reached the opposite shore of the island and found Toby sitting on a waterlogged stump at the lake's edge. He hopped down when he saw them.

"Are we ready to go?" he asked with an unconcern that didn't match the bright curiosity of his eyes.

"If you are," Luck replied.

Toby's presence brought back the easygoing friendly atmosphere that had marked the beginning of the excursion. Not once did Eve feel uncomfortable, yet an uncertainty stayed with her. She couldn't tell whether Luck regarded her as a woman or a friend.

He beached the boat on the shore in front of her parents' cottage and gave her a hand to dry land. There was nothing in his manner to indicate he would accept an invitation to come to the house for a drink, so Eve didn't issue one.

"I enjoyed myself," she said instead. "Thanks for asking me to come along."

"It was our pleasure. Maybe we'll do it again sometime." It was a noncommittal reply, indefinite, promising nothing.

Eve tried not to let her disappointment show as she clutched the picnic basket and the blouse she hadn't worn. After waving goodbye to Toby aboard the boat, she struck out for the road and the log cottage opposite it.

SINCE HE'D LEFT EVE, the frown around his forehead and eyes had deepened. As he walked the path from the lake to his house, Luck tried to recall the last time he'd felt as alive as he had those few brief moments when he'd held Eve and kissed her. The deadness inside him had gone. He worried at it, searching for it in some hidden corner, barely conscious of Toby ambling along behind him.

"Dad?" Toby requested his attention and received an abstract glance. "Why do people kiss?"

That brought Luck sharply out of his reverie. He shortened his strides to let Toby catch up with him and raised a suspicious eyebrow. "Because they like each other." He gave a general answer.

Toby turned his head to eye him thoughtfully. "Have you ever kissed anybody you didn't like?"

Luck knew it was a loaded question, but he answered it anyway. "No."

"If you only kiss people you like, then you must like Eve," Toby concluded. The sharply questioning look couldn't be ignored, and the boy admitted, "I saw you and Eve. I was coming back to see if you were ready to leave, but you were so busy kissing her that you didn't hear me."

"No, I didn't hear you," Luck admitted grimly. The hot rush of emotion had deafened him to everything but the soft sounds of submission she made. He was bothered by a vague sense of infidelity. "And, yes, I like Eve."

"Why don't you marry her?"

"Liking isn't loving." Luck cast an irritated glance at his son. "And I thought it was understood that that subject was closed."

There was a long sigh from Toby but no comment.

LATER THAT NIGHT Toby was sprawled on the floor of the living room, arms crossed on a throw pillow, his chin resting in the hollow of his fists while he watched television. At a commercial, he turned to glance at his father in the easy chair—only he wasn't there.

Frowning, Toby pushed up on his hands to peer into the kitchen, but there was no sign of him. His father hadn't been acting right since the boat ride. That fact prompted Toby to go in search of him.

He found him in a darkened bedroom. The hallway light spilled in to show him sitting on the bed, elbows on his knees and his chin resting on clasped hands. Toby paused in the doorway for a minute, confused until he saw that his father was staring at the framed photograph of his mother on the dresser.

Toby walked up to him and laid a comforting hand on his shoulder. "What's wrong, dad?"

Bringing his hands down, Luck turned his head, paused, then sighed heavily. A smile broke half-heartedly. "Nothing, sport."

But Toby glanced at the picture. "Were you thinking about mom?"

290

There was a wry twist to his father's mouth. "No, I wasn't." Pushing to his feet, he rested a hand on Toby's shoulder. Together they left the room. As they walked out the door, Toby stole a glance over his shoulder at the picture of the smiling tawny-haired blonde. He slipped his small hand into his father's, but he knew it was small comfort.

THE NEXT DAY Toby's stomach insisted it was lunchtime. Entering the house through the back door, he walked into the kitchen. His arrival coincided with his father saying a final goodbye to an unknown party on the telephone extension in the kitchen.

"I'll tell him. Right...I'll be there," Luck said, and hung up.

His curiosity overflowed, as it usually did. "Who was that? Tell me what? Where will you be?" The questions tumbled out with barely a breath in between.

"Your granddad said hello," Luck replied, answering two questions.

"Why didn't you let me talk to him?" Toby frowned in disappointment.

"Because he was busy. Next time, okay?" his father promised, and glanced at the wall clock. "I suppose you want lunch. What will it be? Hamburgers? Grilled cheese? How about some soup?"

"Hamburgers," Toby chose without a great

291

deal of interest or enthusiasm. Hooking an arm around a chair back, he watched his father take the meat from the refrigerator and carry it to the stove, where he shaped portions into patties to put in the skillet. "You said you'd be there. Be where? When?"

"I have to drive to Duluth this Friday to meet with your grandfather," Luck replied, and half turned to instruct, "Put the ketchup and mustard on the table."

"I suppose you're going to ask Mrs. Jackson to come over to stay with me," Toby grumbled as he went about setting the table and putting on the condiments.

"You are absolutely right. I'm calling her after lunch."

"Oh, dad, do you have to?" Toby appealed to him. "Sometimes Mrs. Jackson is a real pain."

"Has it ever occurred to you that Mrs. Jackson might think you are a real pain?" his father countered.

"She always thinks I'm making up stories."

"I wonder why?" Luck murmured dryly.

Toby let the silverware clatter to the table as a thought occurred to hm. "Why couldn't you ask Eve to come over? If I *have* to have somebody sit with me, I'd rather it was Eve."

Luck hesitated, and Toby studied that momentary indecision with interest. "I'll ask her," his father finally agreed.

"You'll call her after lunch?" Toby persisted for a more definite agreement.

"Yes."

EVE WAS HALFWAY OUT THE DOOR with her arms full of suntan lotion, blanket and a paperback for an afternoon in the sun when the telephone rang. She ended up dropping everything but the lotion onto couch cushions before she got the receiver to her ear.

"Rowlands," she answered.

"Hello, Eve?" Luck's voice responded on the other end of the line.

She tossed the suntan lotion on top of the blanket and hugged her free arm around her middle, holding tight to the pleasure of his voice. "Yes, this is Eve."

"Luck McClure," he needlessly identified himself. "Are you busy this Friday?"

"No." She and her mother had tentatively talked about a shopping expedition into Cable, but that certainly could be postponed.

"I have a large favor to ask. I have some business I have to take care of on Friday, which means I'll be gone most of the day and late into the evening. Toby asked if you would stay with him while I'm gone instead of the woman who usually sits with him."

Swallowing her disappointment, Eve smoothly agreed, "I don't mind in the least looking after Toby. What time would you like me to come?"

"I'd like to get an early start. Would eight o'clock be too early?" Luck asked.

"I can be there by eight."

"Thanks. Toby will be glad to know you're coming," he said. "We'll see you on Friday."

"On Friday," Eve repeated, and echoed his goodbye.

Toby would be glad she was coming, he'd said. Did that mean that Luck wouldn't? Eve sighed wearily because she simply didn't know.

ON FRIDAY morning her father dropped her off at the lake house a few minutes before eight. As she got out of the car, he leaned over to remind her, "If you need anything, you be sure to call us. Your mother or I can be over in a matter of minutes."

"I will. Thanks, dad." She waved to him and hurried toward the house.

Toby had obviously been watching for her because the front door opened before she reached it. He stood in the opening, a broad smile of welcome on his face.

"Hi, Eve."

"Hello, Toby." Her gaze went past him to the tall figure approaching the door as she entered.

The fluttering of her pulse signaled the heightening of her senses. Eve had never seen Luck in business clothes, and the dark suit and tie altered his appearance in a way that intensified the aura of male authority, dominating and powerful.

"Right on time." He smiled in an absent fashion. "I left a phone number by the telephone. You can reach me there if you have an emergency."

"Which I hope I won't," she replied, trying to respond with her usual naturalness.

After a glance of agreement, he laid a hand on Toby's head. "Behave yourself. Otherwise Eve will make you stand in a corner."

"No, she won't." Toby dipped his head to avoid the mussing of his father's hand.

His smile held a trace of affection and indulgence toward his son when Luck turned to Eve. "I shouldn't be too late getting back tonight."

"Don't worry about it," she assured him. "Toby and I will be all right."

"You know how to reach me if you need me," Luck reminded her, and she tried not to be disappointed because the remark held no underlying meaning. It was a straightforward statement from a father to a sitter. "I have to be going," he addressed both of them and smiled at his son. "See you later."

"Tell granddad hi for me," Toby instructed.

"I will," Luck promised.

To get out the door, Luck had to walk past Eve. His arm inadvertently brushed against hers, sending a little quiver through her limbs. When she breathed in, she caught the musky scent of his male after-shave lotion, potently stimulating as the man who wore it. The essence of him seemed to linger even afer he'd walked out the door.

With Toby standing beside her on the threshold, Eve watched him walk to the car. She returned his wave when he reversed out of the driveway onto the road and felt a definite sensation of being part of the family—standing at the doorway with her "son" and waving goodbye to her "husband."

Eve shook the thought away. It was that kind of dangerous thinking that would lead to heartbreak. It was definitely not wise. She was a baby-sitter—that's all.

Fixing a bright smile on her mouth, she looked down at Toby. "What's on the agenda this morning?"

He shrugged and tipped his head back to give her a bright-eyed look that reminded her a lot of his father. "I don't know. Do you want to play catch?"

"Do you think we'll break a window?" Eve teased.

"I hope not," Toby declared with a grim look. "I had to spend half the money I was saving for a minibike to pay my share of the damage to your windshield. Dad paid for most of it 'cause it was mostly his fault for throwing the ball too high, but he wouldn't have been playing if it hadn't been for me. We share things."

296

"Yes, I can see that," she nodded, because the two seemed to have a remarkable relationship, unique to anything she'd come across in her meetings with parents at school.

"Do you want to play catch?" he repeated his suggestion.

"Sure," Eve agreed, even though she didn't feel obligated to entertain him. The idea of being active appealed to her. "Go get your ball and glove."

"I'll bring dad's for you," he offered. "Sometimes I throw it pretty hard—" Toby warned "—and it stings your hand when you catch it."

The driveway seemed the safest place to play catch since there weren't any windows in the line of fire. When Toby tired of that, they walked down by the lake, where he gave her lessons in the fine art of skipping stones on the lake's surface.

At noon they returned to the lake cabin. "What would you like for lunch?" Eve asked as they entered through the kitchen door.

"A peanut butter sandwich and a glass of milk is okay." He didn't sound enthused by his own suggestion.

"Is that what you usually have?" she asked.

"It's easy," Toby shrugged. "Dad and I aren't much for cooking."

"How about if I check the refrigerator and see if there's anything else to eat?" Eve suggested, certain that Toby would like something more imaginative if she offered to fix it.

"Go ahead," he agreed, then warned, "There's not much in there except some frozen dinners in the freezer section of the icebox."

When she opened the refrigerator door, she discovered Toby was right. The shelves were nearly bare, except for milk, eggs, bacon and a couple of jars of jam.

Toby watched her expression. "I told you," he reminded her. "Dad fixes breakfast and sometimes cooks steaks on the grill. Otherwise we eat out or have frozen dinners. They're pretty good, though."

Eve found a package of cheese in the dairy drawer of the refrigerator. "Do you like grilled cheese sandwiches?" she asked.

"Yeah," he nodded.

While the skillet was heating to grill them, Eve searched through the cupboards and found a lone can of condensed tomato soup. She diluted it with milk and added a dab of butter. When she set the lunch on the table, Toby consumed it with all the gusto of the growing boy that he was.

"Boy, that was good, Eve!" he declared, and leaned back in his chair to rub his full stomach. "You sure are a good cook."

"Grilling a sandwich and opening a can of soup isn't exactly cooking," she smiled. "I was thinking that I might call my father and see if he would drive us to the store this afternoon and pick up some groceries. I'll cook you a *real* dinner tonight. Would you like that?"

"You bet!"

CHAPTER SIX

AFTER A FEW INQUIRIES Eve was able to discover some of Toby's favorite dishes. Being a young boy, he had simple tastes. Dinner that evening consisted of fried chicken, mashed potatoes and gravy and some early sweet corn-on-the-cob. For dessert she fixed fresh strawberry shortcake with lots of whipped cream.

"I can't ever remember eating food that good," Toby insisted. "It was really delicious, Eve."

"Why, thank you, sir." With her hands full of dirty dishes to be carried to the sink, she gave him a mock curtsy.

"I'll help wash the dishes," he volunteered, and pushed away from the table. "Dad usually dries them."

"You don't need to help." She had already learned while she was preparing the meal that Toby was accustomed to doing household chores. His sense of duty was commendable, but he was still very young and needed a break from it once in a while. "You can have the night off and I'll do them."

"Really?" He seemed stunned by her offer.

"Yes, really," she laughed.

"I'll stay and keep you company." He dragged a chair over to the kitchen counter by the sink.

"I'd like that," Eve said, and let the sink fill with water, squirting liquid soap into it.

Kneeling on the chair seat, Toby rested his arms on the counter and propped his chin on an upraised hand to watch her. "You know, it'd really be great to have a mother. It's getting to be a hassle cleaning the house, washing dishes and all that stuff."

"I can imagine." She smiled faintly as she began washing the dishes and rinsing them under the running faucet, then setting them on the draining board to dry.

"I'd sure like to figure out how to find someone for dad to marry." Toby sighed his frustration. "I thought about putting an ad in the paper, but dad really got upset when I mentioned it to him."

Her initial pang of envy came from the knowledge that she coveted the role of Toby's mother—and Luck's wife. It wouldn't take much encouragement to fall head over heels in love with Luck. She was already more than halfway there now.

But after the brief envy came amusement and sympathy for Luck's plight. The idea of advertising for a wife had to have come as a shock to him.

"It would have been a little embarrassing for your father, Toby," Eve murmured, the corners of her mouth deepening with the smile she tried to contain.

"Dad seemed to think that, too." He grimaced in resignation to the decision. "I told dad that you'd make a good mother and he should marry you."

"Toby, you didn't!" She nearly dropped the dish in her hand, a warm pink flooding her cheeks.

"Yes, I did," he assured her innocently. "What's wrong with that? He likes you. I know he does. I saw him kiss you."

Eve became very busy with the dishes, trying to hide her agitation and embarrassment with her work. "Just because you kiss someone doesn't necessarily mean you want to marry them, Toby."

"Yeah, that's what dad said," he admitted.

She hated the curiosity that made her ask, "What else did your dad say when you suggested he should marry me?"

"Nothing. He told me the subject was closed and I wasn't supposed to discuss it anymore, but we need someone around here to take care of us." The comment revealed he hadn't let go of the idea. "There's too much work for a boy like me to do, and dad's busy. Somewhere there's a girl that dad will marry. I just gotta find her."

"Toby McClure, I think you should leave that to your father," Eve suggested.

"Yeah, but he isn't *trying* to find anybody," Toby protested. "I thought I'd have better luck." Then he laughed. "I made a joke, didn't I? Better luck for Luck."

"Yes, you did." Her smile widened into a grin.

"That's my name, too, you know," he declared, and settled his chin on his hand once more.

"No, I didn't know that." Her brown eyes widened in vague surprise. "I thought it was Toby—Tobias," she corrected it from the shortened version.

"That's my middle name," Toby explained. "My real first name is Luck—like my dad's. My mom insisted on naming me after him when I was born, but dad said it was too hard growing up with a name like that. He said I'd wind up getting called Little Luck, and he didn't like the idea of being Big Luck. So they called me Toby instead."

"I think that was probably best," Eve agreed with the decision.

In her experience at the school, she'd seen how cruel children could be sometimes when one of the members had an unusual name. Sometimes they teased him unmercifully. As a rule children didn't like being different. It wasn't until later, when their sense of individuality surfaced, that they showed a desire for unique names.

Yet she couldn't help remembering when she had first been introduced to the father and son, and Luck had explained the family tradition of his name. At the time she had wondered if there was a "little" Luck at home to carry it on. It was slightly amusing to discover it had been Toby all along.

After the dishes were done, she and Toby went into the front room and watched television for a while. At nine o'clock she suggested that it was time he took a bath and got ready for bed. He didn't argue or try to persuade her to let him stay up until Luck came home.

Spanking clean from his bath, Toby trotted barefoot into the living room in his pajamas. He half flopped himself across the armrest of the chair where Eve was sitting.

"Are you going to tuck me into bed?" he asked.

"I sure am." Eve smiled at the irresistible appeal of his look. Toby was just as capable of twisting her around his finger as his roguish father was.

Toby led the way to his room while Eve followed. He made a running leap at the bed, dived under the covers and was settled comfortably by the time Eve arrived at his bedside. A white pillowcase framed the mass of dark brown hair as a pair of bright blue eyes looked back at her.

She made a show of tucking the covers close to his sides while he kept his arms on top of them. Then she sat sideways on the edge of the mattress.

"You don't have to read me a story or anything," Toby said. "I'm too old for that."

"Okay. Would you like me to leave the light on for a while?" Eve asked, referring to the small lamp burning on the bedside table. She already suspected he was "too old" for that, too.

"No." There was a negative movement of his head against the pillow.

Her glance had already been drawn to the night table, where it was caught by the framed photograph of a beautiful blond-haired woman with sparkling green eyes. A vague pain splintered through Eve as she guessed the identity of the smiling face in the photograph.

"Is this a picture of your mother?" she asked Toby for confirmation, her throat hurting.

"Yes. Her name was Lisa." Toby blithely passed on the information.

"She's very beautiful," Eve admitted, aware that Luck would never have called this woman a "brown mouse." She was golden—all sunshine and springtime. Eve despised herself for the jealousy that was twisting inside her. But she didn't have a prayer of ever competing with someone as beautiful as this girl—not even with her memory. It was utterly hopeless to think Luck would ever love her.

"Dad has a picture just like that in his room," Toby informed her. "He talks to it a lot...although he hasn't lately," he added as an afterthought.

"I'm sure he loves her very much." She tried to smile and conceal the awful aching inside. "It's time you were going to sleep."

"Will you kiss me good-night?" he asked with an unblinking look.

"Of course." There was a tightness in her throat as Eve bent toward him and brushed his forehead with a kiss. She longed for the right to do that every night. She straightened, murmuring, "Have a nice night, Toby."

"Good night, Eve." With a contented look on his face, he snuggled deeper under the covers.

Her hand faltered as she reached past the framed photograph to turn out the light. Standing up, she moved silently out of the room. Bitter tears burned the back of her eyes. She regretted more than she ever had in her life that she had been born plain.

In the living room Eve turned down the volume on the television set and picked up a magazine lying on the coffee table. Curling up in the large armchair, she tried to force herself to read the articles it contained. The clock on the fireplace mantel ticked away the time.

IT WAS AFTER MIDNIGHT when Luck pulled into the driveway, much later than he had anticipated. Switching off the engine, he grabbed his briefcase and his suit jacket from the rear seat. The briefcase he carried in his hand as he climbed out of the car; the jacket he swung over his shoulder, held by the hook of a finger. His tie was draped loosely around his neck, the top buttons of his shirt unfastened.

The tension of a long drive and the mental fatigue from a full day of business discussions cramped the muscles in his shoulders and neck. Weariness drew tired lines in his tough rakehell features.

As Luck walked to the front door of the cabin, he noticed the light burning in the window. The edges of his mouth lifted in a faint smile at the welcoming sight. When he opened the door, he heard the muted volume of the television set. There was a warm run of pleasure as he realized Eve must have waited up for him to come home.

Setting his briefcase down just inside the door, he walked into the living room and paused. Eve had fallen asleep in the big armchair, with a magazine in her lap. His smile lengthened at the sight of her curled up like a velvety brown mouse. Luck tossed his suit jacket onto the sofa along with his tie and walked over to turn off the television set.

Silence swirled through the room as he approached the chair where she was sleeping. He intended to wake her, but when he looked down at her, the tiredness seemed to fall away from him. In repose, her serene features reminded him of the gentle beauty of a madonna—or a sleeping beauty waiting to be wakened with a kiss. The latter was a tantalizing thought.

Leaning down, Luck placed his hands on either armrest of the armchair. He felt alive and whole, renewed by her presence. He lowered his mouth onto her lips, stimulated by their sweet softness. At the initial contact, they were unresponsive to the mobile pressure of his kiss. Then Luck felt her lips move against his. Raw emotions surged through him, an aching pressure building inside him.

Eve stirred with the beginnings of wakefulness and he pulled back, not straightening but continuing to lean over her. The desire was strong to pick her up and carry her into his bedroom where he could give rein to those feelings that swept him.

Her lashes slowly drifted open and he watched the dawning light of recognition flare in her brown, nearly black eyes. His blood was warmed by the pleasure at seeing him that ran wild in her look.

"You're home," she murmured in soft joy.

"Yes," Luck answered huskily, because it seemed he had come home. It was a sensation he couldn't quite explain, not even to himself.

One minute he could see the welcome in her eyes and in the next it was gone, as a sudden rush of self-consciousness hid it from him. She lowered her chin, a vague agitation making her restive.

"I must have fallen asleep." She brushed a hand across her eyes, then reached for the opened magazine in her lap.

Faintly irritated by her sudden remoteness, Luck pushed himself erect, withdrawing physically from her as she had withdrawn from him. He saw the flicker of her hurt in the velvet darkness of her eyes. Luck regretted the day he'd ever called her a brown mouse. Her sensitive nature had found the phrase offensive when he had actually used it with teasing affection.

All Eve knew about what he was feeling she saw in the displeasure written on his features. There was a vague sensation that he had kissed her, but she thought she had dreamed that.

"What time is it?" There was a crick in her neck from sleeping in the chair. She rubbed at the stiffness as she uncurled her legs.

"It's nearly one." His answer was abrupt. "I'm sorry I was so late getting back."

"It's all right." Eve smiled in his direction without actually meeting his gaze.

"You didn't have to wait up for me." It almost sounded like a criticism. "You should have lain down on the couch."

"I didn't plan to fall asleep. I was reading and...I guess I dozed off," she explained self-consciously.

"Let me check on Toby, then I'll drive you home," he said.

Luck disappeared into the darkened hallway leading to the bedrooms as Eve forced her cramped body out of the chair. She noticed his suit jacket and tie on the sofa when she retrieved her purse from the coffee table. She remembered how incredibly handsome he'd looked when she'd opened her eyes and seen him standing there, bent over her to wake her. He must have seen the rush of love she'd felt. There didn't seem to be any other explanation for the way he'd withdrawn from her—his sudden shortness. He probably thought she was going to start fawning all over him and didn't want the embarrassment of her unwanted attentions. She resolved not to let him see the way she felt toward him, not again.

When he returned to the living room, Eve managed to appear very calm and controlled— and very casual. Yet there wasn't any approval in his inspecting glance.

"Ready?" he asked.

"Yes." She had to look away from him before she was affected by his blatant masculinity. "Is Toby all right?"

"He's sound asleep," Luck replied. "He'll be okay alone until I get back."

"Of course," she murmured, and moved toward the front door.

Outside, a full moon bathed the night with its

silvery light and the sky was atwinkle with stars. A breeze whispered through the pines, scenting the air with their freshness. Eve paused beside the passenger side of the car while Luck opened the door for her.

Nervousness made her say, "It's a lovely evening, isn't it?" The ambience seemed too romantic for her peace of mind.

"Yes, it is," Luck agreed, and waited until she was inside before closing the door.

Her gaze followed him as he walked around the car and slid behind the wheel. When he started the motor, Eve faced the front. Her nerve ends quivered with his nearness, making the silence intolerable.

"How did your business go today?" she asked, to make conversation.

"Fine." It was a noncommunicative answer, but Luck made it easier by asking, "Did Toby give you any trouble today?"

"None," Eve assured him. At this time of night there was no traffic on the road to her parents' lake cottage. They had it all to themselves. "We played catch—and didn't break a single window," she added with feigned lightness.

"You're luckier than I am." He slid her a brief glance, one side of his mouth lifting in a half smile, his voice dry with amusement.

"We were careful about the area we picked," she explained, relaxing a little under the humorous overtones of the subject matter.

It was a short drive to the cottage. Part of her regretted the quickness with which they covered the distance, and another part of her was relieved. When they drove in, Eve noticed her parents had left the porch light burning.

"I hope they weren't worried about you," Luck commented as he stopped the car.

"I doubt it," she replied. "They've accepted that I'm a big girl now. My hours are my own."

Letting the engine idle, he shifted the gear into the park and half turned in the seat to face her. "How much do I owe you for staying with Toby?"

She stiffened at the offer of payment for her services. "Nothing," Eve insisted.

"I didn't ask you to stay with Toby with the intentions of getting a free baby-sitter. If you hadn't come, I would have had to pay someone else," Luck reasoned.

"Please don't ask me to take money for this," she appealed to him, not wanting to be paid for something she had done gladly. "Just consider it a favor from a neighbor."

"All right." He gave in reluctantly. "I won't argue with you."

"Thank you." Eve looked away to reach for the door handle, but she was kept from opening it by the staying hand that touched her arm.

Almost against her will, she looked back at him. The sheen of the moonlight bronzed the masculine angles and planes of his face, giving them a rugged look. A hunger rose within her that she couldn't deny.

"Thank you for staying with Toby." His voice was pitched disturbingly low, vibrant in its rich tone.

"You're welcome," Eve whispered the reply, too affected by his touch and his nearness to speak normally.

Nor could she draw away when his head bent toward hers. She trembled under the possession of his hard lips, her resolve shattering into a thousand pieces. His hand spanned her rib cage just below the uplift of her breast and silently urged her closer.

Eve arched nearer, trying to satisfy the hunger she tasted in his kiss. The blood pounded in her ears with a thunderous force as she let him part her lips to savor the completeness of her response. A soft moan came from her throat at the ache Luck aroused in her.

He was everything. Her senses were dominated by him. The feel of his rock-hard muscles excited her hesitant hands, which rested lightly on his chest, warmed by the heat generated from his male body. That combination of scents—tobacco smoke, musky cologne and his own male scent—filled her lungs with its heady mixture. And the taste of him was in her mouth.

The world was spinning crazily, but Eve didn't care—as long as she had him to cling to. Kissing him was both heaven and hell. But regardless of the consequences, she seemed to be condemned to loving him.

Luck dragged his mouth from her lips and let it moistly graze over her cheek, trailing fire. Her breath was so shallow, it was practically nonexistent. He combed his fingers into her hair as if to hold her head still.

"And thanks for waiting up for me, Eve," he murmured thickly against her sensitive skin. "It's been a long time since anyone has done that. I can't explain how good it made me feel."

"Luck, I . . . ." But she was afraid to say the words. Then he kissed her again and she didn't need to say anything.

But this time it was brief, although she had the consolation of sensing his reluctance when it ended and he drew away.

"I've got to get back. Toby's alone," Luck said, as if he needed to explain.

"Yes." This time he made no move to stop her when she opened the door. "Good night," she murmured as she stepped out of the car.

"Good night, Eve," he responded.

She seemed to glide on air to the lighted porch, conscious that Luck was waiting to make sure she got safely inside. Opening the door, she turned and waved to him. She watched the red taillights of his car until they disappeared onto the road.

It would be so easy to read something significant into his kisses. Eve tried desperately to guard against raising false hopes. Thinking about the photograph of his late wife helped. That, and the memory of the time when he had intimated he was lonely.

As she undressed for bed, Eve berated herself for being such a fool as to let herself love him. It was very difficult to listen when she felt so good.

THIS TIME there were no lights burning to welcome him home when Luck entered the cabin. He didn't bother to turn any on as he made his way down the hallway in the dark.

"Dad?" Toby's sleepy voice called out to him.

"Yes, son, it's me." He paused by the doorway to his son's room.

"Did you take Eve home?" Toby asked.

"Yes. I just got back," he explained. "Are you okay?"

"Yeah." There was the rustle of bedcovers shifting. "How was granddad?"

"He's fine," Luck assured him. "It's very late. You go back to sleep, Toby. We'll talk in the morning."

"Okay, dad," he replied in the middle of a yawn. "Good night."

"Good night, Toby." Luck waited until he heard silence from the room, then entered his own.

The moonlight shining in through the window

illuminated the room sufficiently, allowing him to undress without the need of turning on the bed lamp. Unbuttoning his shirt, he pulled it free from the waistband of his pants and shrugged out of it to toss it into the clothes hamper.

He sat down on the edge of the bed to take off his shoes. The moon laid its light on the framed photograph sitting on his dresser. Luck stopped to gaze at it.

"We had a good thing, Lisa," he murmured. "But it was a long time ago." There was an amused lift to his mouth, a little on the wry side. "Why do I have the feeling that you don't mind if I fall in love with someone else?"

But she didn't answer him. It had been quite a while since she had. Luck wasn't haunted anymore by images from the past. And he didn't feel any guilt that it was so.

CHAPTER SEVEN

THE AFTERNOON SUN burned into her oiled skin
as Eve shifted her position in the reclining
lounge chair. Dark sunglasses blocked out most
of the glare, but the scarlet swimsuit exposed
her body to the sun's tanning rays. The straps
were unfastened so that they wouldn't leave any
white strips on her shoulders.

When she reached for her glass of iced tea sitting under the chair in the shade, Eve held the
bodice in position with her hand so that the top
wouldn't fall down when she bent over. The sip
of tea momentarily cooled and refreshed her.
She'd promised herself to walk down to the lake
for a swim, but so far she hadn't found the
energy.

The front screen door creaked on its hinges
and Eve turned her head toward the lake cottage
as her mother stepped onto the porch. She saw
Eve and smiled.

"There you are," she declared. "I was ready
to hike down to the lake. You're wanted on the
telephone."

"Me?" She almost forgot about the untied

straps of her swimsuit as she sat up abruptly. A quicksilver run of excitement sped through her nerves. "Who is it?"

"It's Luck McClure," her mother answered.

"Tell him I'll be right there," Eve urged.

Her fingers turned into thumbs as she tried hurriedly to knot the straps behind her neck. While she struggled with that, the leather thongs refused to cooperate with her attempts to slip her bare feet into them. She heard the screen door swing shut behind her mother.

The message was being passed to Luck that she was on her way to the phone, but Eve was afraid he'd get tired of waiting if she took too long. When she finally had the straps tied and the shoes on, she ran to the cottage.

The telephone receiver was off the hook, lying beside the phone on the table. Eve grabbed it up, mindless of the amused glances exchanged by her parents.

"Hello?" She was winded from her panicked rush to the phone—and the breathless excitement she couldn't control.

"Eve? You sound out of breath," Luck's voice observed, and she closed her eyes in silent relief that he hadn't hung up.

"I was outside." She swallowed in an attempt to steady her breathing.

"Your mother told me that she thought you were down by the lake," he admitted.

"Actually, I wasn't," Eve explained. "I was out front, sunbathing."

"Wearing a skimpy little bikini, I suppose," Luck murmured.

"No." She half smiled. "I have on a very respectable one-piece bathing suit."

"I should have guessed." His voice was dry with contained amusement.

The reply stung her sensitive ego. She knew exactly what he was thinking. A one-piece suit was precisely what a brown mouse would wear. After all, they weren't very daring creatures.

"Why are you calling, Luck?" She supposed he wanted her to stay with Toby again. It was really quite a bargain when baby-sitters could be paid with a kiss. After last night what else could he think?

"I called to ask you to have dinner with us tonight. Since you wouldn't let me pay you anything for staying with Toby, I thought you might accept an invitation to dinner," he explained.

If he hadn't added the explanation, she would probably have leaped at the invitation, but he stole the pleasure from it.

"I told you last night that I was just being a friendly neighbor," Eve reminded him stiffly. "I don't expect anything in return. And you certainly aren't obligated to take me to dinner."

"I'm not asking out of any sense of duty,"

Luck stated on a note of tolerance. "Toby and I *want* you to come over for dinner tonight."

"Thank you, but I—" She started to refuse politely for her pride's sake, but he interrupted her.

"Before you turn me down, you'd better hear the terms of the invitation." A faint thread of amusement ran through his voice.

"Terms?" Eve repeated with a bewildered frown.

"Ever since Toby got up this morning, he's been bragging about what a great cook you are," he informed her. "It's been a long time since I've had a home-cooked meal, so I decided to ask you over to dinner tonight and find out if Toby knows what he's talking about."

She was a little stunned by the implication of his reply, and faintly amused. "Do you mean you're asking me to dinner and you're expecting me to cook it?"

"Only part of it," Luck assured her. "I've got some steaks, so I'll take care of the meat course. The rest of the menu I'll leave to you."

"You have a lot of nerve, Luck McClure." But she couldn't help laughing.

"What do you say?" he challenged. "Is it a deal? Will you come tonight?"

"What time?" she asked, and smiled at the mouthpiece of the receiver.

"I'll pick you up at six o'clock. Is that all right?" he asked.

"That's fine," Eve nodded. "I'll be ready."

"I'll see you at six," Luck promised, and rang off.

Her smile lingered as she replaced the receiver on its cradle and turned away from the phone. She happened to glance at her father and caught the merry twinkle in his hazel eyes.

"I take it that you're going out to dinner with Luck," he guessed from the one side of the conversation he'd heard. "You've been seeing quite a bit of him lately. Maybe I should have a chat with him when he comes to pick you up tonight and find out his intentions."

He was only teasing, but Eve reacted just the same. "Don't you dare," she warned, and he laughed.

As PART OF HER NEW IMAGE to rid herself of the brown-mouse label, Eve wore a white blouse of eyelet lace that scalloped to a vee neckline and buttoned down the front. With it she wore a pair of cornflower-blue slacks in a clingy material.

Promptly at six o'clock, Luck drove up to the cottage, accompanied by Toby. Ready and waiting, Eve bolted from the cabin before her father had a chance to tease her further by carrying out his threat to "have a little talk" with Luck.

Toby whistled like an adult wolf when he saw her. Eve flushed a little. She hadn't thought the different style and color of clothes made that much difference in her appearance—enough for an eight-year-old to notice.

When Toby hopped into the rear seat so Eve could sit in front beside Luck, she was subjected to a wickedly admiring rake of his blue eyes. Her cheeks grew even warmer.

"Not bad," Luck murmured his approval.

Compliments from him were something she couldn't handle, so she tried to turn it aside with a self-effacing remark. "You mean, it's not bad for a brown mouse," Eve corrected.

"No, not a brown mouse anymore. A blue one," he declared with a glance at her slacks. After checking for traffic, Luck reversed onto the road.

"Did dad tell you we're going to have steaks tonight?" Toby leaned over the top of the front seat.

"Yes, he did," she admitted.

"How do you like yours cooked?" Luck asked.

"Medium rare." Her sensitive nerves felt just about that raw at the moment, ultraconscious of the man behind the wheel.

"I guessed you were the red-blooded kind." He allowed his gaze to leave the road long enough to send a mocking glance at her. The innuendo seemed to hint she had a passionate nature, which only served to heighten her awareness of him.

"That's the way we like ours, too, isn't it,

dad?" Toby said, unconscious of any hidden meaning in the talk.

"It sure is," Luck agreed, a smile playing at the edges of his mouth.

"You have to watch him, though," Toby told Eve. "Or he winds up burning them."

"Now wait a minute," Luck said in protest. "Who's the cook around here?"

"Eve," his son was quick to answer.

A low chuckle came from Luck's throat. "That's a point well taken." He slowed the car as they approached the drive to the cabin.

Preparations for the evening meal became a family affair. Luck started the grill in the backyard and cooked the steaks, while Toby took care of setting the table and helping Eve. She fixed a fresh spinach salad and wild rice to go along with the steaks. There were enough strawberries left over from the previous night's shortcake dessert to add to other fruit for a mixed fruit sauce as a light dessert.

When they sat down at the table, the meal seemed flawless. Eve wasn't sure whether it was the food or the company that made it all taste so good, but all three of them ate every bite of food on their plates.

"Didn't I tell you Eve was a good cook?" Toby stayed at the table while they lingered over their coffee.

"You certainly did," Luck agreed. "And you were right, too."

"Your father deserves some of the credit," Eve insisted. "I don't know about yours, but my steak was perfect."

"Thank you." Luck inclined his dark head in mocking acceptance of the compliment. Thick strands of rich brown hair fell across his forehead, adding to his rakish air.

"Mine was good, too," Toby assured him, then took away the compliment. "But all you had to do was watch them so they wouldn't burn. Eve really did the cooking."

"And an excellent job, too." He didn't argue with his son's summation. The magnetic blue of his eyes centered on her, lazy and disturbing. "You certainly know the way to a man's heart."

All her senses went haywire at that remark, throwing her into a state of heady confusion. She struggled to conceal it, quickly dropping her gaze and busying her hands with the dessert dishes still on the table.

"Don't bother with the dishes," Luck instructed. "We'll just stack them in the sink for now."

"Nonsense." There was an agitated edge to her voice that betrayed her inner disturbance. "It will only take a few minutes to do them and they'll be out of the way."

"In that case, we'll all help." He pushed out of his chair. "You can clear the table and stack the dishes by the sink, and Toby can wash them while I dry."

They seemed to get them done in record time. Eve finished wiping the stove, table and counter tops a little before Toby and Luck were through.

As the trio entered the living room, Toby turned to walk backward and face them. "Why don't we start a fire in the fireplace, dad?"

"It's summer, Toby," Luck reminded him with an indulgent look.

"I know, but it would be fun," he shrugged. "We could toast marshmallows."

"You can't still be hungry," Eve laughed.

"No, but I'll eat them anyway," he replied, and she understood that most of the pleasure came from toasting them, rather than eating them. "Please, dad. Just a little fire."

"Okay," Luck gave in. "Just a small one."

While Toby dashed back to the kitchen for the bag of marshmallows and a long-handled toasting fork, Luck built a small fire in the stone fireplace. When it was burning nicely, the three of them sat on the floor in a semicircle around the hearth.

Toby did the actual toasting of the marshmallows, passing around the finished product in turns. Half a bag was consumed—mostly by the fire—before he finally tired of the task. All of them had to wash the sticky gooey residue from their hands. Once that was done, the flickering flames of a fading fire drew them back to their former positions.

A contented silence settled over the room, broken only by the soft crackle of the burning wood. Outside, darkness had descended and the soft glow of the fire provided the only light in the front room. Sitting cross-legged between them, Toby yawned loudly.

"Gosh, I'm tired," he declared. "I think I'll go to bed."

Luck wore a look of vague surprise that his son was actually volunteering to go to bed. A little thread of self-consciousness laced its way through Eve's nerve ends at the prospect of being alone with Luck.

"I guess it is your bedtime," Luck remarked as his son pushed to his feet with apparent tiredness.

"Yeah." Toby paused to look at Eve. "Thanks for cooking dinner tonight. It was really good."

"You're welcome." Her mouth trembled a little in its smile.

"Good night," he wished her.

"Good night," she returned.

"I'll be in shortly," Luck promised.

"You don't need to. You can stay with Eve," Toby said, then partially turned to hide the frowning look of reproval he gave his father from her. She heard him whisper, "I'm big enough to go to bed by myself. Don't embarrass me in front of her."

A slow smile broke over Luck's features at his son's admonition. "Get to bed." He affectionately slapped Toby on the behind to send him on his way.

When he'd gone, Luck slid the lazy smile in Eve's direction, encompassing her with the warmth of its casual intimacy. There had been an ease between them. Eve had definitely felt it, yet without Toby's presence to serve as a buffer, it started to dissipate. She became conscious there was only the two of them in the room. The silence that had been so pleasant and comfortable began to grow heavy. She'd never had the knack for making idle conversation, but the situation seemed to demand it.

"He's quite the boy," Eve remarked under the strain of silence.

"Unfortunately he's grown old before his time." His smile twisted into a regretful grimace that held a certain resignation.

"I don't think he's suffered too much from it," she replied, because Toby did appear to have achieved a balance between his boyhood and his sense of responsibility.

"I guess he hasn't." Luck stared at the fire and seemed to lose himself in the tiny yellow flames darting their tongues over the glowing log.

Eve couldn't think of a response, and the silence lengthened. She supposed that he was thinking about his late wife, probably remembering past moments shared.

No more sounds came from the direction of Toby's bedroom, and the tension ran through her system. Her legs were becoming cramped by her curled sitting position, but Eve was reluctant to move and draw attention to herself. She didn't want Luck to look at her and mentally compare her to the beautiful blonde in the photograph.

At that moment he seemed to rouse himself and become aware that he wasn't alone. "That fire is becoming hypnotic," he said, explaining away his preoccupation.

"Yes." Eve pretended she had been fascinated by it, too, when the only fascination that existed within her was for him.

Luck made a move as if to stand, then paused. "Was there any coffee left?"

"Yes." She rose quickly to her feet. "I'll heat it up for you. It will only take a minute."

"I can get it." But Luck didn't protest too stridently, willing to let himself be persuaded to remain where he was.

"No, you stay here," Eve insisted. "I've been sitting so long I'm starting to get stiff. I need to move around a bit." Which was the truth, although the greater truth was a need to be alone and get herself together. She had to stop being torn apart by this unrequited love for him.

"Okay." Luck didn't argue the point further, remaining by the fire. "If you insist."

Activity helped as she buried herself in the kitchen, turning the coffee on to warm it through and setting out cups for each of them. Yet she couldn't forget that another woman had once brought him coffee and kissed his son good-night as she had done the previous evening. The latter thought prompted Eve to check on Toby while she waited for the coffee to heat.

When she entered the hallway, it was at the precise moment that Luck entered it from the living room. Eve stopped, a little guiltily.

"I thought I'd see if Toby was all right," she explained.

The slight curve to his mouth captivated her with its male charm. "That's where I was headed, too," Luck replied, lifting a dark brow in arching inquiry. "Shall we go together and both be satisfied?"

He took her agreement for granted, linking an arm around her waist to guide her down the darkened hallway. The sensation was much too enjoyable for Eve to resist. She was becoming satisfied with the crumbs of his attention— something she had believed her pride would never let her do.

The doorway to his room stood open and they paused in its frame, standing side by side. In the semidarkness they could see his shining face, all youthful innocence in sleep. His dark hair waved across his forehead like a cap. Deep affection for the sleeping child tugged at her heartstrings.

"That's about the only time he's quiet," Luck murmured softly.

A faint smile touched her mouth as Eve turned her head to look up at him in silent understanding. Toby was always doing, saying or up to something. She could well imagine the wry truth in Luck's comment.

When she met his downward glance, something warm and wonderful shone in his blue eyes. There was a caressing quality in the way they wandered over her upturned face. It started her heart pounding at a rapid speed.

He bent slightly toward her, brushing her lips in a light kiss that stirred her senses and left her wanting more. That desire trembled within her, not letting itself be known. Nothing invited it to show her wants, and Eve lacked the aggression and confidence to assert herself.

"Do you suppose the coffee's hot yet?" Luck murmured, not lifting his head very far from hers.

"It should be," she whispered, and doubted if her voice had the strength to speak louder.

As they turned to leave the doorway, neither of them noticed the little boy in bed cautiously open one eye, or the satisfied smile that smugly curved his mouth.

Luck accompanied her to the kitchen and carried his own cup of hot coffee into the living room. He walked past the sofa and chairs to the fireplace, lowering himself to sit on the floor in front of the dying fire. Reaching out, he pulled a couple of throw pillows from the sofa closer to his position and patted them to invite Eve to join him. She sat on one, bending her legs to the side and holding her cup in both hands.

"Toby likes you a lot, Eve," Luck remarked, eyeing her with a sidelong glance.

"I like him a lot, too," she admitted. "So I guess it's mutual."

"Toby and I have led a bachelor's life for a long time," he said, continuing to regard her steadily. "I always thought we managed very well." He paused for a brief second. "Tonight I realized there were a lot of things we've been missing. I'm glad you came to dinner this evening."

"I'm glad you asked me," Eve replied, and guessed at his loneliness.

His actions and words had proved that he liked her, that he even regarded her as reasonably attractive. She knew she should be happy about that, but there was a part of her that wished he could be insanely in love with her, wanting her above all other women. It was silly to wish for the moon when she had the glow of the firelight.

"What I'm trying to say is that meeting you has been one of the best things that has happened to us in a long while." Luck appeared determined to convince her of something, but Eve wasn't sure what it was.

She couldn't help noticing the way it was always "we" or "us," never "I" or "me." He was coupling himself with Toby. It was her effect on "them"—not "him." She lowered her gaze to the cup in her hands.

"I'm handling this badly, aren't I?" His voice held a sigh of self-amusement.

"I can't answer that because I don't know what you're trying to handle," Eve said, attempting to speak lightly but unable to look at him.

"It's really very simple." He curved a hand under her chin and turned it toward him. "I want to kiss you. I've been wanting to do it all evening, but I never found the opening. So I was trying to make one."

Her heart fluttered at the disturbing hint of desire in his blue eyes. Luck had finally said "I," and her senses were on a rampage, wild with the promise that the word held. With a total lack of concern for the deliberateness of his actions, he took the coffee cup from her hands and set it on the stone hearth beside his.

Her composure was so rattled that she wondered how Luck could go about this all so calmly. Anticipation had her trembling on the brink of raw longing for his embrace. The sensation was becoming so strong that Eve didn't think she could hide it.

When his hands closed on her arms to draw her to him, Eve abandoned herself to the emotional needs and wants searing within. The fire in the hearth was dying, but the one inside her was kindled to a full blaze by the sure possession of his hard male lips.

His hand burrowed into the thickness of her brown hair, holding its mass while he supported the back of her head as his driving kiss forced it backward. Her arms went around his middle, her sense of touch excited by the solidness of his muscled body, so hard and firm and virile.

A mist of sensuality swirled itself around her consciousness and made any thought of caution a hazy ill-defined one. His hand roamed along her spine, alternately caressing and urging her closer. Eve strained to comply and arched nearer. The unyielding wall of his body flattened her breasts, but it wasn't enough.

Her breathing was so shallow it was almost nonexistent when Luck dragged his mouth from her lips to nibble at her throat and trail its way up the pulsing vein to the sensitive hollow below her ear. Eve quivered with the intensity of the passions he was arousing.

"I've needed this for so long, Eve," he declared in a voice thick with desire, the heat of his breath inflaming her skin. "I've been so empty. Fill me up, Eve. Fill me up."

But she didn't need to be urged. Her hunger and emptiness had been as great as his. Her eagerly parted lips were already seeking his when his mouth came back to claim them. The whole weight of him was behind the kiss, bending her backward farther and farther until she slipped off the pillow onto the carpeted floor.

Within seconds they were lying together, and the hard pressure of his male body was making itself felt on every inch of hers. No longer needing to hold her, his hands were free to explore the soft curves that had been against him.

When Luck shifted his position to make a more thorough discovery, a shirt button caught in the eyelet lace of her blouse. He swore under his breath, impatient with the obstacle as Eve was. There was a reluctant delay as Luck paused to free the button. When his knuckles rubbed against a breast, Eve couldn't help breathing in sharply at the inadvertent contact, a white-hot rush of desire searing through her veins.

Her reaction didn't go unnoticed. The instant he had rid himself of the impediment, his hand covered her breast and a soft moan of satisfaction trembled from her throat. He kissed the source of the sound and unerringly found the pleasure point at the base of her neck that sent excited shivers over her skin.

With her eyes closed to lock the delirious sensations of supreme joy forever in her memory, Eve caressed the taut muscles of his shoulders. His deft fingers unfastened the front of her lace blouse and pushed the material aside. When his hand glided inside her brassiere and lifted a breast from its confining cup, she was a churning mass of desire.

Her clamoring needs were almost beyond endurance as his mouth traveled downward from her collarbone to nuzzle the slope of her breast. His leg was hooked across her thighs, and she was rawly conscious of his hard need outlined against her hip. The ache in her loins ran wild when his mouth circled the sensitive peak of her breast. She was writhing inside.

"I thought you told me only married people did that, dad."

CHAPTER EIGHT

TOBY'S VOICE shattered the erotic moment into a thousand pieces. Both of them froze at the sound of it. Then her fingers dug into his muscled arms in embarrassed panic when her suddenly widened eyes saw the pajama-clad boy leaning casually over the back of the couch.

Luck reacted swiftly, using his body as a shield to hide her nakedness while he quickly pulled her blouse over her breast. Eve had a glimpse of the savage anger that took over his hard features before he turned his head to glare at Toby.

"What the hell are you doing out of bed?" he demanded harshly.

"I woke up 'cause I was thirsty, so I came out to the kitchen to get a drink," his son explained, unabashed by the intimate scene he had interrupted and apparently oblivious to the awkward situation he was causing. "How come you were doing that if you and Eve aren't married?"

"You've got two seconds to get into your

bed," Luck warned. "Or, so help me, you won't be able to sit down for a month!"

"But I was only wondering—" Toby began to protest, frowning in bewilderment.

"Now!" Luck snapped the word and brought a knee up as if to rise and carry out his threat.

Toby pushed off the couch and started toward the hallway, grumbling to himself. "You keep telling me I should ask questions when I don't understand. I don't know why you're yelling at me for doing it."

"Go to your room and stay there." The line of his jaw was iron hard.

The response from Toby was a loud sigh that signaled compliance. The instant he was out of sight, Luck sat up and combed a hand through his hair before casting a grimly apologetic glance at Eve's reddened face. She sat up quickly, half turning from him to button her blouse, nearly mortified to death by the incident.

"I'm sorry, Eve," Luck sighed heavily.

"It wasn't your fault," she murmured self-consciously, and tried to restore some semblance of order to her tousled clothes.

She wasn't sure which embarrassed her more—what Toby had seen or what he might have seen if he'd come a few minutes later. She had been lost beyond control, her sense of morality completely abandoned.

337

"I'm going to have a talk with that boy." Irritation vibrated through his taut declaration.

"You shouldn't be angry with him." Despite the embarrassment Toby had caused, Eve defended his innocent role in the scene. She scrambled to her feet the minute she was decent, and Luck followed to stand beside her. She was too disconcerted by the incident to meet his eyes squarely, so her sidelong glance fell somewhere short of his face. "Toby didn't mean to do anything wrong."

"I wouldn't be too sure about that," Luck muttered, more to himself, as he sent a hard glance toward the hallway to the bedrooms.

Then he was bringing all of his attention back to her. She stiffened at the touch of his hand on her shoulder. There were still yearnings within her that hadn't been fully suppressed and she didn't want things to get out of hand twice.

"Eve—" he began in a low tone that seemed to echo the buried wants inside her.

She knew she didn't dare listen to what he wanted to say. "I think you'd better take me home, Luck," she interrupted him stiffly.

Even without looking at him, she sensed his hesitation and trembled inwardly at the thought of trying to resist him if he decided to persuade her to change her mind. She didn't think she'd have the strength of will for a long struggle.

"All right, I will." He gave in grudgingly and removed his hand from her shoulder.

"I think it's best," Eve insisted faintly.

"Of course." There was a clipped edge to his voice. "Give me a minute to tell Toby where I'm going."

"Yes," she murmured.

He moved reluctantly away from her and Eve shuddered uncontrollably when he was out of the room. She had known she loved him, but she hadn't guessed at the depth of that emotion. She had nearly lost all sense of morals for the sake of the moment. It was sobering to realize she would probably do it all over again, given the opportunity.

When Luck entered the bedroom, Toby looked at him with affronted dignity. The urge to grab the boy by the shoulders and shake him hard still rang strong within Luck. It was all he could do to hold onto his temper and not let it fly.

"I'm taking Eve home." The anger was there in his abrupt tone of voice. "When I get back, you and I are going to have a talk."

"Okay," Toby agreed with equal curtness. "But I don't see what you're so uptight about."

"Don't say another word," Luck warned. "Or we'll have that talk now."

339

Toby pressed his lips together in a thin straight line that showed his resentment for the browbeating tactics. Pivoting, Luck walked from the room.

His anger came from an unbridled instinct to protect Eve. It had run strong and hot within him, imposing the need to shelter her body with his own and later to lash out at his son for the mental harm he'd caused.

When he rejoined her in the living room, Luck noticed how much further she had withdrawn into her shell. His senses remembered the way she had responded to him without inhibition. They craved it again, but after the way his own son had embarrassed her, he couldn't bring himself to impose his desires on her to know again that wild feeling she had aroused.

Without a word she turned and walked to the door, avoiding his look. Left with no choice but to follow her, he turned his head to the side in a grim kind of despair. Powerful feelings began to make themselves known to him. Uppermost remained the need to right whatever damage had been done to her sensitive nature.

A RAW TENSION dominated the drive to her parents' lake cottage. Eve sat rigidly in the passenger seat, staring straight ahead. Luck had made a couple of attempts at conversation, but her short one-word answers had ended it. She felt that she didn't dare relax her guard for a second or all her inner feelings would spew forth.

She could only thank God she was adult enough to recognize that Luck could want to make love to her without being in love with her. Her embarrassment would have been doubled otherwise.

Luck stopped his car behind her father's sedan. This time he switched off the engine and got out to walk around the hood and open her door. He silently accompanied her to the front porch.

"Good night, Luck." Eve wanted to escape inside the cabin without further ado, but he wasn't of the same mind.

His hand caught her arm near the elbow. "I'm not letting you go inside feeling the way you do," he said.

"I'm all right," she lied.

His other hand cupped the side of her face, a certain grimness in his expression. "I don't want Toby's interference spoiling those moments for us."

"It doesn't matter." Eve tried to evade the issue.

"It does matter," Luck insisted. "It matters a great deal to me."

"Please." It was a protest of sorts against any discussion of the subject.

His hand wouldn't let her move away from its touch. "I'm not ashamed of wanting to make love to you, Eve," he declared. "And I don't want you to be, either."

His bluntness seemed to weaken her knees. After avoiding his gaze for so long, she finally looked at him. His steady regard captured her glance and held it.

"Okay?" Luck wanted her agreement to his previous statement.

"Okay." She gave it in a whisper.

He kissed her warmly as if to seal the agreement, then lifted his head. "You and I will talk about this tomorrow," he said. "In the meantime, I've got to go back and have a little father-to-son chat with Toby."

"All right." Eve wasn't sure what he wanted to talk about, and that uncertainty was in her voice.

Luck heard it and seemed to hesitate before letting her go. "Good night, Eve."

"Good night." She called softly after him as he descended the porch steps to his car.

Returning to the cabin, Luck went directly to his son's bedroom. He switched on the light as he entered the room. Toby sat up and made a project out of arranging his pillows to lean against them. When Luck walked to the bed, Toby crossed his arms in a gesture that implied determined tolerance.

"Sit down, dad," he said. "I think it's time we talked this out."

Luck didn't find the usual amusement in his son's pseudoadult attitude and had to smother a fierce rush of irritation. "I'll sit down," he stated. "But I'm going to do the talking and you're going to listen."

"Whatever you say." Again there was an exhibition of patience with his father.

"Do you have any idea how much you embarrassed Eve?" Luck demanded, taking a position on the edge of the bed.

"You kinda lost your cool, too, dad," Toby pointed out calmly.

"I said I was going to do the talking," Luck reminded him sternly. "It wasn't so bad that you walked in when you did, Toby. The part that was wrong was when you stayed."

"I wanted to find out what was going on," he explained with wide-eyed innocence.

"It was none of your business," Luck countered. "There are certain times when a couple wants privacy."

"But you told me that happened when the two people were married." A faint light gleamed in Toby's eyes, betraying his supposed naiveté.

"That is beside the point." The line of his mouth became grim as Luck's gaze narrowed on his son. "Right now, I want you to understand

343

that what you did was wrong and you owe Eve an apology.''

''Was what you and Eve were doing wrong?'' Toby inquired.

''Toby.'' There was a warning in his father's voice not to sidetrack the conversation with his own questions.

''Okay,'' he sighed with mock exaggeration. ''I'll apologize to Eve,'' Toby promised. ''But since you like Eve and you want to do things with her that married people do, why don't you marry her? Did you find out if she has staples in her stomach?''

''Staples?'' Luck frowned, briefly avoiding the first question.

''Don't you remember when we met that real sexy blonde on the beach and you said you didn't want to marry anyone with staples in her stomach?'' Toby reminded him.

It took Luck a minute to recall his reference to the centerfold type. ''No, Eve isn't the kind with staples,'' he replied.

''Then why don't you ask her to marry you?'' Toby argued. ''I'd really like it if she became my mother.''

''You would, huh?'' He tilted his head to one side in half challenge. ''After what you pulled tonight, she might not be interested in becoming your mother even if I asked her.''

A look of guilty regret entered Toby's expression. "She was really upset, huh?" He was worried by the question.

"Yes, she was. Thanks to you." Luck didn't lessen the blame.

"If I told her I was sorry, maybe then she'd say yes if you asked her," Toby suggested.

"I've already told you that you're going to apologize to her in the morning," he stated.

"Are you going to ask her to marry you after that?" Toby wanted to know.

"I don't recall even suggesting that I wanted to marry Eve," Luck replied.

"But you do, don't you?" Toby persisted.

"We'll talk about that another time." He avoided a direct answer. "Tonight you just think about what you're going to say to Eve tomorrow."

"Will you think about marrying her?" His son refused to let go of the subject as Luck straightened from the bed. Toby slid under the covers to lie down once again while Luck tucked him in.

"I'll think about it," he conceded.

"Good night, dad." There was a satisfied note in Toby's voice.

"Good night."

Luck was absently shaking his head as he walked from the room. After checking to make sure the fire in the fireplace was out, he went to his own room and walked to the dresser where Lisa's photograph stood. He picked it up and studied it for a minute.

"You know it isn't that I love you any less," he murmured to the picture. "What we had, I'll never lose. It's just that my love for Eve is stronger. You would have liked her."

He held the photograph for a minute longer, saying a kind of farewell to the past and its beautiful memories. With deep affection he placed the picture carefully inside one of the dresser drawers. He had not believed it possible to fall in love twice in a lifetime, but he had. Once as a young man—and now as a mature adult. By closing the drawer, he turned a page in his life.

A ROUND BEVERAGE TRAY was precariously balanced on Toby's small hand as he quietly turned the knob to open his father's door. The orange juice sloshed over the rim of its glass, but he miraculously managed not to spill the hot coffee. With both hands holding the tray once more, he walked to the bed where his father was soundly sleeping.

When he set the tray on the nightstand, Toby noticed something was missing. His mother's photograph was gone from the dresser. A smile slowly began to curve his mouth until he was grinning from ear to ear. He tried hard to wipe it away when he turned a twinkling look on his father.

"It's time to get up, dad." He shook a bronze shoulder to add action to his summons.

His father stirred reluctantly and opened a bleary eye. He closed it again when he saw Toby.

"Come on, dad." Toby nudged him again. "Wake up. It's seven-thirty. I brought you some orange juice and coffee."

This time both sleepy blue eyes opened and Luck pushed himself into a half-sitting position in the bed. Toby handed him the glass of orange juice and crawled onto the bed to sit cross-legged.

After downing the juice, Luck set the glass on the tray and reached for the pack of cigarettes and lighter on the nightstand.

"You are certainly bright-eyed this morning." There was a trace of envy in his father's sleep-thickened voice as he lit a cigarette and blew out a stream of blue gray smoke.

"I've been up awhile," Toby shrugged. "Long enough to make the coffee and have some cereal."

Luck picked up the coffee cup and took a sip from it. "After last night, I think it would be a good idea if you started knocking before walking into somebody's room."

"You mean, so I won't embarrass Eve when she starts sleeping in here after you're married," Toby guessed.

"Yes—" The affirmative reply was out before he realized what he'd admitted. The second he heard what he had said, he came instantly awake.

Toby laughed with glee. "You did decide to marry her!"

"Now, you wait just a minute," Luck ordered, but there wasn't any way he could retract his previous admission. "That doesn't mean Eve is willing to marry me."

"I know." Toby continued to grin widely. "You haven't asked her yet. When are you going to propose to her?"

"You will have to apologize for last night," Luck reminded him. "You aren't getting out of that."

"We can go over there this morning, just like we planned." Toby began laying out the strategy. "I'll apologize to her, then you can ask her to marry you."

"No, Toby." His father shook his head. "That isn't the way it's going to happen. We'll go over there and you'll apologize. That's it."

"Ahh, dad," Toby protested. "You're going to ask her anyway. Why not this morning?"

"Because you don't ask a woman to be your wife while there's an eight-year-old kid standing around listening," his father replied with mild exasperation.

"When are you going to ask her, then?" Toby demanded impatiently.

"I'm going to invite Eve to have dinner with me tonight," he said. "You're going to stay home and I'll have Mrs. Jackson come over to sit with you."

"Mrs. Jackson?" Toby cried with a grimace of dislike. "Why does she have to come over?"

"We've been through this before," Luck reminded him. "You aren't going to stay here by yourself."

"Well, why do you have to go out to dinner with Eve?" he argued. "Why can't she come over here like she did last night? I'll leave you two alone and promise not to listen."

His father sighed heavily and glanced toward the ceiling. "How can I make you understand?" he wondered aloud. "When a woman receives a marriage proposal, she has a right to expect a few romantic touches along with it—a little wine and candlelight. You don't have her come over, cook dinner, wash dishes, then propose. It just isn't done like that."

"It sure sounds like an awful lot of fuss to me," Toby grumbled. "Eve wouldn't mind if you just asked her without going through all that."

"I don't care whether she doesn't mind. I do," Luck stated, and crushed the half-smoked cigarette in the ashtray. "Off the bed," he ordered. "I want to get dressed."

"Are we going to Eve's now?" Toby hopped to the floor.

"Not this early in the morning," Luck told him. "We'll wait until later."

"But it's Sunday. She might go to church," he protested.

"Then we'll drive over there the first thing this afternoon."

"Aw, dad." Toby sighed his disappointment and left the bedroom dragging his feet.

IT WAS NOONTIME when Eve and her parents returned to the lake cottage from Sunday church services. Dinner was in the oven, so they were able to sit down to the table in short order. By one o'clock the dishes were done and Eve went to her room to change out of her good dress.

"Eve?" The questioning call from her mother was accompanied by a knock on the door. "Your father and I are going for a boat ride on the lake. Would you like to come with us?"

Zipping her jeans, Eve went to the door and opened it. "No, thanks, mom." She smiled at the woman with graying brown hair. "I think I'll just stay here and finish that book I was reading."

She didn't mention that Luck had indicated he would see her today. No definite arrangement had been made. Eve preferred that her parents didn't know that she was staying on the off chance he might come by or call.

"Is Eve coming with us?" her father asked from the front room.

"No," her mother answered him. "She's going to stay here."

"I'll bet she's expecting Luck McClure," he

declared on a teasing note, and Eve felt a faint blush warming her cheeks.

"Don't mind him," her mother declared with an understanding smile. "He's remembering the way I sat around the house waiting to hear from him when we were dating." She made a move to leave. "We probably won't be back until later this afternoon."

"Have a good time," Eve said.

"You, too," her mother called back with a wink.

CHAPTER NINE

TOBY WAS SLUMPED in the passenger seat of the car, a grimly dejected expression on his face. "Boy, I wish Mrs. Jackson had been busy tonight." He grumbled the complaint for the sixth time since Luck had phoned her to sit with him.

"She's coming and there's nothing you can do to change that," Luck stated, looking briefly away from the road at his son. "I don't want you pulling any of your shenanigans, either."

Toby was silent for a minute. "Have you thought about how expensive this is going to be, dad?" He tried another tactic. "You not only have to pay Mrs. Jackson to stay with me, but you've also got to pay for Eve's dinner and yours. With the money you're spending tonight, I'd have enough to buy my minibike. It sure would be a lot cheaper if you just asked her this afternoon."

"I don't want to hear any more about it." They had hardly been off the subject since this morning, and his patience was wearing thin.

"But don't I have some say in this?" Toby argued. "After all, she is going to be my mother."

"I wouldn't bring that up if I were you," Luck warned. "You haven't squared yourself with Eve about last night. She might not want to be the mother to a boy who doesn't respect other people's private moments."

"Yes, but I'm going to apologize for that," Toby reasoned. "Eve will understand. I'm just a little kid."

"Sometimes I wonder about that," Luck murmured to himself.

TAKING THE ICE-CUBE TRAY out of the freezer section of the refrigerator, Eve carried it to the sink and popped out a handful of cubes to put in the glass of tea sitting on the counter. The rest she dumped into a plastic container and set it in the freezer for later use. She turned on the cold water faucet to fill the ice-cube tray. The noise made by the running water drowned out the sound of the car pulling into the drive.

As she carried the tray full of water to the refrigerator, she heard car doors slamming outside. Her heart seemed to leap at the sound. In her excitement, Eve forgot about the tray in her hands and started to turn. Water spilled over the sides and onto the floor.

"Damn," she swore softly at her carelessness, and set the tray on the counter.

Hurriedly Eve tore some paper towels off the roll and bent down to sop up the mess. Her pulse raced with the sound of footsteps approaching the cottage. Her haste just seemed to make it take longer to wipe up the spilled water.

A knock rattled the screen door in its frame. She carried the water-soaked wad of paper towels to the sink, a hand cupped under them to catch any drips.

"I'm coming!" Eve called anxiously, and dropped the mess in the sink.

Her glance darted to the screen door and the familiar outline of Luck's build darkened by the wire mesh. She paused long enough to dry her hands on a terry towel and run smoothing fingers over her gleaming brown hair.

There was a wild run of pleasure through her veins as she hurried toward the door. Reflex action adjusted the knitted waistband of her carnation-red top around her snug-fitting jeans.

Eve didn't notice the shorter form standing next to Luck until she was nearly to the door, and realized he'd brought Toby with him. Not that she minded; it was just that Luck had indicated he wanted to talk to her privately. Toby's presence negated that opportunity. And there was the embarrassing matter of last night's scene. She was naturally modest, so there was a sense of discomfort in meeting Toby today.

"Hello." She greeted them through the screen and unlatched the door to open it. There was a nervous edge to her smile until she met the dancing warmth of Luck's blue eyes. It eased almost immediately as a little glow started to build strength. "Sorry it took so long, but I had to mop up some water I spilled."

"That's all right. We didn't wait that long," Luck assured her. The admiring run of his gaze over her face and figure seemed to give her confidence. She could tell he liked what he saw, even if she wasn't the type to turn heads.

"Hello, Toby." Eve was able to smile at the young boy without any strain as he entered the cottage at his father's side.

"Hi." His response seemed a little more subdued than normal, as if his mind were preoccupied with other matters, but his bright eyes were just as alert as they always were.

"Come in," Eve invited. "I just fixed myself a glass of iced tea. Would you two like some?"

Refusal formed on Luck's mouth, but Toby was quicker with his acceptance. "Yeah, I'd like a glass."

"And some cookies, too?" Eve guessed.

"Chocolate chip?" he asked hopefully, and she nodded affirmatively. "I sure would."

"What do you say?" Luck prompted his son to show some manners.

"Thank you," Toby inserted, then frowned. "Or was it supposed to be 'please'?"

"It doesn't matter," Eve assured him with a faint smile. "You've got the idea." Her glance lifted to the boy's father. "Did you want a glass of tea and some cookies?"

"I'll settle for the tea," he replied, changing his mind in the face of his son's acceptance.

The pair followed her into the small kitchen. Toby crowded close to the counter to watch her while Luck stayed out of her way, leaning a hip against a counter top and lighting a cigarette. Eve never lost her awareness of his lean masculinity, even though he wasn't in her line of vision. Her body's finely tuned radar was aware of his presence.

She fixed two more glasses of tea without any mishap and even managed to put the ice-cube tray filled with water in the refrigerator's freezer section without spilling any. Lifting the lid of the cookie jar, Eve took out three chocolate chip cookies and placed them on a paper napkin for Toby.

"Here you go, Toby." She turned to give them to him.

"Wait a minute," Luck stated, and laid a hand on his son's shoulder to stop him from taking them. "Before any refreshments are passed around, there's something Toby wants to say to you, Eve. Isn't there, Toby?" There was a prodding tone in his voice when he addressed his son.

A big sigh came from Toby as he lowered the

356

hand that had reached for the cookies. "Yes," he admitted, and turned his round blue gaze on Eve. "I'm sorry for embarrassing you last night. I didn't mean to."

"I know you didn't." She colored slightly at the reference to the incident.

"Dad explained about respecting other people's privacy," he said. "I was wrong to stay without you knowing I was there. I'm really and truly sorry, Eve. All I wanted to do was find out what was going on. I never meant to embarrass you."

Toby possessed more than his share of natural curiosity. She had known all along that he hadn't meant any harm. It was obvious he wasn't shocked by what he'd seen, which allowed her to feel that the scene between herself and Luck had been natural and right.

"It's all right, Toby," Eve promised him. "You're forgiven, so we can all forget about it."

His blue eyes widened in a hopeful look. "Then you aren't mad or upset about it?"

"No, not at all," she replied with a shake of her head.

Tipping his head back, Toby turned it to look up at his father. "See?" he challenged. "I told you she wouldn't be."

"I know you did," Luck admitted. "But she deserved an apology just the same."

"Now will you ask her to marry you instead

of—" Toby didn't get the question finished before Luck clamped a hand over his mouth to muffle the rest of it.

An electric shock went through Eve as her gaze flew to Luck's face. Her own complexion had gone pale at Toby's suggestion. His ruggedly virile features held grim impatience and displeasure in their expression, and Eve knew she had been right to doubt that Toby knew what he was talking about. It seemed she had been catapulted from one awkward situation into another.

"Toby, I could throttle you," Luck muttered angrily, and took his hand from the boy's mouth. "Don't you dare say another word."

"But—" Toby frowned his lack of understanding.

"I mean it," Luck cut across his voice with stern reproval. "Get your cookies and iced tea and go outside," he ordered. "I don't want to hear so much as a peep out of you."

"Okay," Toby grumbled, and moved to the counter to take the napkin of cookies and a glass of iced tea. Eve was too frozen to help him.

"You stay outside and don't come walking back in," Luck warned. "Remember what you promised me about that."

"Yes, dad," he nodded, and trudged toward the screen door.

Eve continued to stare at Luck as he snubbed

the cigarette butt in an ashtray on the counter. There was regret in the hard line of his mouth and a grim apology in his eyes when he finally looked at her. She heard the door bang shut behind the departing Toby.

"I'm afraid my son has a big mouth," Luck said.

A terrible pain wrenched at her heart. She turned away to hide it, clasping the edge of the counter with both hands. Dredging deep into the well of her reserve strength, she found a little piece of composure.

"Don't worry about it," Eve declared with forced lightness. "I'm not going to hold you to Toby's suggestion, so no marriage proposal is expected."

Her pulse raced as Luck moved to stand behind her. His hands settled lightly on the rounded points of her shoulders. At the moment she wasn't up to resisting his touch. A tremor of longing quivered through her senses.

"Why not?" he murmured, very close to her.

She pretended not to understand. "Why not what?" Her voice wavered.

"Since Toby has already let the cat out of the bag, I might as well ask you to marry me now, instead of waiting," Luck replied.

She half turned to look at him over her shoulder. He couldn't possibly be serious, but his steady gaze seemed to imply that he was. She was afraid to believe it. She loved him so much that it didn't seem possible her wildest dream might come true.

"Luck, you don't have to do this." She gave him a chance to retract his semiproposal.

That lazy half smile lifted a corner of his mouth, potent in its male charm. "I know I don't," he agreed.

"Then. . . ." Eve continued to hesitate.

"I want you to be my wife," Luck said in an effort to make it clear to her that he was serious. It wasn't any kind of cruel joke. "And Toby wants you to be his mother—although I wouldn't blame you if you have second thoughts about taking on that role. He talks when he shouldn't— he sees things he shouldn't—and he knows things he shouldn't. It isn't going to be any bed of roses."

"I don't mind." She breathed the reply because she was beginning to believe that he meant all this.

"You'd better be sure about that." He turned her around to face him and let his hands slide down her back to gather her closer to him. "We haven't known each other long. I don't want to rush you into something. If you want to think it over, I'll wait for your answer."

Spreading her hands across the front of his shirt, Eve could feel his body warmth through the material. The steady beat of his heart assured her that this was all real. It wasn't a dream.

"It isn't that." Eve hadn't realized that she hadn't got around to accepting his proposal until that minute. "I'd like to marry you."

Luck tipped his head toward her. "Did I hear a but at the end of that?" he questioned.

"No." She hadn't said it, not in so many words; yet it was there—silently. "It's just so sudden. I can't think why you'd want to marry me," she admitted at last.

"I want to marry you for the usual reason." A warm dryness rustled his voice. "I love you, Eve."

The breath she drew in became lodged in her throat. She hadn't realized what beautiful words they were until Luck uttered them. An incredulous joy misted her eyes.

"I love you, too," she declared in a voice choked with emotion.

His mouth closed on hers and there was no more need for words. Her hands slid around his neck and into the thickness of his dark hair as his molding arms crushed her to his length. Eve reeled under the hard possession of his kiss, still dazed that he actually wanted her. But he seemed determined to prove it with action as well as words.

When her parted lips were at last convinced, Luck showered her face with rough kisses. Her eyes, her brows, her cheeks, her nose, her chin, her jaw—no part of her was exempted from his hungry foray. It left her so weak she could hardly breathe. Her racing heart threatened to burst from the love swelling within her.

The searing pleasure of it all was a sweet ache that throbbed through her limbs. His hands leisurely roamed her shoulders, back and hips to caress and arouse her flesh to a fever pitch of delight. For Eve there was no holding back. She gave him her heart and soul in return, and anything else he wanted—her pride, her dignity, her self-respect. It was all his.

A faint tremor went through him when Luck lifted his head an inch or so from hers to study her with a heavy-lidded look of desire. "I thought it would take more convincing than this to persuade you to marry me," he admitted huskily.

"Hardly." Eve smiled at that, knowing she had been his for the taking a long time now.

He withdrew a hand from her back to cup her upturned face. She turned into its largeness and pressed a kiss in its palm. His fingers began a tactile examination of her features from the curve of her cheekbone to the outline of her lips.

"That night I bumped into you outside the tavern, I knew I didn't want to let you go," Luck murmured. "But I didn't dream that I'd eventually marry you."

Even though their first meeting was a special and vivid memory, Eve wished he hadn't mentioned it. She didn't want to remember that he had regarded her as a brown mouse. She closed her eyes to shut it out.

"I thought you were a figment of my imagination," he went on, and slid his hand to her neck, where his thumb stroked the curve of her throat. "Until I finally recognized you that rainy afternoon you came to help Toby bake cookies. And there you were, right in my own home."

"I remember," Eve admitted softly, but she wasn't enthused about the subject.

Luck drank in a deep breath and let it out slowly. "Before I met you, I was beginning to think I wasn't capable of caring for another woman."

There was an instantaneous image in her mind of the photograph of his first wife. A painful sweep of jealousy washed over her because she would never be first in his life. She loved him so much that she was willing to settle for being second as long as it meant she could spend her life with him.

"Toby has been wanting me to get married for some time," Luck told her. "He even chose you before I did. I have to admit my son has very good taste."

Eve smiled faintly. "He's still outside—and probably dying of curiosity."

"Let him." His arm tightened fractionally around her waist. "It's what he deserves." Then Luck sighed reluctantly. "I suppose we should let him in on the news, although he was positive you'd agree to marry me."

"He was right." She basked in the blue light of his unswerving gaze.

"He's never going to let us hear the end of it. You know that, don't you?" he mocked lightly.

"Probably not," Eve agreed with a widening smile.

"We might as well go tell him," Luck finally agreed with her suggestion.

As he turned to guide her out of the kitchen, he kept his arm curved tightly around her and her body pressed close to his side. It was a very possessive gesture and it thrilled Eve.

When they walked outside, they found Toby sitting on the porch steps waiting patiently—or perhaps impatiently, judging by how quickly he bounded to his feet to greet them. His bright glance darted eagerly from one to the other.

"Did she say yes?" he asked Luck with bated breath.

"What makes you think I asked her?" Luck challenged.

He cast an anxious look at Eve, who was trying not to smile. "You did, didn't you?" Again the question was addressed to his father.

"I did." Luck didn't keep him in the dark any longer. "And Eve agreed to be my wife."

"Whoopee!" Toby shouted with glee and practically jumped in the air. "I knew she would," he rubbed it in to his father. "I told you that you didn't have to wait until tonight, didn't I?"

Luck glanced at Eve to explain. "I was going to do it up right. I had it all planned—to take you out to dinner, ply you with champagne, sway you with candlelight and flowers. Then I was going to propose. Unfortunately, blabbermouth jumped the gun."

"Now you don't have to do that," Toby inserted. "And I don't have to stay with Mrs. Jackson. Eve can come over to our place tonight and we'll all have dinner together."

"No, she can't," Luck stated, shaking his head.

Toby frowned. "Why can't she come?"

"Because I'm taking her out to dinner just the way I planned," he said. "And Mrs. Jackson is coming over to stay with you just as we arranged it."

"Dad," he protested.

"I'm going to have to share her with you a lot of evenings in the future, but on the first night of our engagement, I'm going to have her all to myself," Luck declared.

"I'd stay in my room," Toby promised.

"That isn't the same," he insisted, and looked again at Eve. "You will have dinner with me tonight if I promise you you won't have to cook it?"

"Yes." Even if she had to cook it, she would have agreed.

"I'll come over early, around seven, so I can talk to your parents." Luck smiled as he realized, "I haven't asked you how soon you'd like the wedding to be?"

His phrasing of the question—not "when" but "how soon"—nearly took her breath away. For a second she could only look at him, a wealth of love shining in her eyes.

"The sooner the better, don't you think?" she suggested, a little tentatively.

"Absolutely." His answer was very definite as he bent his head to claim her lips once more.

What started out as a brief kiss lingered into something longer. Eve leaned more heavily against him, letting his strength support her. Before passion could flare, they were reminded that they weren't alone.

"I have a question," Toby said, interrupting their embrace.

"What is it?" But Luck was more than a little preoccupied with his study of her soft lips.

"Am I supposed to leave you two alone every time you start kissing?" he asked.

"Not necessarily every time. Why?" Luck dragged his gaze from her face to glance curiously at his son.

"If I did, it just seems to me that I might be spending an awful lot of time by myself," Toby sighed. "And I'd really kinda hoped the three of us could be together like a family."

"We *will* be a family," Eve assured him. "And you won't be spending much time alone."

"Eve's right." Luck reached out to curve an arm around his son's shoulders and draw him into their circle. "Part of the plan was for you to have a mother, wasn't it?"

"Yep." Toby smiled widely.

CHAPTER TEN

THE THREE OF THEM spent the afternoon together, partly to allay Toby's concern about his position in the new family unit and partly because Luck and Eve enjoyed Toby's company and shared a mutual desire to include him. Eve knew she was just imagining it, but the sun seemed to shine brighter and the air smelled fresher than it ever had before.

Her parents hadn't returned from their boat ride by the time Luck and Toby left to go home. Eve had some time alone to think over the unexpected proposal and all that had been said. She finally came out of the wonderful daze that had numbed her to a few home truths.

Luck had asked her to marry him for many reasons. He had said that he loved her, and she didn't doubt that in his own way he did. But she realized he didn't love her as much as she loved him. Another factor was Toby: he had needed and wanted a mother, and he had liked her. He'd undoubtedly had a lot of influence on Luck's decision. That was only natural.

Plus Eve had known he was a lonely man. He

wanted the company of a woman—and not just in a sexual way, for she was sure he could find that type of feminine company. That night in front of the tavern, Luck had said he wanted to talk to her—that she was the kind he could talk to. He needed that in a woman, just as she needed to be able to talk to him. But part of his reason for proposing had to be the desire for companionship.

Then there was the bachelor existence he and Toby led. They needed someone to cook and clean house for them. How much more convenient it would be to have live-in help. Cooking and cleaning would be part of her new role, although naturally both Luck and Toby would help.

There was nothing wrong with any of his reasons. None of them were bad. As a matter of fact there were a lot of couples starting out their wedded life with less solid foundations than theirs. But the realizations brought Eve down out of her dreamworld to face the reality of their future. Luck wanted to marry a comfortable, practical Eve, not a starry-eyed romantic. It was better that she knew that.

It didn't alter the special significance of the evening to come. It was still their engagement dinner. Eve took extra care in choosing a dress to wear and fixing her hair and makeup. The results weren't too bad, even to her critical eye. The rose color of the dress was a little drab, but its lines flattered her slender figure. The soft curls of her chestnut hair glistened in the light.

True to his word, Luck arrived promptly at seven, with a bouquet of scarlet roses for Eve. She hadn't mentioned anything to her parents about his proposal, waiting until he came so they could tell them together.

They were overjoyed at the news, especially her mother, who had despaired that Eve would ever find a man to satisfy her. Her father seemed to take pride in Luck's old-fashioned gesture of asking his permission to marry his daughter. It was granted without any hesitation.

By half-past seven the congratulations were over and they were on their way to the restaurant. Eve realized how difficult it was to keep both feet on the ground when she was with Luck. Her hand rested on the car seat, held in the warm clasp of his.

"Are you happy?" he asked.

"Yes." She could say that without any doubt, even with the facts before her concerning his reasons for wanting to marry her.

"I thought we could drive to Duluth tomorrow," he said. "I need to buy you a ring, but I want to be sure you like it. We'll pick something out together. Is tomorrow all right?"

"Yes, it's fine," Eve nodded.

"I want you to meet my father while we're there. We'll have dinner with him," he stated.

"That would be good," she agreed. "I'd like to get to know him."

"You'll like him." He sent her a brief smile. "And I have no doubt that he'll like you."

"I hope so." But she was secretly concerned that his father would compare her with Luck's first wife and wonder what his son saw in such a "plain Jane." A lot of his friends who had known his first wife would probably wonder about that, also. She wouldn't blame them if they did.

"Would you mind if Toby came with us tomorrow?" Luck asked as he slowed the car to turn into the restaurant parking lot.

"Of course I don't mind," Eve assured him. "If we don't include him, he'll probably become convinced he's being neglected."

"That's what I thought, too," he agreed, and parked the car between two others.

After climbing out of the car, Luck walked around it to open her door and help her out. He lingered on the spot, holding her hand and smiling at her.

"Have I told you that you look very lovely tonight?" he asked.

"No, but thank you." Eve smiled, but she wondered if he was just being kind. Perhaps it was a nice way of saying she looked as good as she could look.

Bending his head, he let his mouth move warmly over hers. The firm kiss didn't last long, but it reassured her of his affection. Eve doubted if that brief kiss disturbed him as much as it disturbed her, though.

When it was over, he escorted her to the restaurant entrance, his hand pressed against the back of her waist. Inside they were shown to a small table for two in a quiet corner of the establishment.

"Didn't I promise you candlelight?" Luck gestured to the candle burning in an amber glass when they were both seated in their chairs across from each other.

"Yes, you did," she agreed with a remembering smile. "You neglected to mention the soft music playing in the background." Eve referred to the muted strains of romantic mood music coming over the restaurant's stereo system.

"I saved that for the finishing touch." The corners of his mouth deepened in a vague amusement.

A young and very attractive waitress approached their table. With her blond hair and blue eyes, she seemed the epitome of everything sexy, without appearing vulgarly so. She smiled at both of them, yet Eve jealously thought she noticed something other than professional interest in the girl's eyes when she looked at Luck.

"Would you like a drink before dinner?" she inquired.

"Yes, we'd like a bottle of champagne," Luck ordered with a responding smile.

Eve would probably have checked his pulse to see if he was sick if he hadn't noticed the blonde's obvious beauty. Yet when he did she was hurt. It made no sense at all. Somehow she managed to keep the conflicting emotions out of her expression.

The waitress left and came back with the bottle of champagne. After she had opened it, she poured some in a glass for Luck to sample. He nodded his approval and she filled a glass for each of them.

When she'd gone, Luck raised his glass to make a toast. "To the love of my life, who is soon to be my wife."

It was a very touching sentiment, but Eve knew it was an exaggeration. He had promised her a romantic evening and he was trying to give it to her, but she would rather their relationship remained honest and did not become sullied with false compliments.

"That was very beautiful, Luck," she admitted. "But it wasn't necessary."

"Oh?" His eyebrow arched at her comment. "Why isn't it necessary?"

"Because—" she shrugged a shoulder a little nervously "—I didn't expect you to pretend that you are wildly and romantically in love with me. You don't have to make flowery speeches."

"I see." The line of his jaw became hard, even though he smiled. "And it doesn't bother you if I'm not wildly and romantically in love with you?'' There was a trace of challenge in his question.

Eve assured him, ''I've accepted it.'' She didn't want him to act the part of a romantic lover when it wasn't what he truly felt.

''I'm glad you have,'' he murmured dryly, and motioned for the waitress to bring them menus. ''I understand the prime rib is very good here.''

The dinner conversation was dominated by mundane topics. The meal was very enjoyable, yet Eve sensed some underlying tension. Luck was pleasant and friendly, but sometimes when he looked at her she felt uneasy. He'd always been able to disturb her physically, yet this was different—almost as if he were angry, though he didn't appear to be.

The dinner had stretched to a second cup of coffee after dessert before Luck suggested it was time to leave. Eve accepted his decision, still unable to put her finger on the source of the troubling sensation.

In silence they crossed the parking lot to the car. Luck assisted her into the passenger seat, then walked behind the car to slide into the driver's seat. He made no attempt to start the car.

''Is something wrong?'' Eve frowned slightly.

''There seems to be,'' he said with a nod, and half turned in the seat to face her.

''What is it?'' She wasn't sure if he meant

something was wrong with the car or something else.

"You," Luck answered simply.

"What have I done?" She drew back in surprise.

"Where did you get this ridiculous notion that I'm not wildly in love with you?" he demanded.

"Well, you're not," Eve stated in defense, then faltered under his piercing gaze. "I believe you when you say you love me, but—"

"That's good of you," he taunted dryly. "If I'm not madly in love with you, maybe you should explain why I want to marry you. I'm sure it has something to do with Toby."

"Why are you asking me?" Eve countered. "You know the reasons as well as I do."

"Perhaps better, since they happen to be mine." Luck stretched an arm along the seat back and appeared to relax. "But I'd like to hear you tell me what they are."

"I can provide some of the things that are missing in your life," she said uneasily, not sure why he wanted her to explain, unless it was to make sure she understood.

"Such as?" he prompted her into elaborating on the answer.

"You need a mother for your son, someone to take care of your house and do the cooking, someone to care about you and be there when you want company...." Eve hesitated.

"You left out bed partner," he reminded her coolly.

"That, too," she conceded.

"I'm glad. For a minute I thought I was hiring a full-time housekeeper instead of acquiring a wife." This time some of his anger crept into his voice.

"I . . . don't understand," Eve stammered.

"You silly fool. There is only one reason why I'm marrying you. I love you and I don't want to live without you!" Luck snapped.

"But Toby—"

"I haven't done too bad a job raising him alone. If he has managed without a mother this long, then he can make it the rest of the way," he retorted. "Believe me, I'm glad the two of you like each other, but I wouldn't give a damn if he hated you as long as I loved you."

"But I thought—" Eve tried again to voice her impressions, and again Luck interrupted her.

"As for the cooking and cleaning, I could have that done. I know you haven't inquired, but I could afford that if it were what I wanted."

"You admitted you were lonely," she inserted quickly before he could cut her off again. "You said it was lonely at home that night outside the tavern."

"So I did," Luck admitted. "Eve, a man can have a hundred women living in his house and still be lonely if none of those women is the right one.''

"Please." She turned her head away, afraid of being convinced by him. "I know how much you loved your first wife."

"Yes, I *loved* Lisa—" he stressed the verb "—but it's in the past tense, Eve. I *did* love her, but I love *you* now. It's completely different."

"I know that," she murmured with a little ache.

"Do you?" Luck sighed behind her, then his hands were turning her into his arms. "I loved her as a young man loves. I'm not the same person anymore. I've changed. I've grown up. I'm an adult male, Eve, and I want you and love you as only a man can—wildly, deeply and romantically."

"Luck." Eve held her breath, finally beginning to believe it could be true.

"Come here." He smiled and began to gather her into his arms. "I want to prove it to you."

She could hardly argue when his mouth was covering hers with such hungry force. And she didn't want to anymore.

What readers say about JANET DAILEY

"The books of Janet Dailey bring joy into an otherwise turbulent world."

B.J.S.,* St. Catharines, Ontario

"When reading a Janet Dailey novel I feel like I'm reading a letter from a dear friend."

S.V., Inver Grove Heights, Minnesota

"I wait to buy each new Janet Dailey book as soon as it comes out."

R.G., Des Moines, Iowa

"The only complaint I have of Janet Dailey's books is that they end."

A.M.W., Belford, Ohio

*Names available on request

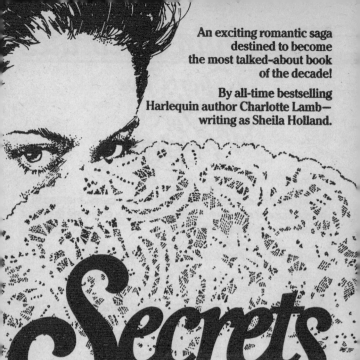

Harlequin Celebrates

Thirty-Five Years of Excellence

...and our commitment to excellence continues. Indulge in the pleasure of superb romance reading by choosing the most popular love stories in the world.

Harlequin Presents®

Exciting romance novels for the woman of today— a rare blend of passion and dramatic realism.

Harlequin Romance™

Tender, captivating stories that sweep to faraway places and delight with the magic of love.

HARLEQUIN SUPERROMANCE™

Longer, more absorbing love stories for the connoisseur of romantic fiction.

Harlequin Temptation™

Sensual and romantic stories about choices, dilemmas, resolutions, and above all, the fulfillment of love.

Harlequin American Romance™

Contemporary romances— uniquely North American in flavor and appeal.